MW01485306

You Weren't Meant to Be Human

You Weren't Meant to Be Human

ANDREW JOSEPH WHITE

SAGA PRESS

LONDON   NEW YORK   TORONTO
AMSTERDAM/ANTWERP   NEW DELHI   SYDNEY/MELBOURNE

AN IMPRINT OF SIMON & SCHUSTER, LLC

1230 AVENUE OF THE AMERICAS, NEW YORK, NEW YORK 10020

First Saga Press hardcover edition September 2025

SAGA PRESS and colophon are trademarks of Simon & Schuster, LLC

For information about special discounts for bulk purchases, please contact Simon & Schuster Special Sales at 1-866-506-1949 or business@simonandschuster.com.

The Simon & Schuster Speakers Bureau can bring authors to your live event. For more information or to book an event, contact the Simon & Schuster Speakers Bureau at 1-866-248-3049 or visit our website at www.simonspeakers.com.

INTERIOR DESIGN BY KARLA SCHWEER

Manufactured in the United States of America

1 3 5 7 9 10 8 6 4 2

Library of Congress Cataloging-in-Publication Data is available.

ISBN 978-1-6680-3807-9
ISBN 978-1-6680-3809-3 (ebook)

For anyone who ever put their
face too close to the fire,
or boiling water, or snapping dogs.

AUTHOR'S NOTE

In addition to a graphic focus on pregnancy, miscarriage, abortion, and child-birth, *You Weren't Meant to Be Human* contains explicit depictions of extreme violence and gore, suicidal ideation, intrusive thoughts, self-harm, sexual assault, and abuse—sometimes alone, sometimes combined, sometimes indistinguish-able one from another. A detailed list of warnings is available on the author's website at AndrewJosephWhite.com.

First
Trimester

One

Crane doesn't know this yet, but he's been pregnant for almost three months already.

TWO

Crane didn't say *yes* to this, though maybe that isn't the best choice of words. Crane doesn't say anything if he can help it. And he wouldn't have written it out, either, scrawled proof of consent like an exploited porn actor under duress, *I agreed to this I swear.* He stopped speaking for a reason. Writing it down defeats the point.

But Levi is still putting him over the manager's desk, a hand to the back trapping him between a broken printer and the security camera monitor, and his jeans are down to his thighs and there are bruises under his jaw, and he can't bring himself to care about if he agreed or not.

Behind him, Levi mumbles, "Stay down."

Is Levi still smoking back there? He doesn't think so but it smells like it. God, that'd be hot, if he was—use the dips between the vertebrae as an ashtray, fuck up the cheap tattoo there with a scar, it'd look so good. Levi's body heat warms the bare backs of Crane's thighs.

Crane whines. It's pathetic.

There are sticky notes pasted around the security camera monitor, little things for him to focus on while Levi unbuckles his belt—the telltale jingle of metal on metal, the low rasp of the zipper. *Last feeding June 2. Reorder cigs. Y'all stop dying or we won't have no one to work the day shift.* That last one's a joke. Or Crane thinks it is. The gas station's never kept regular hours.

Then there're the camera feeds. The front lot with the gravel and pumps, the dark smudge of the road almost visible after nightfall but not quite. The sales floor with the register and self-serve coffee machines, currently unattended. The manager's office camera looking down at their backs. The locked room with the hive of worms and flies.

Levi grabs Crane's hips and pushes inside him. No condom, no lube, no foreplay to get him wet, besides the hand around his throat thirty seconds ago. It hurts. Crane lurches forward, gasps, nearly knocks the monitor off the desk. Levi steadies it. His thumb is on the screen by the hive, covering where blood's gummed up the tile grout.

"Easy," Levi says with that throaty rasp guys get when they're finally inside halfway-decent pussy. "God, you feel good."

He's right. It feels good. It stings, burns the way it does when you're unprepared as hell, but that's half the point, and Crane watches himself get fucked raw on the security camera monitor because he can't get off unless he feels sick to his stomach about the whole thing.

That's how it's gone for as long as they've been together. Levi shoving him against a wall, pushing fingers between his teeth, and Crane taking it whether he wants to or not, because it's not as good if he gets a choice. Levi smells like Marlboro Reds and the gun cleaner he uses on his Mossberg 12-gauge. When he fucks, his dog tags clink together. Crane gets the idea that Levi likes the sound of it, and that's okay, he does too. Fine, he'll spread his legs as much as he can, hobbled by his jeans, whimper like a bitch in heat, reach down to get himself off. He can be a man while there's another man's cock in his pussy, if that's what he wants to call himself. Sure.

Something moves on the security camera, and it's not them.

Crane scans the cameras in a blur, tries to clock where he saw it but can't. He reaches behind him to get Levi to stop, hold on, he *saw* something, but Levi grabs his wrist and wrenches it behind his back. It throws Crane off-balance. He slams cheek-first into the desk, and his teeth cut the inside of his mouth.

"The hell you fighting for?" Levi rasps, suddenly so close to his ear. Still fucking him. Doesn't even break rhythm. God, that feels good, *please*— "Thought you liked when it hurt."

He does. He does he does. Never mind the screen, it doesn't matter, it can't be that important. He wants Levi to use the bruises on his throat as a map of where to put his hand again, squeeze until his vision goes black at the edges. Or, or he can struggle again, make a fuss, see if Levi might call him a *faggot*, because there's nothing quite like a slur to really make his cunt throb.

Unfortunately, when the monitor flickers again, he catches it.

A person. An indistinct column with a head and four limbs at the edge of the front lot camera 1, shambling up the gravel drive from Corridor H to the pumps.

And, on back room camera 5, the hive is awake.

Shit. Shit, *shit*.

Crane straightens up. Shifts his weight back, jams his free elbow against Levi's ribs. *Let go.* But Levi doesn't get it; doesn't see the monitor, doesn't grasp the situation, whatever. He grunts, "What are you—" and slaps a hand over Crane's face to hold him still.

So Crane bites.

"*Jesus!*" Levi pulls out with a sudden wet sound, backs away, and yanks up his pants like there're other things Crane might be keen on biting.

There aren't. Crane is too busy catching his breath, trying to cover up.

Crane's going to regret this later, but that's fine. He's looking forward to it.

"What?" Levi barks. As if shocked that the autistic guy he's been using as a sex toy for two years is acting like an autist. A mark is blooming on Levi's hand. The imprint of each tooth is already black. "What the fuck is wrong with you?"

Crane points to the security camera monitor.

Levi strong-arms him out of the way and tilts the screen to a better angle. While Crane readjusts the padding of his sports bra and zips up his jeans, Levi inspects the feed of the manager's office, the two of them in the dark surrounded by files and old boxes and cleaning supplies, then the front lot, then the hive.

Levi says, "New girl, huh?"

Crane is not the best person to greet a terrified and potentially unwell stranger, but better him than Levi. Levi talks about putting down defectors the same way hunters brag about bagging deer. He drinks too much. He'd been dishonorably discharged and only ever mentioned it to bitch about getting caught; what he did, Crane refuses to ask, but when he comes home with blood on his shirt, it's hard not to mull over the possibilities.

In comparison, then, Crane is the safer option. The boyish half-androgyny of twenty months' testosterone therapy—sparse facial hair, yesterday's eyeliner, almost-but-not-quite flat-chested, and a little too feminine around the mouth—places him squarely in the territory of *not a threat, probably*. It's just the dull stare and unblinking silence that throws people off and, well. This person will have to deal with it.

The girl is halfway across the parking lot when Crane steps out to meet her.

She's barefoot and glassy-eyed, one tank top strap slipping off her dirty shoulder. Hasn't showered in a while, given the state of her hair. The shitty fluorescent lights make it difficult to tell bruises from shadows. She's limping too. Feet are bleeding.

She walked here, then. From where? The closest town is a few miles up the mountain, but if she was from Washville, he would've recognized her.

She sees him and stops.

He waits a moment to see if she starts talking. She doesn't.

Down the gravel driveway, on the easternmost stretch of West Virginia's Corridor H, a truck grumbles past, headed toward the state line. To one side of them, there's old forest; one minute's walk to the other, the condemned livestock exchange. Nobody else for a good long while.

Crane's stomach hurts. He'd been in her place once, three years ago. Creeping too close to his eighteenth birthday, drunk for the first and only time in his life in the high school parking lot, striking matches and letting them burn out. He'd accepted a spot at a top state school earlier that year—majoring in political communication—and graduated salutatorian that morning. The packing list for his dorm was taped to the fridge, and while his classmates kicked off the rest of their lives at the school-sponsored YMCA grad party, there he was in the dark alone, trying to figure out the logistics of self-immolation.

All his childhood prayers had fallen through. There'd never been a car accident or building fire to do the hard part for him. Time was up. Childhood was over, the real world was knocking on the door, and he was tired. He was too scared to die, but he needed it to stop, and it was then or never.

But even after years of fantasizing and hoping and begging God, he still didn't have the guts to do it.

That's when the swarm found him. Because that's what happens: it finds you. By the time it makes you an offer, it already knows you won't say no, and then you end up in front of a strange building, hours from home in the middle of the night, with blood in the back of your throat and burns on your fingertips.

Same story every time, it seems.

Crane takes one cautious step forward, then another. The girl in the parking lot wavers, looking warily over her shoulder like she's thinking of running. Nope. She made her choice. Running won't do her any good.

He clicks his tongue to get her attention and holds up a bottle of water. *Here*, the gesture says.

"Who—?" she says, sounding sick, like she has a head cold.

The bottle gets a shake. *Come on. For you.*

She blinks, then picks her way through the sharp gravel to accept it. It takes a few tries to get the bottle open, but when she does, she sucks it down like she hasn't had a drop for days. When she has to stop to wheeze for air, she pours some onto her face. She splutters, blinking, and aha, there she is. Wild with hunger and confusion. Alive.

She starts to cry.

He'd cried too.

"Thank you," she sobs, "thank you," and Crane stands in the dark, looking past her to the road and rubbing the scar on his wrist, because he can't stand to look someone in the eye.

If he'd actually gotten the guts to do it that night, to actually set the match to something instead of shaking it out every time the flame licked his fingers, how would it have gone?

His burning—*Sophie's* burning, the brown-haired girl in a Forever 21 dress, the sweet female-thing that had existed in Crane's place for so many years—had been premeditated to a degree worthy of institutionalization. She knew she wanted only the face to burn. That was the most bang for her buck, or more accurately, the most visible damage in the least amount of time. She also knew she was a coward, and did not have the willpower to go up in stoic silence like a monk or the activists lighting themselves up in rows on the Capitol steps. The face was enough; it would have to do.

Maybe she would've siphoned gas from the car's tank to smear across her cheeks, or the liquor she'd been choking down would work. The logistics weren't important. What's *important* was that she burned. The scars would be permanent, and she would be free. She'd already written a speech in her Notes app for her future doctor, explaining exactly why she didn't want reconstructive surgery. It's expensive, she'd say, and extra stress on a delicate part of a human body, and it's not worth it, and *I don't want you to do it, please don't fix it, if you fix it I'll do it again, I'll do it again I swear I will.*

She'd say, *I'm sorry I didn't have the words to say it any other way.*

Crane leads the girl inside, turns off the OPEN sign, and locks the door. She's worse up close. White face discolored like it'd been beaten in, fingers bloody and broken-nailed. Her feet track a red-brown mess.

Is Levi still in the office? Thank god. Give her a second to get it together without him.

"Sorry," she sniffles. "You probably just mopped, too. I'm Jess."

Crane shrugs, because that statement presumes he isn't used to cleaning up bodily fluids, and reaches behind the register to bring out the basket. His manager, Tammy, put it together a decade ago, and some of the stuff is still that old: wet wipes, bandages, Neosporin and tweezers, fresh socks and snacks and dry shampoo and mouthwash.

Jess watches it warily before he nudges it toward her, offers some semblance of permission. She immediately snatches up every calorie she can find.

"Thank you," she says, hands full of cheap granola bars. "Uh. Can you talk?"

Crane nods.

"Oh."

It's been a while since the hive brought in somebody new. Used to be two other guys who worked here, Mike and Harry, but Mike died of mouth cancer and Harry started screaming about botfly larvae and tapeworms in his belly, so Levi had to put him down. Cleaning blood and bone pieces off the floor was bad enough, but the impact on Crane's work schedule for the past few months rubbed salt in the wound. He cannot wait to show this girl how to work the register.

While she finishes her water and demolishes the granola bars, Crane texts Tammy. Texting doesn't count as writing things down, as long as it's a situation in which any normal person would text. Otherwise it's a no go. It drives Levi up the wall.

Crane: Got a new one. Let me know when ur up.

That's followed by, *Did u know?*

Tammy will get the girl a phone and some clothes, set her up in the guest room in the back of Tammy's too-old house, the sparse and drafty room that used to be Crane's. Some woman from a Georgia hive will build a fake ID and ship it up in a few weeks. Whoever Jess was before will shrivel away, and a new person will molt—so to speak—into its place. There's a lot of work to do.

But before any of that, fake IDs or instructions on how to clean the coffee machines, she needs to get those feet to stop bleeding.

Crane gives her the milk crate he sits on for slow shifts, and she slumps onto it, hoisting up a foot to assess the damage. Not as bad as it could be; more mud than blood, what with the summer rains coming through the mountains. Crane cracks open another water bottle to soak a paper towel and presses it into her hands. Clean up.

Her face nags at him, to the point he starts chewing on his lip ring. She's familiar in a way he can't put his finger on.

"Um." Scrubbing her feet, Jess takes stock of her surroundings: the cramped sales floor, dirty coffee machines, cigarettes behind the counter. She's adaptable, then. Even struggling through tears, she's trying to keep a cool head. Good. "What's your name? Can you write it down?"

"His name's Crane."

Jess whips around with a yelp. It's just Levi, though, leaning against the door to the employee area, nonchalantly pulling a cigarette from the pack and popping it into his mouth. Jess studies him. The muscles in her neck are taut.

"Like the bird?" she says.

"He's a mute. He ain't silent or nothing, makes all kinds of noise when you get him going—" He grins, using the beat of silence to produce a cheap lighter and get the flame going. Crane's face burns. "But besides that, good luck getting a word out of him. I'm Levi. You smoke?"

"No."

Crane doesn't make a habit of smoking, either, but he still makes a low noise in the back of his throat and holds out a hand. Even an inconsiderate roommate-slash-fuckbuddy-slash-boyfriend-is-too-strong-a-word-but-the-closest-they-have like Levi catches the drift. He comes over to place a fresh cigarette in Crane's mouth and lights it with the gruff homoerotic flair possessed only by ex-soldiers, cocking an eyebrow at the door.

We're gonna finish what we started, right?

Crane breathes in so the flame catches. Of course they are.

Levi, content with that answer, snaps his lighter shut and slings an arm over Crane's shoulder. "So. You look like shit, missy. Where you walk from?"

"My boyfriend's place," Jess says cautiously. "On the other side of the lumberyard."

Five miles as the crow flies; longer if she stuck to roads. Hell of a trek to make with no shoes. Still doesn't explain why Crane's never seen her, though.

"This about him?" Levi says.

Jess hesitates, but nods.

"We can work with that. You need anything?"

Jess inspects her fucked-up hands. The worms or flies don't give a shit about morals, but it doesn't seem like this boyfriend of hers will be missed any.

She says, "Can—can I see them? I want to say thank you."

Of course, Crane thinks. He'd wanted to see them too; an animal desperation to meet the first things to understand him, no matter how horrific they were. So he helps her to her feet, steadying her when she hisses in pain, and Levi takes the key from under the register, and together they walk her across the sales floor through the manager's office, to the heavy iron door set into the dark back wall.

Jess holds tight to Crane's arm.

Levi fights with the lock for a moment, muttering under his breath before it gives way, and . . .

Oh child, the hive says with its thousand chattering jaws and the buzzing of a thousand wings; the flesh flies swarming in thick mats, the wet bodies of soft worms hiding in piles of regurgitated bone-pulp. The smell is revolting. ***Our cherished one, hello, hello, hello.***

As if only half-aware of what she's doing, Jess takes one step forward, then another. Crane, out of instinct, or maybe like a child, covers the scar on his wrist. He still remembers the sting, how for a moment he thought the worm would dig itself into his arm and never come out.

You've made it. You are safe. You are home.

Levi takes Jess by the arm and turns his own hand to show the ugly mark bitten into his skin. "Look at that," he says. "You're gonna get your own. Hold out your— There we go. Don't flinch. You can take it."

A singular, dripping worm extricates itself from the mass. Jess breathes in and nearly chokes on the rotting stink.

When it bites down, she screams only a little.

You will feel the sun on your face when we cannot.

Three

It's been a week, and according to Tammy, Jess hasn't tried to run away or kill herself yet—mainly just slept in the spare bed and crammed down every ounce of food she could find in Tammy's cabinets—so looks like the girl is here to stay.

Levi's gone on a work trip, headed to a hive that's rooted itself in an impound yard just outside McDowell County. Crane couldn't get the details before he left, but Tammy says a girl from down there asked after him. That hive is about to have a shit time, then. His F-150 in a parking lot is the equivalent of a pirate's black spot.

"He bought bullets, didn't he?" Tammy says as she gathers up the accounting books. Half her fingers are arthritic and permanently straightened into sticks. Crane, chewing on a toothpick behind the register, wonders if she got to choose which position her hands would stay in for the rest of her life, or if her joints decided for her. His stomach's been turning all day and the toothpick kind of helps. "Thought I saw him at Walmart with a box of slugs. The price on them is getting real bad, ain't it?"

Crane makes a little noise: *I'm not interested in how inflation is affecting the price of ammunition, Ma.*

"Last I heard from down there," Tammy continues, "the old bitch that runs the impound lot—Beth, you remember her? She came up last year. She was getting into it with Billy. Now, I don't agree with the way she does things, but the way Billy reacted, that was just uncalled for." She bats away Crane's arm to pluck the large-print calculator from behind him. "And if word gets out and cops start sniffing around, that's no good."

Crane makes another noise, this one derisive. If a cop gets too close to this hive, he'll handle it. He's done it before.

"Exactly. So I think your man's just headed down to knock some sense back into him." She falls silent for a moment, propping her hands on her hips. "You doing good without him? You look a bit—hmm. You feeling alright, sweetheart?"

He feels no worse than usual, which is always a little bad. He gestures her away from the register. She has more important things to do than nag at him, like cook the books so the franchise owner down in Florida continues to ignore them.

"Fine," Tammy says. "I'll leave you be. I know how you kids are."

As soon as she's shuffled off and closed the door to the manager's office, Crane grabs his phone to open the encrypted messaging app.

In the group chat, Aspen and Birdie are talking about the latest rash of Supreme Court rulings. Their tendency to natter back and forth via text used to confuse him; they're married, live in the same DC-suburb townhouse, and have no problem with mouth-speech, so it seemed like an odd choice. But Aspen said they want Crane to feel included, so the group chat it is.

Talking to people outside the hive is the sort of thing defectors do. But it's not like that. He swears. He's not going to leave— seriously, why the fuck would he, he's not leaving the hive, even if it kills him.

Aspen and Birdie are worried about him. That's all.

Crane: It's fucking LATE. Dont yall have real jobs

Birdie: real jobs don't schedule people on holidays, it's the fourth???

He checks the calendar. Shit, it rolled over to the Fourth of July a few minutes ago. Washville really must be dying if nobody started cracking off fireworks at midnight sharp.

Birdie: but yes this country continues to be a nightmare

Aspen: I'm still reading, gimme a second. Some coworkers think it's not as bad as it sounds but we'll see. While I do that, how are you holding up? We still good for this weekend?

Oh *shit*, he'd completely forgotten he'd agreed to a—what did Aspen call it, a "proof of life" this week. But three hours down the mountain, three back up, this stomachache, Tammy's joints flaring up, and Jess to keep an eye on? Even with Levi across the state, it's not going to work.

Crane: Manager thinks I look like shit but I'm fine lmao. Also we got a new trainee last week. Can't leave her alone for too long so. Can't come down. Sorry

Birdie: that sucks :(are you sure youre okay? we can do a video call instead if you want

Aspen: We'll miss you, but remember the drive isn't that bad if Birdie or I can get the day off. Anything you need at all, just let us know.

The idea of one of them coming up here makes his stomach turn.

Crane: I know

Aspen: Also I finished the release and yeah, it's bad. States' rights all the way, unless it's abortion in which case fuck us, right?

Birdie: ngl I miss the year where we actually had like three success-ful assassinations or whatever. bring that energy back!!! where is it!!!!

Crane stops responding, but Aspen and Birdie keep talking. They know it's tough for him. He turns the phone on vibrate so he can feel it buzz in his pocket, a reminder that he's being included in some way.

Maybe not visiting is for the best if he looks as bad as Tammy says. No need to freak them out worse.

Though it can't be *that* bad. He leans around the cigarette case to check his reflection in the dark mirror of the window, pulls down an eyelid, and wiggles the toothpick between his teeth. Besides the bruises Levi left a few days ago, finishing that unfinished business from the manager's office with a belt around Crane's neck, there's only the usual eyebags and unbrushed hair. That, and his most recent ink: a centipede above the left elbow. He's covered from his ankles to the back of his neck, a sketchbook for whatever artist is doing shitty flash work for cheap.

Birdie thought she'd seen through it all the first time she'd met him. The tattoos, the dozen piercings scattered across his ears and face, it was all clear to her. "It's gender-affirming, obviously," she'd said like she'd cracked the code. "I mean, look at you."

Crane hadn't had the heart to correct her and say that if he hadn't been able to set himself on fire, he'd needed to change *somehow*.

Either way. It's good to see yourself through someone else's eyes. He leans closer to the reflection and tries to step into another pair of shoes, inspect himself as if he was a stranger. It's not easy. A total lack of self-image, he's heard, is an autism thing. Or a trauma thing, Aspen would point out.

But he's not traumatized. A walking collection of bad decisions, sure, and a masochist with way too many messy kinks, absolutely. *Traumatized?* That word is for veterans and rape victims, not him.

After all, the hive saved him.

His phone buzzes one more time. Right. Might as well check out Aspen's official review of the country's current sociopolitical situation.

It's not them.

Jess: Hi, is this Crane? Sorry, I should've told you Tammy gave me your number

Jess: I think I killed my boyfriend

Jess: I don't know what to do

As soon as Crane barges into the office and shows Tammy the message chain, she's shoving car keys into his hand. "Lord above, did she *walk* there? Go get her before she does something stupid. *Git!*" So now he's pulling eighty-five on an empty stretch of Corridor H past Washville, ignoring the upset whine of his achy old Camry and turning up the radio until high notes of some Top 40 song sting his eardrums.

Levi should be doing this. Crane is queasy and pissed about it. This is supposed to be *Levi's* job, and the son of a bitch is in *McDowell*.

Jess: Past the lumberyard, once you cross the one-lane bridge. You know where that is? Has a chest freezer on the porch, Chevy in the driveway, light's on

Jess: Jesus Christ

Jess: I'm gonna be sick

Jess: Oh shit I think he's moving

The lumberyard isn't technically in Washville, it's closer to Crane and Levi's apartment in the greater Wash County unincorporated area, but it's still the Washville lumberyard because there aren't any other landmarks for miles. Mike used to work there before the swarm found him. According to the stories, so many people ended up with nails in their hand that the injury was given the shorthand *crucifixion*, as in, *Did you hear that John got crucified last week?*

Jess: Yeah he's still breathing oh my god

Crane doesn't like it, but that doesn't mean he can't do it. Levi made sure of that.

Five miles, five minutes later, and Crane is in front of the house—this one-story gray thing plunked on the side of a dirt road—throwing the Camry into park and grabbing his go bag from the front seat.

Jess stumbles out to the concrete steps. She's a ghost backlit by the grainy porch light smothered with moths and skeeter-eaters, leaning against the chest freezer to keep her balance. It makes Crane feel like a horror movie monster: carrying a bag of murder equipment, tightening heavy-duty gloves, walking up to a girl in a cabin where neighbors would maybe only hear if she screamed.

He tries not to think about that last part too hard. Her hands have only just started to heal.

"I thought—" Jess tries. She's swaying nervously, keeps staring at the bugs swarming the porch light. She's following their panicked buzzing against the glass with her too-familiar eyes. "They said I should do it. I thought I—"

Crane catches her by the upper arms, squeezes, breathes in slowly to get her to do the same. She gets the hint, scrambles to follow his cue. He breathes out. So does she.

Easy, it says. Slow the heartbeat, get the lungs under control. It's what Levi told him when he was eighteen, covered in the shit-smelling pulp that spills out of a cut intestine. You can't lose your cool. You panic and you get stupid, and when you get stupid you get hurt.

She says, "I thought I hit him hard enough."

Good thing there's a fix for that.

Inside, the house is all wood paneling, crusty beige carpet, absolutely trashed. FOX News mutters on the TV, a corner of the screen exploded into a rainbow mess of pixels. A bowl of Cheerios sits uneaten on the coffee table. Crane casts around for an idea of what they're dealing with and finds it in a hunting photo on the wall: four guys in blaze orange with guns and bucks.

If Levi was here, he would've clocked the photo in an instant and put a finger against Jess's temple like a cold metal muzzle. "You find that gun cabinet and you keep an eye on it, girlie. If that poor fucker gets to it before you do: *pshew.*" Gunshot noise from the corner of the mouth. "You're out."

Crane is studying it too closely. Jess clears her throat. "You, uh. Won't have to worry about that."

Fine. Time to show her the ropes.

This son of a bitch, as it turns out, is currently on the bedroom floor trying to get on his feet; key word being *try* because it's not going well. Crane wouldn't be surprised if he's being puppeteered by adrenaline alone. There can't *be* much else. His skull is dented, and the swelling is trying to squeeze his pale little eyes out of his face.

The latest attempt to stand fails. Gross, Crane thinks.

Jess wraps her arms around her ribs. She won't come into the room. She stands in the hall, toes barely crossing where the vinyl floor cuts to cheap carpet, studying the torn-up doorframe and old plywood nailed over the windows. There are too many locks on the door. Some of them are broken.

"Yeah," Jess says when Crane gives her a quizzical frown, making sure that this is: one, her boyfriend; and two, the state she left him in, not a total surprise. "Bad, right."

Those words—or maybe Jess's voice itself—sets him off. As much as someone can be *set off* with most of their brain destroyed. He swings his head around, tries to get an arm under him, can't manage it. Saliva drips from his cockeyed mouth.

"Jess," he slurs in the way half-dead people have a tendency to. "Jess."

If they wanted to, they could wait this out. That head trauma, that's something else. Seriously, what did she use? Crane sidesteps to check the room and finds a dumbbell halfway under the bed. It'd be funny if it wasn't such a bad decision. This is why she was supposed to wait for Levi—he'd have talked her through it. He'd have handled it like a soldier. He's not here, though, so the two of them could honestly shut the door, head to the living room, flip through the TV channels, and check back in half an hour.

But any risk is too much, and Jess has to learn.

Crane sets the bag down on the bed, digs out a hammer, and flips it into his hand.

This guy must have some sense left in that brain, must be able to see something, even with all his gray matter scrambled up, because he starts moving again. Trying to get away. Prone on his belly, he grabs the foot of the bed, hauls himself forward an inch, leaving a slick wet trail where he can't pick his head up properly.

Crane plants a booted foot on the lower back—no, none of that, thank you—and nods Jess in. Let's make it quick.

Levi would be explaining the situation right now. Every detail, starting with whatever weapon was in hand that day. It has to be a weapon with plausible deniability, he'd say, in case you bump into the law. Mike used to keep a nail gun in his truck at all times; Harry carried a knife in the same bag as a pair of antlers and a hunting permit; Levi's Mossberg shotgun is a self-defense model perfect for a rural county where 911 doesn't pick up half the time. A hammer's an easy sell to a cop, so it's perfect for a mute.

Jess steps cautiously into the bedroom like it has teeth—to her, it might—and tries to breathe through the mouth instead of her nose. There we go. The man squirms and Crane puts more weight on him, clicking his tongue to keep Jess's attention. Don't look at the windows, don't think too much about what's happening. It's already halfway done, and once you do it the first time, it's easier all the others, promise.

Hammer in hand, pinkie outstretched, and crouched a bit over the struggling mess, Crane traces the path for her. Sketches where the damage has already been done, where she won't have to hit as many times. Right here.

"I don't know," Jess whispers.

Crane gives her a stern look—or something to that effect, expressions are tough for him. Yes, it's difficult. She has to do it anyway. The hammer goes into her hand, fingers pressed around the handle and rotated so she's holding it the correct way, clawed end down. Think of the guy on the floor as a stubborn nail she has to pull out and discard. That's all.

The man, his swollen eyes drying out and pink foam bubbling out of his mouth, manages another word, or a vague approximation of English: "No," it sounds like, "no." Or maybe "oh," over and over.

Whatever it is, it makes Jess stumble. It makes her push the hammer away, her eyes panicked-horse whirling.

"I can't," she says.

The fuck is she talking about. She can't? The hive chose her for a reason. The flies wouldn't have crawled into this room as a horrible shimmering mass and coated the walls and buzzed in a disgusting cacophony if they didn't want *her*. Now she's here, they saved her, and hives don't appreciate it when their chosen people don't return the favor.

He gets up. Takes his foot off the worm-food. Grabs her.

She makes the smallest, most terrified sound he's ever heard.

It's not happening, he realizes. He can't force her—and if he does and it cracks something in her, shatters an irreplaceable piece of her psyche, then he's not going to be the one to put her down. No way in hell.

24

Fine. He'll do it himself.

To her credit, Jess doesn't think she can get away with not watching it happen. She's plastered herself to the threshold, fingertips resting perfectly along the claw marks marring the splotchy wood, but she does not turn away. Her eyes are trained on the hammer and the place it will come down.

Aspen and Birdie would be disgusted with Crane if they knew.

Crane hoists a leg over the man on the bedroom floor, puts all his weight on the back of the neck, and brings the clawed end of the hammer down twice.

Four

Jess, apparently, processes her feelings out loud.

Crane already has a stomachache and has spent the past few minutes developing a gross knot of nausea in the crux of his throat. Now, on top of checking his rearview for stray cops wandering in from the next county over and staring daggers at the speedometer— commit only one crime at a time, never crack forty-five while there's a body in the trunk—he has a headache too.

He puts the collar of his shirt into his mouth to pick at a thread that's come loose from the stitching. Sure, murder would make anyone nervous. He can't fault Jess for handling it in a way that happens to be annoying.

But he cannot deal with this right now.

"And this is normal for you?" Jess asks, addressing Crane for the first time since she started talking. "You're used to this?"

Well, yes. Mike and Levi made sure of that. Getting locked in the trunk of a car with a corpse in the middling heat of a West Virginia summer, with all the choking death-stink, Levi with a timer and Mike sitting on the trunk to keep it closed—that would do the trick.

What had Mike said when he pulled Crane out of that trunk by the hair? *"The hive's got no use for scared little girls."*

In the grand scheme of things, Crane is being downright kind.

Jess scrubs a hand over her face, tugs at her cheeks, squeezes her nose like she's trying to get feeling back in her body. "Okay," she says. "Okay. It's just that—you didn't hesitate. Sean's dead. You just did it. Oh my god. Okay."

Crane doesn't look at her, just huffs, hopes the message that comes across is, *Of course I did.*

Jess says, "And what happens if I can't do it? If I decide nope, I'm out, I take it back?"

Crane hits the brakes.

The Camry screeches to a halt at a red light, the only stoplight in Wash County, where it's just them in front of the Dollar General. The lumberyard looms in the distance.

A single sentence in the Notes of Crane's phone: *We kill you.*

He shows it to her. He looks at her like, *Do you see this? Do you understand what you've agreed to?* Was the swarm unclear, was the bite on your wrist not enough to drive the point home?

Would you rather be in that house, with that man, with whatever he did to you?

Would you rather be out there in the world alone?

No. Of course not.

The light turns green.

"I wasn't going to," Jess says weakly. "I just wanted to ask."

He shouldn't be such a bitch. Think about what the man on the bedroom floor—Sean, apparently, as if he deserves a name—must have done to her to put her in the path of a hive. To make her face down the swarm of white-striped, red-eyed flesh flies crawling in through the gaps of her makeshift prison cell, swallowing the walls and popcorn ceiling with that mind-killing hum:

Oh child, your hands—your bruises—oh child, what has he done to you? When is the last time you saw the sun?

Think about what must have been done to her, to make her look at *that* and say *yes*.

In the face of that, what gives Crane the right?

Because nobody even did anything to him. He had never been hurt, never abused, never molested, never beat. He'd been pretty, and smart, and so very good at smiling through the urge to self-immolate. Hell, his parents had even loved him.

It's just that, at some point in his mother's womb, through no fault of hers or his father's or his own, he'd been put together incorrectly.

Oh child, this world was not made for ones like you. Come with us, come with us, come with us.

He shouldn't be such a bitch, but he looks over at the girl in the shotgun seat with her dark hair and skinny lips and bags under her eyes all just like his own, and no, can't manage it. Sorry.

If that's all he can do, Aspen and Birdie would say, that's alright for now. Just try to be a better person tomorrow.

Crane kills the car's engine by the delivery entrance at the back of the gas station, pops the trunk, and storms over to Jess's side of the car to bang his hand against her window. *Get out.* She flinches but does as she's told, standing away from him in the gravel lot the way she would if a wild animal wandered too close.

She can dislike him all she wants. He's doing her a favor.

In the trunk, the body bag has curled up on itself where it's been disrespectfully jammed between jugs of motor oil and antifreeze. The head was a bit of a mess, but the guy is still in one piece, so Crane counts this as an easy hunt. Still, the sick bolus in his throat won't dislodge. Nausea's been chasing him for days now. Weeks, actually. It's just that he's been bullying through it like he's done all his life.

Be a big boy and get over it. He nods Jess to him, has her grab the handles by the feet. *Let's get this son of a bitch up.*

Inside, Tammy is waiting for them, attempting to appear frustrated and not doing a very good job. As soon as the door closes and the two of them drop the body onto the floor beside the crates of beer waiting to go into the drink cooler, she's rushing over. Or the closest she can get to rushing with her knees so bad. She grabs Jess by the cheeks—Jess is taller than her by a good half foot, though that's not difficult—and checks her over. Her jaw, her mouth, her temple.

"You got all your pieces?" Tammy demands. "Not hurt nowhere, are you? Look at me, let me check your eyes."

"I'm okay," Jess says as her eyelids are unceremoniously pulled apart.

"Uh-huh." Next, Tammy takes Jess's wrists, turns them to inspect the bruises and scabs. "The bastard didn't put a hand on you?"

"I'm okay, I promise."

Tammy needs a few more seconds to believe her, but as soon as she's assured that the poor girl is all together and okay, she gives Jess a sharp granny-tug on the ear.

Jess yelps. "Ow!"

"What'd you go and do something like that for?" Tammy demands, gesturing at the door. Jess visibly scrambles to keep up with the one-eighty. "Did you *walk* to his house? All the way across the county? You're going to give an old woman a heart attack, you hear me?"

"Yes, ma'am," Jess whispers. "I just—I thought—they said I could."

Tammy's face softens for half a second. "I know, sweetheart. You've had a rough week. We'll get this done and we can go home." Then she turns on Crane. "And *you*."

For his trouble, he receives a pinch straight on the nose and a shake of his entire head. Crane gives an undignified squawk.

"At least the boys gave you a month to settle in!" she snaps. "Trying to get her to do it herself already, I cannot *believe* you."

Crane rubs his nose. Did Jess text Tammy to tattle on the drive back? Holy shit, what is she, five?

"Anyway." Tammy jingles the key. "Grab that body, let's get the worms fed."

The first time Crane saw his hive, it was an incomprehensible horror. The sight was so alien, he couldn't put the pieces together: scraps of clothing and chunks of hair, bones gnawed apart to scrape nutrients from the marrow, ossified calcium vomited into a wasp's nest taking up the entire storage closet. The flies slept in clumps and the worms pulsed like neurons under a microscope, or what Crane imagined that might look like.

These days, when he sees his hive, it's a moment of peace. He doesn't understand much, but he does understand this.

Children, the hive croons. **Hello, hello, hello.**

Today is different.

When Tammy opens that door, the smell hits like a brick. It's a meat freezer left unplugged, the trunk of Mike's car with the sunbaked corpse. Jess's eyes are watering; she's breathing through her teeth like she can filter out the rancid particles in the air. That's fine. She's not used to it. But Crane's stomach completely betrays him. His mouth waters, saliva lurching forward to protect the teeth and soft tissues from incoming stomach acid.

No, he is *not* going to throw up in front of Jess. He tries to swallow the mess of spit, but that makes it worse.

You care for us, and we care for you in turn.

This needs to be over with. Before he makes a mess. He drops the bag to the floor, making Jess hiss when the rough plastic strap is ripped from her hands, and fumbles for the zipper.

You treat us so kindly, children. You offer us so much. We are so lucky to have you.

Together, with Tammy watching because she doesn't have the strength for this anymore, they shove the corpse out of the body bag and onto the floor, spilling blood and brain matter across the tile. One arm ragdoll-flops onto the floor with a gross *smack.*

We thank you. We love you.

The hive descends. Chattering worms lunge from their calcium-keratin-synthetic fiber mound to burrow into the softest parts of Sean's body they can find. The cheek, under the jaw, crawling up the shirt into the stomach. The youngest worms are small, maybe as thick as Crane's thumb and a foot long, and quick as fuck. They crawl and chew and swallow, leaving behind a series of gaping wounds for their bigger, slower elders to follow them into the meat. Once the worms are done, then the flies will come down and pick the rotten parts clean, lay eggs to replenish the swarm. The cycle of life.

And as the worms feast, the flies talk about the space beyond the dark, stinking storage closet. How the sky is such a lovely shade of blue, then gold, then pink, then the deepest, richest purple. How the mountains are ancient and alive. How they are all so hungry and this little corner of the world is so perfect in the light.

"Holy shit," Jess breathes.

The room is the color of a cut-open stomach.

Crane can't keep it down anymore.

He stumbles out of the room—"Crane?" Tammy says—and can't open the delivery door properly, just slams into the push bar and lurches outside before he vomits.

It's the kind of throwing up that feels like getting punched in the stomach, that's so violent he can't get a breath in between one retch and the other. His lungs lock up. His throat collapses. He catches himself on the hood of the Camry, doubles over, makes that sick croaking sound that comes up with puke.

Once his stomach is empty, a string of drool falls from his lips to the gravel. His mouth tastes like sand and bitter, burning acid.

He gasps for air. Fuck. *Fuck.*

Behind him, the delivery door clacks shut.

"Crane?" Tammy says again. "Oh Lord, what a mess."

He spits, and she puts a hand on his chest to ease him upright.

"I was telling you," she murmurs, "you ain't been looking good."

He shakes his head. He's fine. It won't happen again.

Tammy won't take that for an answer. She sits him on the curb beside the ice cooler, presses the back of her hand to his forehead, tries to suss out a possible fever. There's nothing. The neon

CLOSED sign shines in the window. An ad for Camels stares across the empty lot.

"Hold tight," she's saying, "give me a moment."

Crane drops his head between his knees and spits again. He's fine. Yes, he's been feeling off lately, but he's always off. He spent most of his childhood vaguely nauseated. And he's tired, and his head hurts, and his stomach's been upset for so long. He's fine. He's *fine*.

Tammy comes back a minute later with a bottle of water: a godsend. "Here." He takes a mouthful and swishes before dribbling it out into the gravel. Stomach acid warps the taste, turning it so bizarrely sweet that he flips the bottle over to see if it isn't some newfangled sugared stuff, or maybe flat soda.

"And this too."

Tammy taps a box against his shoulder.

It's a pregnancy test.

Crane shoves it back at her. Stumbles to his feet, coughs like he's trying to get something out of his lungs. Absolutely not. He—no, it doesn't work like that. He's been on testosterone for almost two years, he hasn't had his period in nearly as long, there hasn't even been any spotting or anything.

You can't get pregnant on testosterone. It doesn't work like that.

Right?

Crane realizes, slowly, that he's not sure.

Tammy regards him like he's a child, and it makes him hate himself a bit. "Just take it," she says. Crane shakes his head. "Sweetheart, I am sixty-five goddamn years old. Believe me when I say I've seen my fair share of girls in denial. Not that I'm saying you're a girl, but I'm saying I know it when I see it."

She holds the box against his chest until he gives in.

All Crane can think is that pregnancy tests, for a minuscule while, had been gender neutral. There'd been a whole campaign about it when Sophie was in high school. Nobody had been asking for much—just, could companies please say pregnant people instead of pregnant women, and maybe could there not be so much pink on the box?

It'd worked, for a time. A few companies made the switch, taking the opportunity to turn a minuscule packaging decision into a sweeping promotional campaign celebrating their progressiveness, their inclusivity, their whatever. One commercial even showed a man looking down at his (flat) belly while a handsome husband rubbed his shoulders. How wonderful. After decades of fighting tooth and nail, a trans guy got to see himself on TV for three seconds.

But it backslid quick. None of it had made the companies more money, because of course it hadn't, and some far-right fuckface posted a video on social media with a gun, talking about finding the marketing execs responsible and executing them in Times Square. So this box in his hand is bright pink and says *women* so many times that it feels like groveling. *See? We're reasonable people who know what a woman is.*

He can't be pregnant. He can't.

Five

The first time Crane let Levi fuck him, it was the first time he'd let anyone fuck him. He'd been eighteen, and if he had to guess, Levi had a decade on him, and yes, that *was* part of the appeal—he'd been thinking about Levi fucking him for a while, and an age gap had become integral to the fantasy.

Looking back, Crane is unsure what Levi had seen in him. That was what he considers to have been his *try-hard* era: where a trans guy trying to look too much like a man simply embarrasses himself in the process. The haircut situation was in limbo, none of his thrift-store clothes fit the way they should, he hadn't lost the baby fat on his cheeks. He wouldn't even start testosterone for another few months.

Levi hadn't minded that, though. Or the silence. Levi knew what he wanted, and he knew Crane was going to give it to him. Maybe Crane had been obvious. Maybe it'd written itself on his face without his permission. He thought about Levi fucking him when Levi shared his cigarettes, offered hand-me-down camo jackets, and took him behind the store to teach him how to use the shotgun. He thought about it when Levi sat him up in the dirt after he'd been pulled from the trunk, and he thought about it when Levi shoved him to his knees in front of maggot-infested roadkill and told him to get in there with his hands. He was sick and terrified, and he wanted Levi to shove fingers down his throat.

Turns out if you treat the mute behind the counter like a real man, he'll do whatever you want.

When it finally happened, Levi had his jeans down to his thighs in the back of the F-150, saying he'd be gentle, it'd only hurt at first. Crane had blood on his face. He was shivering. Ten minutes ago, a cop had seen the security monitor and panicked, and Crane killed him; Levi was proud, he said, he kept saying how proud he was. Crane's job was to defend the hive and he'd done the right thing. In the back seat, Crane's tits were bitten red and black and he was having trouble breathing. He'd done it. He was scared. When the cop was dead, Levi had taken him outside and let him cough and wheeze, and he couldn't quite remember how he'd ended up in the truck with his bra shoved up and his boxers caught on one ankle.

But while Levi opened a condom wrapper with his teeth, Crane typed a sentence on his phone and pushed it into Levi's face.

Get me pregnant and I'll kill you.

What he'd meant was *I'll kill myself.* He just hadn't been able to type it out.

Big words for a man who couldn't even work up the nerve to set himself on fire.

Crane drives to the apartment just outside Washville with the box of pregnancy tests in his shotgun seat like another passenger. The radio is stressing him out. The country station runs sermons between songs: *"Do you have a personal relationship with Jesus?"* NPR reports on the wildfires choking out every inch of sky west of the Mississippi and an increase in deadly foodborne infections. The late-night host on the Top 40 station thinks disabled parking spots are stupid. He turns it off.

He'd known from a young age that he didn't want kids. It started as a general revulsion toward children and motherhood; hell, he hadn't liked kids when he was a kid. In elementary school, when the news ran sob stories about newborns abandoned in dumpsters or left behind in hospitals, he never understood why those mothers were called monsters. If he ever had a baby, he thought, that's what he'd do.

When he was older and he learned the mechanics of it all, it certainly didn't change his mind. A fetus cannibalizes the mother. It crushes organs, saps nutrients, would starve its host to death if biology allowed it. "Birth is a miracle," a health teacher claimed, but all Sophie could see was the blood. That night, she googled birth complications until she fell asleep, dreaming of uterine rupture and postpartum psychosis.

Then, the final nail in the coffin: Crane is a man. Sure, whatever, trans men can have babies and want them and love them, he doesn't give a fuck. *Do you understand that if there is a parasite inside me I'll kill myself?*

According to Aspen's review of the last slate of Supreme Court rulings, abortion is not only banned but now officially a murder charge in ten states. Including West Virginia. Effective immediately.

In the parking lot, Crane shivers. He can't swallow right anymore.

The apartment complex is less a complex and more a line of run-down, flat-faced squares built into a hill. When he and Levi moved in together, they weren't being picky. Just trying to get out of Tammy's guest bedroom and off Mike's couch, respectively. But the rental ad sounded decent. Cheap, close to the gas station, hardwood floors. The ad had not, however, detailed the pest problems and constant utility failures. This year, Crane is keeping a log—*July 2nd, no hot water, had to boil a pot on the stove to wash hair*—in hopes that he can get rent knocked down upon renewal, though he has a sneaking suspicion that nobody monitors the leasing office's email account anymore.

It takes five minutes to bully himself out of the car and into the complex. Someone's left a mess in the laundry room. The second washing machine is broken again, the lid wrenched off and propped up in the corner. And through the too-heavy apartment door, their one-bedroom shitbox isn't much better. Stained gray couch, cheap flat-screen set on a table pulled off the side of the road; clothes rack shoved into the corner because the dryer is three dollars a spin, next to the big black gun safe.

Crane dumps his go bag in the galley kitchen and locks himself in the bathroom, even though Levi's all the way across the state. The pink of the box is jarring here. The bathroom is all-white tile, stained mirrors, too-bright lights.

The anxiety is making him overheat. He strips off his shirt and stands there in his sports bra.

In the Schrödinger's space before he takes the test, there is both one line on the display and two. He is both pregnant and not. There is a universe where he gets a negative result and, he imagines, bursts into relieved tears. He'll collapse into bed, text Aspen and Birdie about how stupid today was, and pass out until noon. It'll be a bad day, that's all. He's had a lot of those.

In the universe where it's positive—

What? What is there? Besides static, a TV turned to a dead channel?

The smart thing to do in that situation would be to go to Tammy. Put the test on the table between them in a wordless cry for help. She would be able to fix it. She can do anything. But, god, the idea of showing up on her porch in a self-destructive panic, the way she'd look at him and know she'd called it—

Crane rips open the box and pries out the thin white stick like it's already a biohazard.

He chugs water from the sink even though his bladder doesn't need the assistance, squats over the toilet with the test, and leaves it on the edge of the counter to process for the required five minutes.

Five minutes ticking down on his phone's timer is an eternity. To distract himself, he sits on the edge of the tub to reread the instruction packet. He wonders if, when the company reneged on their inclusive packaging, and the abortion crackdowns really went wild, the wording on this booklet got changed, or if it'd always been this unnerving. Or he's overreacting. They're just instructions.

If POSITIVE, schedule an ultrasound with your healthcare provider. Prenatal and maternity care improves birth outcomes for both mother and child.

Fuck off.

Not for the first time, Crane wants Levi. Or, no, that's not right. *Want* is incorrect, too imprecise, and autism harbors a deep disdain for imprecise things. Crane wants Levi a lot, but in the way he wants the ache of a bruise around his neck. What he wants is Levi here. Sitting on the bathroom floor across from him, sucking on a cigarette while they both wait for the timer to run out. Crane would reach for that cigarette and take a drag to have something to do with his mouth.

Levi would not be comforting. He would not be nice about this. He'd get pithy, say it's Crane's fault this is happening. *"Did you skip a shot,"* he'd demand. *"Did you not inject enough, what did you do?"*

But that motherfucker would be here having to deal with it. He'd have to think about the split in the future and chew on it like Crane is doing alone. If it's negative, he'd growl *thank fuck* and storm out of the room. And if it's positive, he'd have a friend up north where it's all legal, can call in a favor, can get misoprostol and mifepristone across state lines. That's the whole point of this. Hives take care of their people.

If it's positive, maybe Levi would remember the note Crane typed and feel the same pit in his stomach.

The timer goes off.

Crane picks up the test and turns it toward the burning lightbulb, like he's not seeing it correctly, or he's looking at it from the wrong angle.

It doesn't change. The world doesn't work like that; the curve of the universe does not shift because he wants it to.

Crane wonders if he should feel something. He doesn't. He's just cold.

Six

spen and Birdie live in an HOA-approved townhouse three hours down the mountain, thirty minutes outside Washington, DC, all butterfly gardens and pride flags surrounded by soccer moms and SUVs. They bought the place when Birdie learned her brother was wanted for terrorism and turned over his info, dropping the reward on a down payment and bathroom repair. (The bathtub was leaking into the ceiling; sold as is.)

"I hate the feds as much as the next bitch," she'd said during one of the times Crane had found the time to visit. He was keeping her company while she potted flowers in a pink sundress, neckline plunging down to the scar her brother had left the first time he'd tried to kill her. Crane had taken to playing in the dirt. "But he's in prison and I have a house, so! Fuck it."

Crane has a key to the front door. It's on his key ring right now. He still knocks and waits for an answer.

Considering the situation, Crane thought he'd be having a worse reaction. Shouldn't he be having a meltdown? Completely losing his shit? Trying to DIY a hysterectomy, or whatever it is vets do when they spay cats and scoop out whatever half-formed kittens they find to toss into the biohazard bin?

He decides he's in shock.

Granted, when Aspen opens the door in boxers and an oversized T-shirt, rubbing sleep from their eyes, he does get pretty close to crying.

"Oh shit," Aspen says instead of hello, then hollers up the stairs: "*Birdie!*"

"*What?*" Birdie calls back.

"*Crane.*"

It must be something about being a father that allows Aspen to load a name with so much weight and concern that it needs no further explanation. Birdie rushes down the stairs with their three-year-old daughter Luna on her hip as Aspen guides Crane inside.

"Crane!" Luna says, though at her age it comes across more as a situationally inappropriate *Cwane.*

Birdie puts a hand on Luna's head to shush her. "Hey," she starts, eyeing him carefully because she's the person in the room most familiar with suicidal breakdowns. "Is it bad?"

Crane nods—and there it goes. He's sniffling in the foyer, then sobbing, and Aspen leads him into the living room with a pitying hum. "Okay, come on, let's go," they say, setting him onto the couch and fetching the weighted blanket to drape around his shoulders. Crane wraps it tighter. He needs the pressure. "There we go. Let me get—the iPad, where is it—here."

Aspen sits on the coffee table and holds out the tablet. Across the room, Birdie prompts Luna to pay attention to the TV, but Luna isn't having it, instead trying to figure out why Crane gets the device and not her. "Over here," Birdie whispers to her. "Let's give Crane a moment."

The tablet is open to the AAC app. A keyboard, a collection of pre-pared phrases, the saved history of sentences too complex to convey through facial expressions: *"Please." "Thank you." "I don't like that food." "How's the restraining order holding up?" "Did you hear about the queer center that got bombed last week?"* The usual.

Crane takes it, reacquainting himself with the screen through blurred vision. There's always a pang of guilt when he looks at this. AAC apps are expensive; what was this one, over a hundred dollars? And it's not like he had a stroke. He's not nonverbal. He could talk if he wanted.

"Can we ask?" Aspen says. "What happened?"

Whatever he types, the app will parrot in its synthetic voice. The cursor blinks invitingly. It is incapable of judgment.

He writes, *"I'm pregnant."*

Birdie says, "Oh fuck."

The thing about Aspen and Birdie is that they seem convinced they can "save" him. Why not? They managed to save themselves.

From what Crane has pieced together, the two of them barely made it to their mid-twenties alive. Birdie, for example, was raised by a drove of rich fascists alongside a brother who'd tried to off her at least twice. She transitioned in homeless shelters, catching glimpses of her family only when her father showed up on TV dog whistling the Great Replacement and white genocide.

"Please let him be one of them," she'd muttered once, wine drunk and doomscrolling, refreshing her feed in hopes she'd find her dad's name in the list of the dead. Reports were coming in from the Virginia State Capitol Building that afternoon—a homemade IED had taken out a few Democrats, with a singular Republican as collateral damage. Conservatives began the martyrdom process before the fumes cleared, and liberals weren't doing shit. Crane, who had no idea at the time that Birdie's brother was the culprit or that her father was a state senator, stared at her blankly. "God, do you think it was Dad's idea?" she said. "You think he's in on it?"

The courts must've decided that Birdie's father was not, in fact, in on it. Crane could pull up the Wikipedia page for the Virginia State Senate and find her father's name still on the roster.

And Aspen. Crane gets the sense he should know more about Aspen than he does, considering they went to the same high school. Saying they went to school *together* wouldn't be quite right, since there was only an overlap of one semester, but the point stands. To Crane, Aspen exists in three distinct pieces: there is Aspen the father, of course, who cares too much and collects floral tattoos as scar cover-ups on their wrists. There is Aspen the high school senior, who read gay porn in class and screamed at substitutes who read their legal name during roll call and spent a lot of time crying in the school darkroom.

Then there's Aspen the tangled knot of trauma that is not discussed under any circumstances. Crane's stumbled across threads he wasn't meant to find and never knows what to do with them. Aspen detransitioned and married the first guy they dated so their parents wouldn't have legal control over them anymore. Aspen didn't go to high school graduation because their husband-of-two-months wouldn't let them. Aspen didn't finish college and, in the eyes of the law, hadn't technically kidnapped Luna because she hadn't been born when Aspen bailed, but it'd been a whole thing. It's better these days, Aspen insists. With the restraining order and all.

Now the two of them see Crane and, Crane thinks, they see a bizarre remnant of what they'd been. A chance to help some version of themselves.

It's not that simple.

"Okay," Aspen says again, with forced calmness this time. "Okay. When did you find out?"

Crane types, "*This morning,*" then, "*Last night,*" then, "*2am I think.*"

"Luna baby," Birdie whispers. Luna, who is reasonable for a toddler in Crane's experience, looks up at her curiously. "Why don't we let Dad and Crane talk for a bit? Let's make breakfast."

"It's Levi's?" Aspen asks, as if Levi isn't the only person Crane has ever fucked in his life.

Crane nods.

"Does he know?"

Crane shakes his head.

"Are you safe?"

There's no good way to respond, no matter what version of the question Aspen is asking. Crane can see two branching implications. *Are you safe from that boyfriend of yours?* That question is fine, and has an answer, even if Aspen doesn't like it: yeah, sure. Crane can handle Levi. He's been handling Levi for a while, and he's good at it, and their relationship actually works, believe it or not. As if anyone else would *want* to fuck Crane. As if anyone else would put up with him for more than a few days or give him what he asks for.

But *are you safe from yourself?* That's another thing entirely.

Aspen's lips draw into a thin line. "How worried do we have to be about you?"

Birdie, overhearing this, hurries Luna off to the kitchen, turning on the fan above the stove to drown out their conversation. Crane clutches the iPad but doesn't type. He can't make his fingers move.

If he goes far enough back in the app history, he'll find the log from when he explained what happened before the swarm came. What he almost did. They know how much time he spent as a child staring into the mirror, trying to pull the skin off his face; they know he has the self-destructive drive.

The cursor on the tablet continues to blink. In the kitchen, Birdie starts the stove, sits Luna up on the counter, shows her how to crack an egg.

"Crane," Aspen says. "You like it when I'm straightforward, so I'm being straightforward: I'm not gonna sit here and guess why you don't talk. It's your disability, not mine."

Crane wants to protest the word *disability*, but on what grounds? He's fucking disabled.

"But you've told me yourself you're verbal, you're perfectly capable of typing, all that. Maybe—and I'm sorry, I'm going to sound like my therapist here—maybe you stopped talking because you felt like nobody listened, or because you struggled for so long to be understood that you said hey, screw this, you're done, it's everyone else's turn to do the hard part. And I get that. Really."

Aspen leans in, settles their elbows on their broad knees.

"But we're meeting you halfway. We've put in the work, haven't we? We're worried about you. So *type something.*"

Crane's fingers hover above the screen.

It takes him a moment—he keeps hitting the wrong keys, fumbling for the backspace button—but eventually the program murmurs, *"You know what I'm going to do."*

It's not much, but it is confirmation of the worst-case scenario. The sort of crisis Aspen must've predicted would come around, no matter how many times Crane tried to deny it.

They're going to use this, aren't they? *You couldn't even tell your boy-friend*; one more item to include in the list of myriad reasons why Crane needs to dump Levi and move away from Wash County. For his own safety.

God, they probably feel so vindicated right now.

Aspen immediately switches into problem-solving mode. "It won't come to that. If you caught this early, which—" Their eyes flit to his stomach. Crane wants to curl up into a ball. "Which you probably did, it'll just be a few pills. Undetectable in the blood, no different from a heavy period. And if it's not early, then we'll figure it out. I'll make some calls, see if I can't get you in somewhere tomorrow. Will tomorrow morning be too late?"

Tomorrow is fine. He can get the abortion and be back in Washville by evening. Nobody has to know.

On the other side of the open-concept first floor, Birdie walks Luna through frying up vegetarian sausage. Luna has Aspen's eyes and a stranger's blonde hair. Crane wonders if Aspen looks at their daughter and tries to convince themself that the blonde is Birdie's, overwriting a terrible history with a better one.

In the harsh kitchen light, Birdie's scar is a bright white line across the expanse of her chest.

The day is slow and soggy with brutal humidity. Crane had forgotten how hot it gets away from the mountains. By noon it's hit the mid-nineties, and the sun is bright enough to hurt; even on the most patriotic of holidays, because somehow it's still the goddamn Fourth of July, the world grinds to a halt and huddles into the shade.

Aspen produces a pregnancy test from the spare bathroom. They're kept under the sink and will continue to be kept there until the family saves up enough money for a hysterectomy or an orchiectomy, whichever insurance will approve first, because Birdie's unmedicated anxiety swears vasectomies aren't foolproof. Aspen insists that Crane take a test one more time. Rule out the possibility of a false positive. He acquiesces and it is immediately whisked away so he won't have to subject himself to the result.

Still, considering that Aspen is on the phone pulling favors from friends they've made as a journalism assistant, Crane can make an educated guess.

In the meantime, Birdie slathers Luna in sunscreen and sets up a tiny pool on their cracked back porch.

"I could use another set of hands with her," she says, "if you want to get your mind off things."

So Crane sits by the kiddie pool under the creaky yard umbrella, hands in the water and playing with Luna's pool toys more than she is. She keeps throwing waterlogged beanbags at him, and he keeps catching them. She's a good talker for her age. He didn't think kids could string together a sentence at three, but what does he know.

Around lunch, Birdie brings out peanut butter sandwiches and cucumbers. Crane doesn't feel great, but he tries to eat anyway.

He takes the tablet from the table—slightly overheating from the ambient temperature—and changes the AAC app from voice-over to large-type before writing, *I didn't think you could get pregnant on testosterone*, and flipping it around for Birdie to read.

She leans forward and nibbles on a cucumber spear. She's gorgeous in her sundress and wide-brimmed hat, heart-shaped glasses perched on the edge of her nose. Reminds him of a kestrel.

"I didn't think so either," she admits. She probably got the same spiel of well-meaning semi-misinformation when she started hormones. It destroys your fertility for good, it's borderline castration, there's time to rethink this permanent mistake, etcetera, etcetera. Turns out, one of the first Google results upon attempting to verify that information is a big all-caps THE DOCTORS DON'T KNOW SHIT. Crane feels deeply stupid.

He types, *Hell of a way to find out.*

Birdie giggles, because she giggles when she's uncomfortable. "Seriously."

After lunch, and after Luna splashes Crane's face and insists he's playing with her squishy crab wrong, whatever that means, Aspen comes out to the tiny backyard with phone held aloft.

"Tomorrow," they announce. "Nine in the morning. We'll be on the road by six."

Nine in the morning. Less than twenty-four hours and he'll be in a doctor's office getting this thing flushed out with a potent cocktail of chemicals and hormones. That means it's practically over.

He bumps his head against Aspen's thigh in thank-you. His hair leaves a wet spot on their shorts.

"I know," Aspen says softly.

"Would you want to stay a second night?" Birdie asks. "Just in case something happens?"

Crane closes his eyes.

If Birdie has one flaw—and sure, she has a few, she's nervous to a fault and insecure and a bit of a pushover—but if she has one, it's that she's obvious.

Stay. You don't have to go back.

He can't blame her for trying. As far as either of them knows, Crane is an old classmate who moved to a small town for a shit job and a shittier boyfriend. They've seen the bruises, read between the lines, asked questions he wasn't sharp enough to catch the true meaning behind. They're following the handbook. *What to do when your friend is in an abusive relationship; what to do when your friend is in a cult.* Bullet point number one: no matter what they're going through, don't let them go through it alone.

If they're pushier than the handbook says they should be, it's only because they're scared for him.

And yes. Sometimes Crane wakes up on their pullout couch and thinks about not going back. Sometimes he opens Aspen's yearbook and finds the picture of him and his parents on freshman orientation night and he considers it: breaking his phone. Dumping the car in a ditch. Hiding in this little townhouse for the rest of his life.

But.

This world was not made for ones like you.

Even if he survived defecting, even if this house would not be hunted and devoured for abetting it, it wouldn't be worth it. Seventeen years as Sophie, as a person, out there? It broke him. Might have killed him if he'd messed up that night in the car, if he'd ever gotten what he'd prayed for.

The hive saved him. The hive gave him permission to cut his hair and change his name and shut the fuck up. It's the hive that gives him a reason to exist, and it's the hive that puts a hand on the back of his neck and tells him what to do and god, *god*, please tell him what to do. Please take all his higher thinking from him. He doesn't want it. Sometimes when he feeds the worms and the flies, he mouths *thank you*, because they're the only things that have ever understood.

Nothing Birdie and Aspen do can change that.

Besides. If they knew everything he's done, they'd hate him.

When Crane shakes his head, Birdie doesn't seem surprised by the answer, but that doesn't mean she likes it. She stares off through the rickety back fence, where some kids are attempting a game of soccer. They keep calling for breaks, sucking down water, lying in the grass under a tall, tall tree shriveling in the heat.

He is vaguely aware that he is using the both of them for their kindness. If he was a better person, he'd ghost them already.

For what it's worth, the rest of the day is nice. When it's time for Luna's nap, she insists Crane tucks her in, which works fine since he immediately falls asleep on the floor beside her. Dinner is pasta, with sauce on the side because tomato sauce is a textural nightmare for half the table, and Luna picks the evening movie. Crane can't keep his eyes open. He realizes it's over only when Aspen nudges him awake, motioning that it's time to make up the couch.

Crane turns the tablet over and tries to decide whether he wants to say this.

"Can I sleep in your bed?"

The bed isn't built for three people, but they make it work. Crane curls up between them—Birdie on one side, Aspen on the other—and Birdie splays her warm hands across the tattoos under his shirt, the way she soothes her daughter on a bad day. The two-headed lamb on his shoulder. The black line down his spine. The clusters of snakes, roses, bugs across his hips and arms. The lines are thin and wobbly, but he likes it that way. He wants to get some on his hands soon.

Once this is done, he'll reach out to that artist in Shepherdstown. Drop fifty dollars on a flash piece. That'd be nice.

Seven

Crane gets sick again that night, which is why he hears the back door open.

He'd always been under the impression that morning sickness wasn't, like, actually a *thing*. A bit of nausea during pregnancy makes sense, sure—there's a lot of reorganizing going on down there, none of which could possibly feel good. But it had taken on such a mythic level of cultural shorthand that he'd become skeptical. Getting sick is movie shorthand for pregnancy, like coughing blood is for dying. There was no way it was legit.

Morning sickness is in fact a thing, he decides, sitting on the cool tile of the en suite bathroom and pressing his forehead against the ceramic of the toilet. He dry-heaves twice and coughs saliva into the bowl. Spits. Wipes his lip with a square of toilet paper.

Only a few more hours left. This will be inside him for only a few more hours.

He scrubs his face, grateful that Aspen took a makeup wipe to his smeared eyeliner the same way they scrub crumbs from Luna's mouth, and he taps his palm to his chest to calm down. He knows the drill. Sophie spent her senior year on the verge of vomiting. Keep moving to distract the gag reflex, but don't touch the neck or turn the head. Keep the jaw locked. Breathe through grit teeth.

A few more hours.

He doesn't want to, but for the first time since the positive test, he touches his stomach. He digs his fingers into the fat that's gathered on his belly since starting testosterone. It doesn't feel any different under there. No hard knotting under the skin where a swelling uterus would be. On the floor, he cradles his phone and looks up the cutoff for a medical abortion. Nine weeks. A little over two months. That should be fine. He caught this early—he thinks. Without a period, there's no way to tell, to count backward or know for sure. But nine weeks? It can't have been longer than that.

After this, Levi has to go back to wearing condoms. Or, at least, he can't cum inside him anymore until they figure out what's going on. Does birth control mess up hormones? He'll look that up later.

When the wave of nausea passes, Crane hauls himself up to the sink and drinks from the faucet. Water splutters from his chin and catches in his pubescent facial hair, a gift from his father's side of the family tree.

Downstairs, the back door grumbles open on its track.

Crane closes the faucet.

Aspen and Birdie have a lot of faith in their sliding back door, and especially in the shoddy latch working in tandem with the don't-kill-me bar jammed into the track. Crane can't remember if the bar was put back in place when they came in yesterday. Is Luna tall enough to reach the latch? She can't be. Unless she's smart enough to drag over a box to stand on.

He waits for another sound.

Thinks he hears *something*.

Shit.

Crane slips out of the bathroom, quiet as he can to avoid waking the two so peacefully in bed, and eases into the hall.

The townhouse isn't huge. There's the washing machine behind a squeaky folding door, the HVAC closet that never closes all the way, Luna's room at the end. Buying a house was a pipe dream, Aspen and Birdie explained once, and the delight of having *their* place is visible on every inch of the walls. The mortgage closing date written in pink Sharpie by the baseboard, Luna's height etched by the stairs, houseplants allowed to anchor themselves to the paint.

Owning a house had always seemed insurmountably nerve-racking to Crane. The property taxes? The repairs? The responsibility? No thank you. He'd never given it more thought than that, though. Growing up, Sophie figured she wouldn't own anything until her parents died and their four-bedroom colonial ended up in her name, maybe, if she could swing said taxes. See what it took for Aspen and Birdie to buy a place? A terrorist attack.

Crane peeks into Luna's room.

She's soundly asleep on her mattress, surrounded by stuffed animals and a glittery princess canopy.

Shit.

He slides the door shut and braves a glance down the stairs.

Nothing on the landing except a thrifted mirror. No light except the streetlamps dotting the parking lot, shining vague yellow that isn't truly enough to see by.

If that's it, then the least he can do is check the back door. Confirm it's locked, that the noise was just the air conditioner churning in the middle of the night, then crawl back into bed. Curl up in a safe harbor until morning. He's a grown man. He can do that.

Crane pads silently down to the landing and opens his phone—no messages from Levi, or Jess, just a few concerned questions from Tammy to ignore—to pop on the flashlight.

There's a man at the bottom of the stairs.

The bullet of fear feels like getting turned inside out.

The back door is wrenched open, the latch is broken, and there's a man staring at him. It's not even Levi. It's some fucker in black work clothes and heavy treads in the fucking July heat, the hood and neck gaiter leaving only a set of beady blank eyes exposed and *watching*.

Except for the thick black gloves. The left one peeled back to show the hive-bite punched into the wrist.

In this moment, paralyzed with phone in hand, Crane is not thinking about the appointment at the Washington, DC, clinic he's not making it to. There's no moment when it clicks for him that he's about to be stuck with a parasite anchored to his uterine lining, that the cells that will eventually become a heart are twitching in the first burgeonings of a pulse.

All he can think is that this is defector behavior. This is what he told Jess in the car last night. *We kill you.*

Aspen and Birdie and Luna don't deserve this.

At the bottom of the stairs, the man who must be from another hive, a hunter from Virginia or rural Maryland, one of Levi's buddies from the northern stretch of the mountains, does not move. The door hangs open like a mouth. It lets in humid summer air and the sound of crickets, the distant rumble of late-night traffic from the highway two blocks west.

When this man speaks, he speaks with the hundred overlapping whispers of the hive:

"Come home."

It's been a while since a hive has had a real, honest-to-god defector. At least, a defector Levi's had to deal with. According to Tammy, defectors used to be more common, but the way she sees it, there's less to run *toward* these days. Put on the news for literally five minutes; who wants to be a part of that? Certainly not her, she said. She was fine staying right here, thank you. But every so often, Levi gets a call to be on the lookout for certain plates, or some poor bastard or another, and he always says he will, even if it hasn't panned out in a while.

The last time it did, it was a boy from Tennessee. Right when Tammy stopped trying to convince Crane that moving in with Levi was a bad idea, when the apartment was still half-unpacked. A hive mother a few hours outside Knoxville—some Southern hives have *mothers*, it's tradition apparently—rang up Tammy, said to let her enforcer know they had a runner. Tammy said we don't got enforcers up here, but we do got a hunter. The hive mother said that'd do.

Lo and behold, Levi caught the guy passing through. Took out the lower leg with buckshot since it was the only ammunition he had on hand that day. Hoisted him up, wrapped up the wound in a garbage bag, and brought the boy home, like a friend who'd been out drinking too long.

Crane had woken up to the commotion, sliding out of their new shared bed (they hadn't bought a used bed frame off Facebook Marketplace yet, so it was just a mattress on the floor) and plodding over to where Levi had dumped the delirious kid in the tub. All Crane could think, even with a sobbing, shred-legged stranger taking up their new bathroom, was that this place was so shitty that maintenance had painted the porcelain, who *does* that, and the blood would fuck up the paint and never come out.

"You want him back?" Levi asked into his phone, jamming it between his cheek and shoulder so he could open a Bud Lite with both hands.

Crane hesitated in the doorway and Levi noticed, mouthed, *Hey, baby.*

"Dunno how picky your worms are," he continued, "if they get territorial or whatever."

"Worms," the woman on the other side of the line groused. Her scratchy voice was audible through the phone speaker, a side effect of Levi's combined affinity for shotguns and disregard for ear protection. *"The lot of you are so disrespectful."*

"They're *worms,*" Levi snorted. "Tammy thought you wanted him back. Do you? Or can I shut him up?"

The Tennessee hive mother did not want him back. Levi shrugged, hung up, and started running the tap because driving this guy out into the wilderness to put him down would take too much time and waste expensive ammo. Plus, drowning makes the least mess.

"Help me with this," Levi said as the defector—who couldn't have been older than nineteen, Crane's age then—started to clue into why, even through the fever of blood loss and pain, freezing water was hitting his cheek. "He's got some fight in him."

Crane doesn't remember how the drowning went. What he does remember is burning muscles and the slip of hands against wet skin, and then stepping out of the tub and Levi shoving him hard against the bathroom wall.

The body was still warm in the water when Crane wiped away the face-fucked slurry of spit and cum that'd smeared down his chin, stained his shirt, left him coughing and crying. "There we go," Levi had said, scooping up the mess with two fingers and shoving it back into Crane's mouth. "That's a good boy."

See? *We kill you.*

On the stairs of Aspen and Birdie's house, Crane thinks, a fly must have followed him to Virginia. Or there's a hive creeping away from the mountains and closer to cities, real population centers, that caught scent of him in the suburbs. He stares at this man—this man with a swarm lodged in his throat. This *thing*, whatever he is, that shouldn't exist. As far as Crane knows.

He wasn't running. He was going to come home.

He'll come home now, actually. Right now. Promise. Swear it.

Just don't go upstairs.

Just give him a second to make it believable.

Crane gets the time he needs, because the worms and the flies and the hive and the swarm are nothing if not understanding. The man watches, waiting, as Crane fetches his clothes from the laundry, resets the back door the best he can, and shoves his feet hard into his shoes. Aspen and Birdie will be confused when they wake up. Paranoid too, when they notice the lock broken. That's okay. As long as they're safe, as long as they don't try to follow. They don't know where he lives. He's never given them a town; he's never even given them a county.

He leaves a note, too. It's simple. *Sorry.* Then he spends a moment considering a whole *don't come looking for me* spiel, before deciding that'd just make it worse.

The note goes onto the coffee table, between a candle and a copy of *The Little Engine That Could*.

What are the chances that Crane has already crossed the line? Already branded himself a defector by stepping foot in this cluttered house and sleeping in the warm bed upstairs? Given how desperately the hive tears its traitors apart, this whole "killing himself" thing might be moot. Oh shit, would Levi be the one to do it? As he takes one look back at the living room, one final inspection to make sure it's all in place, he reviews everything he knows about Levi and tries to decide whether his not-really-boyfriend would insist on being the one to uphold the rules.

As he steps out onto the sidewalk, he fails to come to any kind of conclusion. Levi doesn't love Crane—Crane doesn't love Levi either—though he likes to think they've ended up with a semi-sentimental attachment to each other, the same way you grow fond of a stray cat in the neighborhood.

But the hive will understand. Right? If he tells the hive he's pregnant, they'll understand why he panicked. He'll apologize and they'll fix the problem together and it'll be okay.

He's leaving the house. He's doing what he's told. He's good at that. It's the only thing he's good at.

It'll be fine.

The strange man follows.

The strange man walks oddly, stiffly, as if his body isn't quite his and it's taking some getting used to. He trails Crane like a herding dog. The streetlights glow, and at the mouth of the neighborhood cul-de-sac, a car drives by on a late-night errand.

Aspen and Birdie and Luna are safe. That's what he focuses on, because that's what matters. He did the right thing.

Crane unlocks the Camry and gets in. Is he allowed to be proud of how well he's keeping it together? With how prone he was to melt-downs and tantrums and anxiety attacks as a kid, this is an improve-ment. The repetitive numbness of *am I going to die soon, I didn't mean it I was going to come back, the hive has to understand*—that's better than the alternative of losing his shit.

Aspen would correct him: no, this is called *dissociation*. Or a com-plete removal from the survival instinct, which is in and of itself a form of suicidality. Both are bad.

The man with the swarm in his throat drops into the shotgun seat and swings the door shut.

Silence.

Quiet, except for the blood in Crane's ears and the air in his lungs. The creak of body weight and the shuffling of clothes. He's been wearing this outfit for over twenty-four hours now. The shirt has taken on the distinct over-warmth of clothing kept too close to the body for too long.

Crane puts the key in the ignition, because he is doing as he's told, but does not get the chance to turn it.

The man snatches. Not for Crane, but for the seat-back lever. It falls and Crane falls with it, yelping. And then the man is grabbing him, scrabbling for Crane's legs with his strange, fucked-up puppet-movements, and pulling him and wrenching him until Crane's legs are sprawled over the center console and, oh fuck, no no no, the man is on *top of him.*

What if the man came to kill him instead.

The survival instinct kicks in.

Crane flails. Fights for distance. If he can get some *space*, he can pull the door handle and fall out backward into the parking lot and bolt. Or grab the metal pipe he keeps between the seat and the door. Crane can't get it. Too far back. The man's too heavy and keeps pinning him, putting weight on him. Holding him down.

Levi taught him, though. Hit dirty and hit hard, hit the throat and eyes and nose and make it hurt.

Crane catches the neck gaiter. Twist and it'll cut off the air supply, make it feel like the eyes are going to pop out of the skull, because that's what it feels like when someone's choking you, *really* choking you, and not the fun way. The *I'm going to die* way.

But the gaiter comes down off the face and something's wrong.

Crane figures it out in pieces. Has half a second to sort it out while the fabric is tight in his hands. It's not that the face itself is wrong; he doesn't like that phrasing here, doesn't like the impreciseness of it in this moment. The face is flat and distinctly strange, sure, the features slightly off from where they should be. Like this man was disassembled and put back together in a hurry.

It's what's *under*. Between the muscles and under the skin.

An artery on the neck slithers away from the makeshift garrote.

Crane jerks back. Hits the hard plastic of the car door, and his vision swims. His hips are wrenched at a bad angle. His legs are spread like he's inviting something.

"Stop."

There are worms. There are worms under his skin, and he speaks like the hive. And there are hands gathering up Crane's throbbing head, cradling his skull, holding him tightly but so carefully. So kindly. The gloves are bite-proof, Crane thinks. They have the fresh smell of a hardware store.

"STOP."

Crane stops.

The car is quiet again.

He doesn't know what's happening and he doesn't know what he's looking at anymore. Just do it. Whatever's going to happen, Jesus Christ, get it over with, *please.*

Slowly, the man with the swarm in his mouth and the worms under his skin releases Crane's head. Inch by inch, waiting for Crane to lunge, or bite. Crane doesn't. He was told to stop, and he stopped.

So the man takes the hem of Crane's shirt and pushes it up. Exposes the belly, the sweat to the sweltering air trapped in the car; soft fat, dark hair, the traitorous organ underneath. It rises and falls as Crane breathes. Stutters as his lungs do.

The man, with all the gravity of a religious rite, presses his face to the skin.

Prostrates himself to the altar of Crane's insides.

The hive knows.

Eight

Early morning on the mountain, before the sun starts getting ideas. Wash County is all dark cliffs and zigzag roads and stars, insomniacs, and third-shifters at the lumberyard.

Crane started the drive chewing on a hangnail, and as he turns off Corridor H and into the gas station parking lot—when his swarm says *home* it means here—he's worrying a bloody mess on his thumb. The man with the worms under his skin hasn't moved from the shotgun seat since they crossed state lines. Crane can't stop thinking about the burning-warm face pressed to his belly, gloves holding his hips the way Levi does when they're fucking.

The CLOSED sign in the window is running out of battery. Only the emergency lights are on: one over the register, another by the dumpster.

And Levi's there. Leaning against the truck with a Marlboro between two fingers, 12-gauge propped up against the back tire. Watching the Camry with the half-lidded predatory gaze he usually reserves for worm food.

The emergency lights catch the smoke trailing from his mouth, gives him a strange halo.

Crane parks halfway up the lot and kills the engine.

Right there. There's the motherfucker who did this to him. That's the man who came in him, whose cock knocked him up and put him here.

Does he know? He has to. Why else would he be here.

The man with the worms under his skin and the neck gaiter pulled up, unnaturally still, watches.

Crane is aware that all he needs to do is talk to the hive. Get out of the car and walk into that dark back room and unravel himself. He is such a good follower. He has enacted every order and given every piece of himself to this. He is grateful for everything. *I'm sorry*, his expression will say, *I should have come to you first. Please help me.*

But his teeth are chattering.

He throws open the door and steps out into the gravel.

Levi pushes away from the truck, spreading his hands like Crane's reaction to all this isn't perfectly reasonable or, at the very least, hadn't been telegraphed two years in advance. "So were you gonna just let me find the test in the trash or what?"

He takes the first step into range, and Crane yanks the pipe from the car frame and swings.

The problem is that Crane bought this pipe after Harry suggested he might have an easier time getting lug nuts off his tires with extra leverage, more length on the wrench, so it's long and light and completely hollow. If Crane had thought this through any, he could've gone for the actual lug wrench, or the still-bloody hammer wrapped up in his go bag, but all that is in the trunk and pregnancy brain, hormones, *I'll kill you*, the panic nausea is creeping up his throat and he isn't thinking right.

The first hit connects right at the cheekbone, makes a dull sound, and smacks the cigarette clean out of his mouth. Levi grunts, stumbles, slaps a hand over his cheek where a snag in the iron ripped the skin.

The second hit doesn't land.

Levi bodies Crane against the back door. Smashes him against the car with his full weight. The pipe clangs against the gravel. "What the *fuck*—"

Crane can't fight his way out. Even with everything Levi taught him. He's so tired and Levi is so much stronger, and usually he'd twist this around as a fetish thing—what's that one video he has bookmarked? *Merciless Male Domination*, that—but Levi is actually really for-real *hurting* him, and yeah, most of the time he likes it but—

"Let go."

Levi does. Instantly.

Crane collapses.

"He's fine," Levi says above him.

The man with the worms under his skin is there now, backlit and towering, taller than Levi and broader across the shoulders. Crane presses the heels of his hands into his eyes until they're about to burst.

"He's fine," Levi's saying, and "Wait, you—" and "Fuck, fuck."

Crane knows he's making some stupid animal noise, but he can't stop, can't make himself shut up.

"Look," Levi says, "he's fine. I didn't hurt him, I didn't hurt the baby. See? It's fine."

Crane crams his wrist into his mouth because if he doesn't bite down, he's going to scream. The red marks turn black like the perforated half-moon in the crook of Levi's thumb.

Get me pregnant and I'll kill you.

I'll kill myself.

The man with the worms under his skin shoulders Levi out of the way and gets on the ground, puts himself on Crane's level, and pulls him close. All Crane's muscles are rigid. Curling him up like a bug. He's hyperventilating and trying to get his fingers under the skin of his face to tear it off.

He should've set himself on fire. The swarm should've let him do it.

"Shh," the man says, peeling nails away from skin. *"Shh."*

It's not a baby inside him. It's barely not a blastocyst. According to the website he'd been looking at a few hours ago, a nine-week fetus (it can't have been longer than nine weeks, it *can't*) is a wet insect, a grub waiting for a cocoon. Crane can't rip away his skin, so his hands flap helplessly, over and over. The man doesn't stop him. Just holds him.

You call it a baby only if you want it.

Back over at the truck, Levi's got his shotgun. He makes it cough up all its shells and pockets them, one red cylinder after the other. The sharp glance he cuts at Crane is obvious. Levi's not stupid. He remembered that night in the back seat. A sharp line of blood runs down his cheek.

"You almost done?" he calls, opening the Mossberg's action with a menacing click for a final check before dropping it into the bed. The tone is the same one Crane's teachers used during the last meltdown he'd let himself have. What had it been over, anyway. Something stupid. A kid spilling tomato soup on Sophie's leg in the lunch line. *"She's acting like her foot got amputated,"* the teacher on duty mumbled. (Or maybe it's the tone her first dentist took when he said, *"We can't handle this, ma'am,"* and Mom held down her thrashing child, repeating, *"Sorry, I'm so sorry."*)

When Crane doesn't respond, Levi comes over to the Camry, plucks the keys out of the ignition, and lets himself into the gas station.

"Shh," the man says one more time.

Crane wants to be quiet. He wants to so bad. He's being a child. Grow up. *Stop.* He fights for an ounce of composure and can't get it. He's going to be sick.

He doesn't realize Levi's back until Levi opens a bottle of water and pours half of it over Crane's head.

Crane splutters at the sudden cold. His hair plasters to his face and his shirt is wet. It's *wet.* He wrestles it over his head and throws it because his clothes absolutely cannot under any condition be *wet,* it's cold and it clings and it makes him want to scream. Some of it's splattered onto the man with the worms under his skin, and he doesn't seem to care. What is it like, not wanting to howl and sob when something doesn't feel right. Crane can't imagine. Crane can't think much of anything.

Levi says, "Are you done?"

Half-lucid and half-naked, gulping down air, Crane nods. Yes. He's done. Just don't do that again. Please.

So Levi leans against the Camry and casts his gaze toward Corridor H, scoping out his territory. Crane still is crying, but that's acceptable. He can cry quietly.

In the lot—with stars slowly disappearing in the encroaching sunrise, Crane leaning all his weight onto the man with the worms under his skin—Crane tries as hard as he can but can't recall anyone else in the hive getting pregnant. At any hive, ever. Which is weird, because people have babies. As a species, as a whole, it happens more often than not. It seems like the sort of thing that'd get passed up through the grapevine, even if only via nasty rumors; Levi eating dinner over the sink and calling into the living room to ask if Crane heard about Samantha from outside Chattanooga, who left her kid in a hot car and killed him. *Holy shit, what a dumb bitch.*

Is Crane the first?

He can't be. That's not how probability, or birth rates, or the general human population works.

"I ain't gonna ask where you were," Levi says, "or why. This ugly bastard found you—" The man makes a displeased clicking sound reminiscent of a worm snapping its jaws. "And we've got bigger things to deal with, so. It's water under the bridge. Okay?"

Aspen and Birdie and Luna are safe. Crane doesn't believe in God but thank God. A drop of water falls from his hair onto his bare breast.

"Okay." Levi replaces the cigarette Crane knocked out and fishes in his pocket for the lighter. With the cut on his face slicing through the growing bruise, blood on the corner of his mouth, dog tags dangling down his chest, it's almost lewd. Crane focuses on the blood. He drew blood. *Fuck you.* "Figured this was gonna be rough, but the pipe, that got me. Forgot you had that."

He finds the lighter. Lights up.

Levi says, "Here's how it's going to work. I've already gone through the apartment and locked up anything you could make a mess with. Razors, scissors, knives, bleach—you want anything, you're gonna have to ask me. And you're a smart son of a bitch, so we'll have to keep an eye on you. That's why this motherfucker is here. We're not taking any chances."

The man snorts scathingly.

"Speaking of." Levi looks down at him. "You didn't do anything to it, did you?"

No, of course he didn't get the chance to scrape this thing out of him.

"Good."

Good.

Why does Levi care? Why did he say it like that? *Good.*

Did Levi knock him up *on purpose*?

That can't be right. Crane is aware, vaguely, that there are men out there whose whole thing is getting trans guys pregnant. They get off on it: putting a mutilated woman in her place. Yeah, Levi's an asshole, but he's not like *that*. He didn't help Crane start T, but he never tried to stop him, either. Sure, sometimes when they fuck, Levi calls him a bitch, or a slut, but that's technically gender-neutral, if he ignores the time that *good girl* slipped out too, if he ignores how wet it made him. Levi was the first person to make Crane feel like a man. This couldn't have happened on purpose.

And now he's really thinking about it. Cobbling together the future from books and movies and the pregnant women he looked away from when he passed them in the street. His tits swelling with milk, his belly fat and heavy with a creature he's only ever been able to conceive of as a literal chestburster. He'll have to push it out or cut it out. It's going to hurt. It's going to eat him alive.

He's hyperventilating again. Beating his face with his hands. If he caves his skull in this will *stop*, this will all be over, he won't have to do this, *please don't make me do this, please just let me talk to the hive.*

Levi says, "Shit." Kneels on the ground and grabs Crane's wrists tight. The man with the worms in his head holds Crane to his chest.

He can't do this. He can't he can't he can't.

"I know this is going to suck for you," Levi says. His voice, right

73

now, is the kindest it's ever been. "But listen to me. I'm gonna make myself clear. Alright? The hive wants you to have this baby. You hear me? So you're having this fucking baby."

No, he's not. This was a mistake. The hive will understand he can't do this. It loves him, doesn't it? It always has. He doesn't want to die. It has to understand. It has to.

He tries to stand, reaching for the buzzing emergency light, but Levi gets him under the arms. "Nope," he says, even as Crane sobs and struggles and his feet slip in the loose rocks. "We're going home. You look like shit."

Aspen: Crane?

Aspen: Are you taking a walk or something?

Aspen: We need to leave for the appointment in an hour.

Aspen: Birdie found your note. Are you okay? The door is fucked up.

Aspen: We're not upset. If you need to talk something out I have the tablet. We're not mad at you.

Birdie: I hate that I get it but I did the same thing with my parents when I was ur age. I made the mistake and went back to them. I know it sucks and its bad but I can put money on the fact that u went back because ur scared. and we're scared for u too and we're not mad but please let us know you're not dead in a ditch somewhere or smth. please?

Nine

Out in the living room, muffled by the flimsy door and the drone of the standing fan, Levi's voice: "You still in there or what?"

According to the alarm clock, it's late afternoon. Hard to prove with the blackout curtains. Crane wakes up tacky-mouthed, blankets tangled around his feet, and a gray pillow shunted off to the dirty hardwood.

For a moment—a moment too long—he can't remember how much of the previous forty-eight hours actually happened. There's no physical evidence to show for it. No new bruises, somehow. No swollen stomach. Only a dehydration headache to prove he cried himself sick, and the thin sheen of sweat that means it's time to update the utility failure spreadsheet.

In the living room, again: *"Talk,* motherfucker."

The only response is a boar-like grunt.

Right. The sun-warmed gravel of the parking lot. The man with the worms under his skin. The positive test. All real.

Crane doesn't get up. He puts a hand on his stomach and watches the ceiling. It's dizzyingly blank up there; no overhead light, no fan, no fire alarm. (The alarm went off two nights in a row when they moved in, so Levi ripped it down and threw it into the trash.) Nothing to focus on except the skin under his palm.

No matter how hard he presses, he can't find the thing inside him. It's the same fat and organs as always.

It's not right that he can't feel it. His body shouldn't be allowed to hide itself from him. What did that one website say? *You're starting your third month, Mama!* At nine weeks, because maybe it's been nine weeks probably, the baby is the size of a grape.

No. Not a baby.

Embryo, then. Fetus. Larva. He imagines a larger-than-life maggot or, what is the larval stage of a worm? Just a slightly different worm? That, sitting in the gory slop of his pelvis. Flystrike cranked up to eleven, the sort of thing Harry was going on about before Levi put him down with the shotgun.

"You kill him or just hollow him out?" Levi says out there. He's got that grit-teeth growl he gets when he's mad. "What'd you do to him, huh? How bad did you fuck him up?"

Crane resists the urge to drag his phone from the nightstand and look up pictures of myiasis, human shoulders and dog necks turned into meaty lotus pods. If he does, he'll have to check his messages. All the stressed texts from Aspen and Birdie he knows he'll have, they're going to make him ill. Again.

"Jesus."

The telling *thump-thump* of the noisy floor; someone approaching. Crane buries his face in the pillow before the bedroom door opens and obnoxious yellow light cuts across the bed, pretends he's still asleep.

Not that it matters. Levi takes Crane's head in one big hand and thumbs open an eyelid.

"Making sure you're still breathing," he mumbles as Crane flinches away. He pulls a shirt out of the worn-but-not-noticeably-dirty pile beside the hamper to sniff. A purple-green bruise swallows his entire cheek, punctuated by a fresh scab. "M'going out for slugs. Don't do nothing stupid."

How many bullets did he use down in McDowell that he needs more already? That, or he's stockpiling. He does that when he's nervous.

"Big guy's out there, he'll keep an eye on you. We clear?"

Levi pulls on the shirt, dog tags jingling. He's got a whole mess of scars—some on his hands from soldier shit, couple on the arms from people fighting for their lives, the usual—but the newest is a swollen keloid that looks too much like an incision for a bowel surgery. He came home with it a few months ago, an odd cut right above the waistband of his jeans. Never said a word about it.

"We clear?" Levi repeats.

Crane nods into the pillow.

Levi pats the wall twice. "Good," he says, and walks out.

As soon as the apartment door thuds shut, though, Crane is up. Dragging himself out of bed, reeling against morning sickness even though it isn't morning, *unfair*. He hits the bedroom door too hard and stumbles into the hall.

He yanks open the linen closet.

His testosterone. Levi said he'd gotten rid of anything he could make a mess with. Anything he could hurt himself with.

Did his needles—

Levi's never had an issue with him being on hormones, but Aspen said it'd be a good idea "just in case" so yes, he keeps his injection kit hidden. Split up, too. Three weeks' worth of supplies in a glass Tupperware behind two plastic organizers in the linen closet, with extra syringes under a set of towels, a box of sharps at the bottom of his go bag, the vials themselves in his sock drawer. Crane shoves aside the mess of cleaning supplies and extra toilet paper and reaches down into the spiderweb-choked nook behind the organizer drawers.

There. There it is. He pulls it out, peels off the lid, and counts every piece, heartbeat slowing from its tachycardia pace: 18-gauge needle; 25-gauge needle; syringe; sterile alcohol swabs; Band-Aids. All still here.

Just to make sure, he pops open the tiny cardboard box holding the vial and holds the medication up to the light.

Testosterone is an unassuming clear liquid in a nondescript medical bottle. If there's a tint to it, that depends on the bulbs in the light fixtures. There's only a bit left.

It's here. It's okay. And, even after everything, it's shot day.

He's not missing a dose—no way in hell.

Except the man with the worms in his head makes that boar-grunt noise.

Crane crams the vial back into the box. The man is standing at the end of the hall, where it spits out into the living room. No hood or neck gaiter anymore. Only his smashed-flat face and veiny arms and ripstop pants, like he just walked off a shift at the garage.

Seeing him in the light is strange. He wasn't meant to be looked at in full visibility; it betrays the frayed edges where he's unraveled or wasn't put together right in the first place. Gaps on the tips of his fingers where nails should be but aren't, atrophic scars peppering dents in the skin. Hell, with the egregious lack of living movement that isn't the awful puppet-jerk of, what, a worm manually tugging a tendon, any civilian would have alarm bells ringing at fifty paces.

Keep an eye on you, Levi said.

What is this son of a bitch, then. Besides a stranger who shouldn't exist. Who speaks like a swarm and holds worms between the layers of his body like a hive.

Is he a hive? A bizarre middle ground between the worms and their prey?

Hives understand their people.

The man reaches for the Tupperware with his bare calloused hands, the veins in the wrist searching for a more comfortable position, so fuck it. Crane does the stupid thing and holds it out to him.

Look, the motion says. The man tilts his head curiously, as if the supplies inside make more sense at an angle. Look, it's medication. Most everyone takes medication at some point. (Crane has no idea what effects testosterone will have on a larva, on that embryonic grub inside him. He also has no idea if the thing in front of him knows either.) It's nothing to worry about. If it's anything, it's proof that he isn't built for this anymore. Build a body of evidence. It'll be best for everyone if the hive takes it all back, lets him flush the baby out, puts everything back how it was. No hard feelings.

Here, he'll even show him.

Crane gestures for the man to follow, then eases past—come on, let's fetch an ice pack from the freezer, and a paper towel for a placemat. Sit on the floor. If he wants to see the boy he's here to surveil, wants to get to know him, this is the best way to do it.

The kitchen tile is cool and welcoming, and the man watches.

The man needs a name. He doesn't have dog tags like Levi, and Crane doesn't recognize him, doesn't keep tabs on people in the surrounding hives, if that's what he even was before he was this. And labeling him *David* or *Steve* or whatever would be borderline comical. *Hey, have you seen that giant freak with literal fucking worms inside him? Oh yeah, John's right over there.*

Crane lands on *Stagger*, then. The way he walks, the rigor mortis marionette of it all. The kind of thing a zombie movie would call its zombies when they're contractually obligated to avoid the z-word. Stagger. It suits him.

So Crane sets out one of each item—except the disinfecting alcohol swabs, two of those—and lets Stagger inspect them up close. Injecting looks scary, but it's not that bad. He takes extra care cleaning the top of the vial, locks the 18-gauge needle onto the syringe, and draws out less than his official dose.

Stagger eyes it and Crane spreads his fingers to give him a better view.

He doesn't have a lot of testosterone left. Aspen's been helping with the procuring side of things, but still; a rash of manufacturer recalls, the hive-provided ID nearly getting caught at a pharmacy, his first endocrinologist dropping every trans client with a simpering email about a new law. Plus, getting a refill is a nightmare if you don't talk. Aspen has to make the phone calls, and every pharmacist is on the verge of ringing up the prescriber in a fit of disgust—*Is this mute mentally competent? Who allowed an overgrown child to destroy her body this way?* Crane has a few months' in reserve, but after that. It'll be tough.

Crane swaps the imposing 18-gauge needle for a smaller one and lifts it to the kitchen light to check for bubbles and impurities. None. Good.

Stagger receives the ice pack.

Stagger's mouth pulls into a sort of frown. Crane hikes up his shirt, shuffles down the waistband of his pants, shows the soft patch beside his navel. Here—put it here.

When Stagger continues to hesitate, Crane takes his wrist and brings him closer until they're as close as they were in the Camry. The cold makes contact. Stagger's face is inches away. There we go. Like that.

It's unbearably intimate, being this close. Helping with a medical procedure so integral to Crane's continued existence. Intimate enough that he almost bails, is so glad he stopped speaking because he couldn't bear being expected to put together words in a moment like this. God, when he was nineteen and naïve, in the first months of hormones, he would do his shot and pretend that it was Levi giving it to him. That Levi would take even a baseline interest in the changing of his body, hell, would want to be an active participant in that changing. And the pain, too. Levi wouldn't let him use the ice pack. That would be chickening out. No, he'd make Crane feel the needle as it went in, every millimeter of it. He'd tilt Crane's chin up so he could see the wince, grin lopsidedly as it slid through the skin and layers of fat. It'd be so hot. It'd really be something.

But every time Crane does his injection, Levi's never so much as in the same room. And now it's Stagger here instead.

As soon as the ice pack begins to hurt, Crane eases it away, offering the closest thing he can manage to a smile, a *thank-you*. Then he disinfects the burning-cold skin, takes a pinch of stomach fat, and pushes the needle in himself.

The forty-five-degree angle is flawless. Stagger lets out a concerned whine but look, look, it's okay. The bevel slips right through the meat, burying all the way to the hilt. Just like that. He pushes the plunger, slow and careful, and testosterone cypionate floods under the skin.

A few seconds later, it's done. Crane pulls out the needle and plasters over the injection site with a Band-Aid.

Crane needs this. Without this, what is he? Sophie pressing her small breasts flat with her hands, then propping them up in the mirror. Wearing her hair long to hide behind it, and flinching from the boys in her class even though they were nothing but cordial to her; wondering, if she walked into the wrong locker room after gym class, would they push her against the bench and fuck her? She was fourteen when she first fantasized about it. It made her sick, even though it was so incredibly tame in comparison to what she would think up later.

(Crane should tell Levi about it. Levi would get a kick out of it, and Crane would finally have an excuse not to feel bad about getting off to being called a girl.)

Without this, what would he be except Sophie playing with matches in the back seat of her mom's car?

And without the hive, he's nothing.

Stagger brushes his thumb against the Band-Aid. The knot of liquid sits under the skin, waiting to be absorbed into the body, where it will hasten the growth of dark body hair, and the restructuring of fat, and the swelling of the clit. Can Stagger feel it? Does he want to? Can he feel *this*? Crane grabs Stagger's wrist hard and pushes until the hand is digging into where his uterus might be, into wherever that grub is curled up asleep.

Crane would make a shit father. He can barely handle showering on a regular basis, let alone take care of a creature dependent on him for survival. He couldn't graduate high school without trying to set himself on fire. He's not the right person for this, and the hive has to know that.

So why him?

Can Stagger answer that? After three years of service and love and kindness, why would they subject him to *this*?

Stagger doesn't say anything. Doesn't even give a boar-grunt, or a single clicking, rasping hive-word. He can't be bothered to respond at all.

Crane slaps Stagger's hand away. Gets up. Snatches all the medical trash and dumps it into the garbage except for the sharps, which will go into an old milk jug into the trunk of his car until it's time to dump them at a needle exchange.

This half-dead, half-worm man whose only job is to watch him, keep him on a leash, control him, does not bother to answer. This *thing*, the arbiter of what he can and cannot do, can't say a single word about why, and unlike Levi doesn't even have the decency to offer to fuck him instead.

He needs to talk to the hive. Now.

Ten

As a condition of his suicide watch, Crane is no longer allowed to drive. Because of course. Why would Levi or Stagger or the worms agree to let him behind the wheel when he could crumple it around a tree or send it off a sharp mountain's edge.

Crane is peeved about it on a trivial level. Killing yourself in a car accident has too much uncertainty, too many opportunities to muck it up and survive. Sophie dreamed about it in regard to the whole self-mutilation thing, oh my god did she weigh the pros and cons of being caught in a car fire and being pulled out in just the nick of time. But for this? Not Crane's method of choice.

Besides, it's not like he's going to do it. He won't have to go that far. The hive will understand.

"There's someone here," Levi snarls when Crane nips out of the truck and slams the door. Stagger, attempting to follow through the same door, narrowly avoids getting his thick fingers caught. He protests with an annoyed click. "Hey—"

Yeah, there's a car at the pumps, whatever. Just don't let anyone into the back. They've done riskier stuff with more people around.

The sky is the dull blue of summer twilight, the first violet streaks of sunset splashed across the clouds, the kind of color the swarm would spend hours recounting to the hive, only to fail to do it justice. The bell rings when Crane shoves his way inside. Jess is nearly asleep at the register—her hair put up with a claw clip since she's using the ponytail holder to tie back her shirt, some relief from heat that West Virginia infrastructure is not made for—while Tammy does inventory and a bearded trucker type counts out change for a coffee. It's been on the pot so long it's burnt.

"Crane?" Tammy struggles to her arthritic feet. "Sweetheart, where have you been? Did you get my messages?"

He doesn't answer. Levi doesn't answer for him either, only presents his bite-marked wrist to the man at the counter. "Coffee's on the house, Larry. Take it and get out."

"What?" says Jess as Crane yanks the key from behind the register and makes a beeline for the manager's office.

"Christ, man," says Larry-from-another-hive.

"Levi," says Tammy, "stop your ass right there. The hell is going on? Who is that?" She catches Stagger with a hand to the chest. "Lord almighty, you're ugly."

Crane jams the key into the hive's padlock, dumps the chains to the concrete floor, and closes himself inside the stinking, constricting coffin.

In the dark, before he finds the light switch, he can almost convince himself he's back in the trunk.

The heat. The rancid all-consuming stink. The hum of translucent wings almost like the rush of blood in his ears. And Sean's corpse is in this room somewhere, subsumed into the wretched mess of calcium and regurgitation, covered in fly eggs and worm spit.

Crane lets the rotten air flood his mouth and decides not to turn on the light. The hive doesn't like the light. It's a shit equivalent for the sun, they tell him. They accept no imposters. They want the sun, the sun, the sun, and they can never have it, not in the dark rooms they hide in to survive.

Child.

He kneels. Eyes focused on nothing in the dark. It's what he did when he saw the hive for the first time, seventeen years old and scared. Rocking side to side to soothe himself.

Oh child. Poor little thing.

He'd been so grateful back then. He tries to remember that feeling, tamp down the feral rage swallowing every ounce of patience and kindness he's managed to dredge up. Place that gratitude back into his bones where it belongs.

Remember: without the hive, he's nothing.

You are breathing hard. You are afraid. Why are you afraid?

He places a hand on his stomach.

He would have given the hive—any hive, not just his own, the one in McDowell or any other in the poorest mountains and countrysides—*anything* else if it had asked. What does it need? A tongue? An eye? Some other pound of flesh from his living, breathing body? Done, agreed, in a heartbeat. Without hesitation. Anything but this.

And they have to have known. That's what he gets stuck on every time he tries to pick it apart. Hives understand their people. His hive has always been tender. Even when he messes up, even if he does something as bad as running away. His hive *knows him.*

So why?

Ah.

The little one you carry.

Don't call it that. Don't don't don't.

Does it cause you pain? Does it feel as if something is wrong?

Crane knows those words. Even understands what they mean in that order, technically.

Your body knows so much about itself. If something is wrong with the little one, if you can feel it in your womb, then please. We wish to help.

With all the strength he can muster, he shakes his head. No, nothing is—nothing is wrong with it, he doesn't think. It'd be easier if something *was* wrong with it, actually. He hopes there is a chromosomal abnormality so incompatible with life that the larva feeding off his oxygen supply shrivels and fails and comes out in a bloody lump.

He wants it gone. He wants it out.

Please.

The swarm buzzes. The worms slide over each other in a constant wet undertone, like saliva swishing in the mouth, or—or when intestines squirm about on the operating table. His eyes are adjusting to the dark and some of the worms are watching. Older ones, with dull bodies and heavy jaws.

We see. You are unhappy.

He is.

We imagined this might be your reaction. Gravidity must go against your instincts—a female trying so hard to appear male, to be treated as one, yes, of course.

He nods. Exactly. Of course they understand. He knew they would. His bottom lip quivers.

We know you. We understand you.

Yes.

We know you better than you know yourself.

That's why he's here. Without the hive, he's nothing.

And is this not what you wanted?

Crane tries to breathe in but can't. Thinks he feels his heart stop somewhere in his throat.

All the autonomic functions of the body grind to a cold stop.

You pleaded for us to do as we wished with you, didn't you? To mold you in our image. To give you a place. To make your choices, change your body, make you into something useful. To keep you from being something other than fuckmeat and repulsive lust and fear.

To make the outside match the inside.

How fortunate, then, that we've given you what you want.

Crane doesn't hear the hive door open or the footsteps. Barely feels the hands guiding him away, leathery skin cradling his face and directing it toward the office light.

"What did you do?" Tammy is demanding. Not of him. There's spit on her wrinkled lips. Crane crams his nose into her palm to find her pulse, squeezes his eyes shut, tries to pretend he's a teenager in her guest room again. "One of y'all better fucking answer me."

Our child simply needs time to come around.

"To *what*?"

Levi says, "He's pregnant."

Crane focuses on Tammy's pulse. Tries to match his to hers, even though he feels like he's going to have a heart attack and hers is getting faster, faster.

Jess, somewhere in the office, says, "Holy shit."

"Okay." Tammy sucks in air through her crooked teeth and drags her free hand through Crane's hair. "Okay, sweetheart. I can handle this. We'll just—"

You will NOT.

Tammy flinches.

The little one is ours.

"We're keeping it," Levi says.

Tammy snarls. "Fuck." Then, "Go with them, baby." She hands Crane off to Jess and Stagger. "Sit him down, I'll be right there." Then she's raising her voice at Levi and the hive, and Stagger is leading him to the chair in the corner of the office and Jess is helping him sit.

The gas station tilts under him.

"He can handle it," Levi is saying.

"Hey," Jess murmurs. "Hey. Breathe."

He realizes with sudden clarity that he hates her.

If the hive was going to pick anyone for this bullshit, why couldn't it have been her? She comes here, fucks up her first hunt, and has the gall to stand in front of him and look at him with such big eyes, like she *feels bad* about this. As if she knows him, or cares.

It should've been her. Let her be the one to carry the hive's precious *little one*. Hell, maybe she'd even like it. Maybe they should find out.

Jess takes a step back. "Crane?" she says nervously.

Stagger puts a hand on the back of his neck and squeezes.

Then Tammy is in front of him again. Oh, thank god. Ma is here. He reaches for her childishly and she allows it, presses his hands tight between hers. She's cold. Her skin is paper-thin, fragile like suede, every knot and vein and spot painfully visible. He wonders how many years she has left. Who knows how much time the hive takes from their people.

"How far along are you?" she asks. Jess looks away. "Do you know?" He shakes his head.

She extricates a hand and presses the palm to Crane's stomach. Tells him to lean back a bit, dear. Moves down, nudges aside the waistband of his pants to press her fingers right above the pelvis. Lower than Crane would've thought to go.

"*Almost* feel something." She thinks, puts pressure on a different spot. Hums. "There it is. I'd say—" A sigh. "Eleven weeks. Maybe closer to twelve."

Not just the start of the third month. Three months, in their totality.

The medical abortion Aspen and Birdie had scheduled wouldn't have worked.

"It gets a little easier in the second trimester," Tammy offers. "You stop feeling so sick all the time, if you're lucky." She takes her cold fingers away, leans in. Lowers her voice. "If you want to move back in with me, you let me know. I'll get you out of there. I don't care what I have to say to that boy."

Past her, over her shoulder, Levi is murmuring to Jess, his head ducked to her temple. Her big brown eyes focus anywhere but him. She frets with the frayed edges of her jean shorts. When Levi asks her a question, she makes a face that probably means *no.*

The claw clip is falling out of her hair. Her sneakers are scuffed. There's a blot by her eye where she messed up putting on drugstore mascara—if she didn't steal it from Sean's house while loading up his corpse, she bought it at the Dollar General across from Wash County's singular stoplight.

"Crane?" Tammy says. "You hearing me?"

Sophie was thirteen the first time she wanted to hurt herself.

Or that was halfway decent shorthand for it. If she'd ever bothered to describe the specifics of what she wanted to do, presumably to a mental health professional, that's what it would've been called. Self-harm. Pain-seeking behavior. But even as a young teen, she knew that wording wasn't quite right. The pain would be an unfortunate side effect of what actually had to be done.

The moment it clicked, she was standing outside with her middle school class while the fire alarm blared. It's not as if it was an actual *fire*. Just a faulty wire in the gym that gave off a spark, never got above a flicker. Barely more than a drill. Boring. But Sophie thought about being caught in that school as it burned. Being rescued with second- or third-degree burns obliterating her beyond recognition. In her imagination, the moment when she walked to the mirror to see her melted face for the first time? It was everything she'd ever wanted.

It consumed her. In high school, stuck in the art classroom while Aspen had a meltdown in the hall, she chewed on her eraser and wished for a car accident or a dog mauling. She considered the time she saw a woman on a TV talk show who'd been attacked by a chim-panzee. At night, she pulled blankets over her head and googled burn survivors until her vision blurred. One night, she found a write-up of a fireman recovering from full-body burns. An incident report of sorts, or a case study, complete with photos. From all angles, every piece of him. The glistening, still-fresh wounds and painful skin grafts—they were beautiful. *He* was beautiful. So beautiful to her, in fact, that she thought about him fucking her and masturbated in that awkward fifteen-year-old way. She saved the photos and made an album on her phone, titled *homework*, and looked at them under her desk at school.

Sophie wasn't actually going to do anything to herself. She wouldn't make a plan until she was walking across the graduation stage, and even that wouldn't pan out. Even in her worst fantasies, none of the accidents were her fault. It was always someone else's unleashed dog, or decision to drive drunk. See, she told herself. She doesn't want to *do* it. If *she* wanted to do it, then it would be bad. Obviously.

But as she got older, began creeping toward womanhood, or whatever future was stalking closer by the day, it got worse. Didn't it. The things she thought about.

Disgusting motherfucker. Wanting the boys in the locker room to rape her. Maybe beat her into the bench until she stumbled out broken-nosed and sobbing. She held the kitchen knife in her hand too long. She put her face near the chain-link fence in the backyard, where the neighbor's reactive German shepherd snapped its teeth. She stood there barefoot in the grass, in the sundress she forced herself to wear, breathing hard as the animal paced back and forth, huffing angrily at her presence. She thought about letting that dog fuck her. Horrible, filthy piece of SHIT.

A week before high school graduation—a month after she looked up "female castration" in a fit of disgust at her own libido—Sophie tried on the cute black dress she intended to wear to the ceremony, tied up her hair with a ribbon, and stared at herself in the bedroom mirror.

"I know I bought eyeliner," Mom was saying from the bathroom across the hall. "It's somewhere, I promise!"

Sophie said, "Mom, seriously, it's okay." Her voice was a soprano, sweet and clear. She'd spent most of her school years in choir, mulling over and refusing every concert solo, because she wanted the attention, but the wrong attention made her want to die, and she was pretty sure this would be the wrong kind. She didn't know what the right kind was.

In the mirror, she was busy trying to make the dress accentuate what little chest she had.

Long dark hair. Big eyes, small tits, pale skin.

There should have been *proof* written on her. An imperfection or impurity she could point to as evidence of everything that was wrong with her. There wasn't. She was just a girl.

And what *had* gone wrong? Nothing had even happened to her. Mom, chatting happily from the bathroom, joking about the heat index predicted for the ceremony, could not have been the cause of the crossed wires in her head, the disgusting wants lurking in her lizard brain. Dad, napping off lunch on the couch downstairs, was a kind man with kinder hands, so it could not have been him, either.

And yet. And yet she didn't want this anymore. She was sick of speaking and straight As and expectations and a future she would inevitably crumple under. What she *wanted* was to set herself on fire. She wanted to cut her knee ligaments so she would be forced to crawl on all fours. She wanted to reach into her throat and find her vocal cords and crush them, then let someone take her and break her and use her. Put an ice pick into her orbital socket if she had to. Fuck her up for good. Make the outside match the inside.

Then she'd be happy.

When Mom came out of the bathroom, Sophie was crying.

"Oh," Mom said, dropping the eyeliner she'd finally found. "Oh no. Come here."

While she's sobbing into her mother's shoulder, while Mom runs a hand across her hair and whispers to her, rocking her back and forth like she's a baby again, go ahead. Make eye contact with the mirror. Really look.

Doesn't Jess look a hell of a lot like that.

"Crane?" Tammy says again. "*Crane.*"

Jess stares, and Crane can taste the impending burning-hot bile in the back of his throat.

Fuck her. She doesn't get to do this to him, not now, not like this. It should be her in his place right now. It should've been her. *Fuck her.*

And Stagger is holding him. A hand on the chest, on the shoulder, pressing down. Body curled protectively, close and warm. Murmuring, **"Okay. It's okay. It's okay."**

He'll run, Crane thinks, like he hasn't already failed. He'll defect, he wants to say, as if he is capable of surviving out there in the world alone. They can't do this to him. They can't.

Oh, but they can.

Carry our little one into the sun, the hive says, **where we cannot go.**

Second Trimester

Eleven

There are rules now.

Guidelines for what Crane may or may not do, for his safety.

"And the baby's," Levi said.

One: No driving, as stated previously. The Camry's key has been confiscated and hidden.

Two: He must be accompanied by Levi or Stagger at all times, to avoid instances of drinking bleach, hitting his stomach with random heavy objects, etcetera.

Three: The following items are banned from the apartment—belts, rope, the go bag. The shotgun and all ammunition must be secured in the gun safe at all times. The following items are available only by request, and use must be supervised—kitchen knives, painkillers, scissors, replacement blades for Levi's razor. One day Crane gets back from the gas station and the metal coat hangers have been replaced with plastic. It's so absurd he laughs.

Four: He may no longer assist with or perform hunts on behalf of the hive, alone or with supervision. Not that he ever wanted to. That's fine.

Five: He must agree to weekly check-ins with Tammy regarding the health and growth of the fetus.

Nothing is said about his HRT, and he's not risking it. Crane dismantles the three-week supply kept in the Tupperware, hides each piece of medical equipment individually, and climbs onto a chair with a screwdriver to hide his hormones in the vent. Stagger holds the chair steady.

"Hey," Jess says one day, while Crane is trying to show her the specifics of breaking down the register at the end of a shift. Not that the specifics really matter, but more accurate numbers make for better lying, and Crane is in the process of actively attempting to work himself to death, because everything else is off the table. "Um."

Crane turns to her with a stony glare. *We were in the middle of something*, he hopes his expression says. Jess catches his annoyance immediately, which is the advantage of working with non-autistics. They tend to pick up the carefully crafted social cues he manages to lay down. She shrinks a bit.

"There's," she tries again, "something I wanted to—"

If this is about the hunt, or what she saw last month in the manager's office, he doesn't give a shit. He doesn't want to hear it. Least of all from her.

Third attempt. "How are you holding up?"

She's messed up his counting. He slams the cash drawer shut. Let her figure it out herself.

How the apartment used to be:

Crane's alarm blaring from his phone and Levi coming into the bedroom to yank off the blankets. "Up and at 'em," Levi would say, then snort when Crane would growl and snatch them back. T-shirts with red stains slung over the shower curtain rod because Crane's washed enough period blood out of underwear to clean up better than Levi ever could. Crane stealing Levi's jackets. Levi squeezing Crane's thigh right on a bruise, to watch him squirm. Cobbling together dinner for two from dollar-store rations and getting fucked face down on the hardwood floor. Levi wandering out to the front porch of the apartment complex to grab a smoke, and Crane always going with him, sitting on the concrete in Levi's clothes, leaning against Levi's leg as the lighter clicked.

"Want a drag?" Levi might say, handing the cigarette down. Sometimes Crane would take it. Sometimes he wouldn't.

Once, there was a deer—a buck wandering out from the woods with another buck's severed head stuck on his antlers, the two of them locked together forever. A rutting match ended in decapitation. The rotting head hung like a trophy from the buck's eight-point rack as he picked his way across the parking lot, between the cars and trucks.

Levi nudged Crane's shoulder. "Holy shit. Look at the size of him."

The two of them stayed there, even after the cigarette burned out, until the buck disappeared from view.

Birdie texts sometimes—dinging the group chat with mundane observations. Her legal adoption of Luna has gone through. Pictures of a tortoiseshell stray Aspen's started feeding. Complaints about daycare availability. A happy birthday message at midnight; *I hope 21 is kind to u.* Little things, pebbles dropped into a well, hoping to hear a splash at the bottom and never quite managing.

How the apartment is now:

Stagger sleeping on the couch, or in the hall, or at the foot of the bed. Levi changing the combination to the gun safe every three days. Crane coming home from shifts to eat dinner standing in the kitchen and going straight to bed. Levi won't touch him. Crane brings his phone into the bathroom and jacks off in the tub, watching the grossest porn he can find with the audio cranked so loud in his earbuds it hurts, a desperate attempt to work some of the stress out of his clenched muscles.

It is, admittedly, hard to feel like a man when it takes half a hand up your cunt to get you off.

Twelve

Tammy asks Crane yes-or-no questions in the apartment living room. She feels his stomach and he answers each question with a nod. Yes, he's having trouble buttoning his pants. Yes, he's hungry, which is good because it means the morning sickness is finally cutting him a break, though the dizziness sucks. And yes, dear god, his breasts ache, and the larva is stealing calcium from his bones to build its own, and stripping the oxygen from his blood and pissing into the amniotic fluid. It's disgusting. Yes. That's correct.

In the same vein, Tammy hesitates to divulge details. Probably debating if she should tell him how big the larva is, or what parts of it are starting to form. He imagines its tiny maggot segments are building up from stolen nutrients. She focuses on the important things instead, like how he should be stocking up on liners and extra underwear and drinking more water. For the love of god, put on some weight, and accept he'll go up a cup size. Go get a new bra.

"We'd probably be able to tell the sex," she says. "If we were going to a hospital."

"No fucking hospitals," Levi says, loading his backpack with hunting supplies.

"I ain't talking to you."

Nineteen weeks, she declares.

It's a countdown. Twenty-one weeks left, or thereabouts.

The next morning, right before Levi is supposed to return from his hunting trip to Maryland, Crane stares into the only full-length mirror in the apartment, hung sloppily on the back of the bathroom door.

He's showing.

He holds the hem of his shirt in his mouth, the drawstrings of his pajama pants undone so he can take in the full size of the bump. It's not even that big of a belly. A vague rounding of the stomach and not much more. But it's big enough that he can't pass it off as an unfortunate fat deposit—it's breaking the silhouette of his baggy shirts, shuffling around his organs to make room for itself.

He runs a hand over it. It's softer than he thought it'd be. Only hair and skin, bulging out under the rib cage and distorting the tattoos. He considers the possibility that it's not one giant grub. Maybe it's a mass of them, the way an animal left to rot in the sun swells to bursting with parasites.

Stagger looms in the cramped hallway, as he does.

Crane signs, *What?* He does it one-handed because it still gets the point across. It takes a second for Stagger to recognize it—they haven't had a lot of time to practice their rudimentary ASL, what with Crane picking up extra shifts. If he's too tired to think, then he won't think about how much he wants to die.

"Hurt?"

Not really. Besides the typical pregnancy aches. That's not why he's upset. Come on, buddy, use your worm-infested brain.

Crane takes off his shirt, then the deodorant-stained racerback bra he's worn every day for a year, and turns on the hall light. "Big lights" are usually a hard no in the apartment. This one still has its lightbulb, only because he can't figure out how to remove it. But, see? Look at the belly. Look how big it's gotten.

And, with an overhead light, his tits now cast a shadow across the rib cage. He can grab a handful. That's more than he could do before. A few weeks ago, there was barely enough for Levi to get into his mouth.

Twenty months of testosterone isn't magic. When he hums, the sound rattles at the base of his throat, not quite hitting the low note he hopes for. He's hairy like a tenth-grade boy and sports a thin, patchy struggle of a beard. But it'd done the job well enough. He's tall, and wears Levi's old shirts more often than not, and truckers and hive-bitten strangers passing through have stopped flirting and started calling him *kid*, or *boy*, or just *hey, man* if they're cool like that.

Most importantly, he'd stopped seeing Sophie.

Crane really, really looks in the mirror. Presses his chest flat. Sucks his stomach in.

Sophie is supposed to be gone. She's supposed to be dead, he swears, but now there's something in his stomach and it's growing and it's going to come out and he thinks the first time someone calls him a mother he's going to hit his head against a wall until his skull splits. He's going to pray for an umbilical cord wrapped around its thick grub neck. If he's going to look down one day and see a maggot chewing on his nipple for milk, he might as well take out his own eyes, right?

His distress must be visible. ***"Shh,"*** Stagger murmurs.

Crane mimics him: "Shh." And again. "Shhh."

It's supposed to help. Something about the vagus nerve, he thinks. There we go. Easy now.

In the awkward alcove of the hallway, tucked between the closet and the bathroom door, it's okay. He wants to find whatever worm makes up Stagger's jugular, or carotid artery, and press his forehead against it so he can feel it the way he feels for Tammy's pulse. Align their heartbeats, or whatever passes for a heartbeat in Stagger's body, if he has one, because Crane can't control his pulse on his own. A little kid incapable of regulating emotions without Mommy.

The moment before Crane reaches for him, because god he wants to stop feeling like this, the apartment door whines open and slams shut. Something heavy hits the hardwood.

Crane pulls away quick.

"*Crane*. You here?" Levi's footsteps thump into the kitchen. Cabinets bang one after another. What kind of question is that—where else would he be? "First aid kit. Where'd you put it."

Crane wrestles on his bra and shirt, snatches the kit from the linen closet, and finds Levi in the kitchen, opening a beer with one hand and clutching a wadded-up towel to his shoulder with the other.

"He had a buddy," Levi says, half turning and dropping the towel to show the murder scene swallowing the left side of his back. "Caught me off guard. Hurts like a bitch."

Fuck. Levi's shoulder is black with blood. How long has he been walking around like this? The whole drive back down from Maryland, feeding the hive, everything? Crane kicks over a stool from the shitty dining table they don't use—jabs his finger at it, *sit*—and goes for the kitchen shears to get the shirt off before remembering they were confiscated two months ago. Fine. He peels up a torn edge of fabric from the wound and rips it until he can toss the whole mess on the floor.

Levi hisses. "I liked that shirt."

Too late. There's a perfect four-inch line across the shoulder blade smelling like pennies.

Crane washes his hands, because Levi ending up with an infection isn't high on the list of things he wants to deal with, shooting a pointed glare across the kitchen. Levi sniffs morosely.

"I didn't see him, okay? Sue me." Then: "Hey." Stagger's lurking by the fridge. "Forgot to save a piece for you. Little busy."

Stagger huffs, but Crane shoots him a look too. They can have one of their weird macho stare-downs later, thank you.

Cleaning a wound sucks. It'd be easier in the bathroom, but the room is tiny; easier to avoid staining the grout in the first place than attempt to get down there and scrub it. Bad enough in there as it is. Crane spreads a plastic sheet across the kitchen floor to catch the splatter, but the leaky dribble of homemade saline and diluted blood gets everywhere anyway. At least the wound isn't visibly dirty. Only a few stray towel fibers.

God. The fibers look like the tiny white worms he'd find while helping Birdie with the garden. He plucks one out with tweezers and holds it up to double-check.

Just linen.

The wound's too big for butterfly bandages—doesn't look like it scraped the bone, but it definitely went through all the skin and hit the muscle—and absolutely will not hold with superglue, so stitches it is. Levi winces into his beer but takes it like a champ. Push the needle through the skin, drag the thread through, pull it taut.

Leaving bloody fingerprints across Levi's bare back, Crane seethes.

Levi hasn't even *tried* to help. It'd be stupid to expect Levi to be fully on his side; Levi is always going to put the hive first. That's part of the deal. Crane would put the hive over Levi, too. But *nothing*?

It's not like he wants sappy, saccharine reassurance. If anyone offered soft-boy of-course-I-still-see-you-as-a-man platitudes, spouted "trans men are men" validity circle-jerk shit, or showed him seahorse dad memes, he'd gag. It's that, okay, look, the hottest thing Levi'd ever done to him was shove his head down on his cock so hard he'd nearly vomited, and all Levi said was, "Come on. Thought you'd take it like a man."

Crane yanks one of the stitches too hard. Levi grunts into his beer.

The least Levi could do is that. Give Crane something to take. But Levi hasn't hurt him since that night in the parking lot. Hasn't pushed him to the ground or left a bruise, not with Stagger breathing down their necks.

What it would take to change that.

Push, drag, pull.

He thinks about Levi ducking his head to Jess's shoulder. Her dark hair and thin lips and big eyes.

It's a stretch. It's a low blow. It's nonsense.

It's perfect.

He stitches the last inch, ties off the thread, and cuts it with his teeth because he doesn't know where the scissors are anymore.

And as soon as the needle is back in the first aid kit, he brings his fist down onto the line of sloppy sutures holding Levi's newest hole closed.

Levi choke-screams, *"Fuck."* The only kind of thing you can get out when your vision's gone white at the edges. He rockets off the stool like he's been shot and keels around, grabbing for him uselessly.

In an instant, Stagger bullies into the kitchen. The ever-present protector, of course. Can't let a little domestic dispute go unchallenged. He jams himself between Crane and Levi with that deep-chest snarl, puts an arm out, ducks his head like some big buck in the snow.

Crane is grinning, though. He can feel the blood in his veins again.

"The fuck is wrong with—*fuck*." Levi hunches over, clutches his shoulder, struggles to get his breath. He's glassy-eyed, feet planted in the pink soap-water smearing the kitchen floor. Still holding the beer too, dangling by the bottleneck from his fingers.

He points the bottle at Stagger. "You. Move."

Crane wouldn't mind if Stagger did—let's refresh some bruises tonight—but he doesn't, and that sets Levi off too. *What, you think you knocked him up, big motherfucker you think you are.* That sort of thing. It's been a while since he's gotten to see the good stuff. Crane hadn't realized he'd missed it.

"Get out of the way," Levi snarls, then, "Look at me, the fuck's gotten into you? *Look at me.*"

Oh, he'll let Levi know. That's no problem. He grabs a notepad from the counter and a pen, the same notepad and pen they use for the grocery lists, and writes in big, scrawling letters.

ARE YOU FUCKING JESS

Levi stares at the sentence like there's a chance he's misreading four of the simplest words in the English language.

"Am I—"

He laughs. It sounds like a bark.

"It's the hormones," Levi says. He looks to Stagger as if bro code supersedes the past fifteen seconds, *you seeing this?* Stagger doesn't catch on because he is a bunch of worms stuffed into a human body. "Holy shit, they really do make you crazy."

Stagger identifies the note as a source of tension and crumples it.

"Is this because I didn't take her on the hunt today? *Special treatment?*" Levi's showing all his big predator teeth and Stagger is getting pissed and, you know what, Crane hadn't thought of that, but sure! After everything Mike and Levi put him through during his first months with the hive, this is absolutely because he didn't take Jess on the hunt today, one hundred percent. "You think I wanna babysit some little girl again? Shut the fuck up. Shut the *fuck*—"

Crane's phone rings.

It gets real quiet in the kitchen real fast.

He'd completely forgotten that the damn thing was in his pocket. It still has the janky default ringtone too, because nobody ever calls him.

Both Stagger and Levi watch him—always watching, the kind of cruel and unusual punishment *watching* that would violate the Geneva Convention if he was a prisoner of war—as he pulls the phone out and checks the caller ID.

He tilts the screen. Tammy.

Levi snaps, "Answer it."

He does. Through the haze of his pounding head, he remembers to click his tongue twice to acknowledge that yes, he has in fact picked up.

"Hey, sweetheart," Tammy says. "Sorry about the call, I know how much you hate these things. Just wanted to let you know we got something interesting down at the house you might wanna see, if you can keep your mouth shut."

Tammy snorts dryly at her own joke.

"Anyway. The little girl from the McDowell hive's here. Pregnant, but won't be for much longer. Could use an extra hand with the mess."

Crane is halfway out the door by the time she's done with the last sentence, Stagger pausing only for a moment to grab his gaiter and gloves before trailing behind. Levi only yells a little.

Thirteen

No car keys means walking. That's fine. It's a good day for it.

Tammy lives in Washville proper, tucked against the woods in a ranch house some two decades older than she is. Used to be that Harry would come by every week; cut the grass, hack down the ivy, do the things Tammy can't with her hands so bad and her husband dead. Then he died too, so Crane picked up the slack. Then Crane got knocked up and nobody wants him doing hard work, so now Jess is doing it. Last time Levi and Crane swung by, she was in the yard with gloves, yanking grass out of cracks in the concrete walkway.

For a better part of the twenty minutes down the side of the highway to town, Stagger grumbles about Crane's stunt in the apartment. Crane waves him off—he's distracted, burning with adrenaline, repeating over and over *there's another one, there's another one?*—but Stagger won't let it go. The worms won't stay still.

They need to work on their signing. The only thing Crane can manage is *okay*. The sign for *O*, the sign for *K*. *Okay*. It's okay. He's in one piece, okay? Drop it.

God, he hopes Levi makes him pay for it later.

Washville itself is a collection of shops and old stores branching out from an ill-maintained Main Street, and Crane will absolutely not be seen on its sidewalks during the day. Together, he and Stagger skirt around town and find the gravel residential roads behind the dialysis clinic.

There's a charm to it, living at such a high elevation that the world looks flat and empty forever. Wide clear skies, shoddy yards pitted with puddles, piles of firewood, guesstimated property lines marked by differing grass heights. There're deer tracks in the mud, and a cat at the base of a pine with knobby-knee roots.

Crane likes it here. Hard to believe that he could like something that isn't imminently self-destructive, but whatever. He likes how the cliffs light up orange and red every autumn, and the way fog clings to the treetops. He also likes to think he would've moved up here even if the swarm hadn't found him. He can't say that for certain, but it's nice to imagine.

Finally, the two of them spot 636 Victory Lane slouching alone halfway down the road. Crane doesn't recognize the car in the driveway. He's homesick as he takes the steps two at a time and knocks.

"*Get that*," Tammy demands, muffled, and Jess does as she's told.

Shit. He thought Jess was working today.

Jess hesitates in the doorway, smelling earthy and wet, wound-like. The same thing he's been smelling since Levi got home. Wearing Tammy's hand-me-downs and scabs on her knees.

She says, visibly uncomfortable, "Both of you?"

"Is that Crane?" Tammy calls from the other side of the house.

She calls back: "Yeah. Him and the, uh, other guy." Then, quieter, "Look, can your friend stay outside? In the backyard or something?"

Crane shoulders past her and clicks his tongue for Stagger to follow.

Tammy's house is a comfort. Ugly vinyl floors, wood walls, lace curtains, and ancient white appliances. There is one air-conditioning unit, and it's jammed crookedly into the living room window. Crane used to fall asleep on the brown couch watching World War I documentaries, read the angry letters Tammy's daughter sent in the mail every few months after pulling them from the trash, dig freezer-burned ice cream out from behind mounds of stockpiled venison.

Maybe he should've taken Tammy up on the option to move back in. He'd have to share the space with Jess, but he can grit his teeth through a lot.

Jess, left with no other option, considering she'd just been completely ignored, shuts the door. "The girl is in the back."

A pained sound groans from one of the rooms. Crane's blood goes cold. The last time he heard something like that was when he found a deer with a broken neck on the side of the road. Stagger pulls down his neck gaiter. His nostrils flare. The entire house reeks of injured human.

Tammy bustles out of the hall with arms full of dirty towels.

"Good." She dumps the towels into Jess's arms. "Throw these in the wash and bring new ones. You—" Pointing at Stagger. "Stay in the living room. She's scared enough as it is." Stagger gives a low whine, but even the worms won't contradict an Appalachian granny. "And Crane, with me."

Tammy turns on her heel and leads him to the spare bedroom. Crane's mind turns, turns, turns, sorts through every movie he's watched and book he's read to prepare himself for what might be on the other side of the threshold.

It fails.

The girl kneeling by the bed, face pressed to the sheets—sweat-soaked, shivering, dress rucked up to her thighs—is a fucking *child*.

Watery blue eyes. Hair so blonde it's almost white. Legs stained and hands clasped like she's praying.

Crane stops short in the doorway.

Tammy whisks past him, rustling the plastic sheet she's set over the carpet. (With the amount of blood they deal with, that kind of sheet is standard issue for hive households.) The smell is thicker here, heavier. He can taste it in the back of his throat.

"Head up, girl," Tammy says, taking her by the nape of the neck. "Show me you're still breathing."

"It hurts," the girl whimpers.

"I know. Contractions hurt."

"It's too soon."

"I know," Tammy says again.

She's eighteen at most, though he'd guess lower if he had the capacity to mentally withstand the implications of it. Her belly shows through her dress, barely. Certainly not big enough for this to be anything but a tragedy.

"I don't want a man in here," the girl says. "Tell him to go away."

Tammy shakes her head. "He's a good one. Ain't gonna hurt you.

And look. Look at him. He got himself pregnant, too. *Breathe*, baby. See? Look at his belly."

Crane grits his teeth—silver lining, he passes for male to a terrified little girl—and ducks back out to the kitchen to grab a bottle of water before returning. Bottles of water are apparently how the hive shows affection, or care, or worry. Crane prefers it to speaking. Her hands shake when she tries to drink, so Crane holds it to her lips.

She has faint freckles across her nose. She's striking. So tiny too. He's never been to McDowell, but he thinks he would've heard of her at some point, the distant murmuring of a dozen hive workers about a beautiful thing hiding in a West Virginia impound lot. Or maybe he doesn't pay attention and nobody tells him anything.

She coughs, swallows.

Reaches for his belly.

Says, "Wait." Says, "Crane?"

Crane blinks.

"Levi told me about you." Her voice cracks. The pads of her fingers press against his stomach, right where his shirt goes taut. "You look—just like he said you do."

Levi talks about him?

That can't be right. There's nothing to talk about. Their relationship barely counted as a relationship, even before all this. The sex was good, the rent is halved, there's always someone to leave dinner on the stove or help pull a body out of the trunk. Levi made Crane feel like a man and Crane made Levi feel like a *man*. That doesn't count as anything to talk about, to him.

Crane catches Tammy's attention and pulls a face. A request for context, and a change of subject, if she doesn't mind.

"This is Hannah. Showed up a few hours ago," Tammy says.

She picks up a notepad by the side of the bed, checks her watch, jots down the time. "Stole a car from the impound lot and drove up herself. In labor the whole time. Figured I was her best bet." She glances over. "You said nobody at McDowell knew? Not even the hive?"

Hannah whispers, "I thought Beth'd be mad."

Beth. The old bitch who runs the impound lot. Hannah must've been layering on the sweatshirts and sucking in her stomach hard to get through it. And if even the McDowell hive had no idea? Jesus.

"You probably thought right," Tammy mutters. "Given she called me a minute ago to ask if I'd seen hide or hair of you."

Hannah looks up in a panic.

"I didn't tell her. You got enough to deal with right now." Tammy kneels with a groan, carefully wiping down the girl's shaking thighs with a warm washcloth. "Though now that I'm thinking about it. Who was it? Was it Billy?"

Hannah moans a weak "No," and thank god. Crane's never met Billy, but from Levi's stories, the guy's a piece of work. A retired hunter pushing fifty, the kind of man Levi keeps having to push around. He sounds like the type.

"Then who's the daddy?"

No response. Hannah squeezes her eyes shut, blows out hard through her teeth.

"Because if you didn't want this, we can tell Levi. You give us a name, we'll see if we can't get his man"—Tammy nods to Crane—"to take care of the bastard."

"No," Hannah says. "No."

Tammy stays there for a moment in silence, then says, "You change your mind, you tell us. We'll handle it."

According to Tammy, Hannah is approximately twenty weeks pregnant; if they go with that number, she's a single week further along than Crane is. Also according to Tammy, being born at twenty weeks is a death sentence. It barely counts as a stillborn at this point. *Late-term miscarriage*, that's what she says.

Crane has never been more jealous in his life.

Jess returns with fresh towels and takes to braiding Hannah's hair while Tammy checks dilation, dictating her notes to Crane. But that doesn't last forever. Labor takes a long time. It's a slow, painful slog. Most of the time there's nothing to do except be there with her, and Crane is bad at that.

That's how he ends up on the back porch with a peanut butter sandwich, while Stagger busies himself breaking down a pallet for firewood. There are a few big wooden pallets in Tammy's shed, for some reason—old people just find themselves in possession of random shit. Nobody will need firewood for a moment, but it stores easier broken down, so Stagger is ripping apart the pallet with his hands and stacking the pieces neatly.

Sometimes, Stagger stops for a moment and watches the window to the guest bedroom. The curtains are drawn and there's nothing to see, but he's fixed on it.

Crane snorts at him. Gotta feel weird knowing there's a baby on the way and it's not even his.

"Little one," Stagger says.

Crane nods. Yep.

Truth is, he's strangely relieved. This whole mess is raising more questions than it's answering—how did Hannah's baby slip the hive? Why doesn't she get her own gross flesh guardian?—but at least he'll get to see what comes out of her. Some curled-up grub the size of a fist. A bolus of larvae. Whatever. No reason it wouldn't be the same as what's in him.

He'd like one piece of certainty, if the world didn't mind.

"Okay?"

Okay, Crane signs.

The back door slaps shut, and Tammy steps out onto the porch with a glass of iced tea. She gives Stagger the stink eye, but folds up her creaky limbs to sit beside Crane on the dirty stairs, and spends a moment recovering from it by sighing and letting the breeze toss her straw-gray hair.

"That brute treating you alright?" she asks.

Crane isn't sure if she's referring to Levi or Stagger, so he makes a noncommittal noise.

"Mm. Dunno why I even bother asking." She's kidding, though, he thinks. "And when's the last time you cut your hair. Look like a shaggy dog."

Don't remind him. A few more weeks of growth and he'll start getting dysphoria about that too, but with everything going on, he's lucky he's brushing his teeth once a day, or showering at all. He rolls his eyes and she seems to get the message. She looks out over the yard, at the big rhododendron bush at the edge of her property where she buried the pistol that killed her husband. That must've happened, what, forty years ago?

The worms have been here awhile.

Tammy says, "Sweetheart, can I be honest with you for a second?"

It's not like he's going to tell her no. She takes a sip of her iced tea.

"For the past two decades," she says, "give or take, my job was to make sure that a single baby wasn't born to the hives around here."

Oh.

Crane is struck with belly-deep pain so sharp and sudden he almost doesn't recognize it. He grasps for it, mentally fumbling like he always does with feelings.

"Babies are nothing but trouble for the worms," Tammy says. "They're a mouth to feed, they draw attention, they're a liability. Plus, you know, sometimes they kill their mothers, and we can't have that."

Crane stares into the distance. At the dark tree line, where Washville devolves into wilderness.

"Didn't happen all that often," Tammy continues. "We're an antisocial bunch, ain't we. Not one of us fit for wanting babies, let alone raising them. But accidents happen. Bad things happen too. And used to be that I could take money out of the till, bring them to a clinic, and pay under the table to make it all go away. When that didn't work, I found them an antibiotic and a muscle relaxer, got them stinking drunk, and dug in there myself with something sharp."

What the hell is she doing, then? Why is she still talking? Why are they both just sitting here? They could sneak away from Levi and Stagger both, skip the alcohol, he'll grit his teeth through a procedure in the kitchen. Let her pull out whatever tools she uses, force open the cervix with whatever's on hand, give him a rag to bite on.

Tammy must see all that on his face.

"A few months ago," she says, "the worms told me to stop. Stop traveling, stop checking on girls, everything. My job was just to stay here with you."

She purses her lips, sucks on her crooked teeth, can't seem to get over the rancid taste of the words forming in her mouth.

"So first you, then her. Your brute shows up. The worms want whatever it is that's inside you. I don't—" She gestures. "I see the pieces, but can't figure out what the hell to make of them. All I know is that I don't like it."

She says, "And I'd make it as right as I can, but I ain't looking forward to dying."

And then she's getting up. Groaning as she goes, cursing her old knees and the weather and the rain that's just passed through.

All this time Tammy has been getting rid of babies, and she won't do it for him. Not for the kid she took under her wing, considers more of her child than her actual daughter. Because the hive told her no.

"Oh," Tammy says with a snort. "How long you been there, Jess?"

Jess, on the other side of the screen door, shrugs. "Not long," she says, but even Crane can tell that's a lie.

First-time births take forever. Muscles struggle, organs refuse to stretch, the cervix thins weakly like it isn't quite sure if this is what it's supposed to do.

When Hannah finally starts pushing in earnest—when her body's wrenched itself open enough to allow it—she's stumbled her way out of a hot shower, towel wrapped desperately around her shoulders in an attempt to preserve what's left of her modesty. Her wet braid smears down the center of her back.

"I can feel it," she whimpers, reaching between her legs to plug it up and make it stop.

Jess fetches warm water and more washcloths. Tammy reminds her to breathe. Hannah stares at the bed, then asks if she should get up there and lie down on her back, because that's what they do on TV. Is that the right thing to do?

It's a demeaning position, Crane thinks. And counterintuitive. Going against gravity.

Tammy says, "This ain't no hospital. You can push this out standing, if it's easier."

Hannah does decide on standing. Crane can't blame her; there's a sort of defiance to insisting on staying upright though the pain. But the windowsills are too narrow to brace herself on, the nightstand too low, the bed too soft to offer any real support.

Alright. Crane gets Hannah's attention and gestures her to him. He'll hold her up. Come on, come here.

She studies him. The gears in her head turn for a moment, then whatever she's weighing must come out on the side of yes because she steps closer, lets Crane gather her up, braces herself against his chest. She fits neatly under his chin. She's burning hot. He's got her. It's okay. The next wave of contractions seizes her muscles and her moan rattles his teeth.

"Push," Tammy says.

There are so many ways this could go wrong. Sophie was obsessed with them all. Women used to write wills before childbirth. Tearing, hemorrhage, infection; try not to picture this child bleeding out onto the tarp. Try not to think about the stained towels in Tammy's arms.

Hannah wails into his shirt, and he cradles the back of her head like a newborn.

"Almost there," Jess whispers as Tammy reaches down to check her progress. "It's almost over."

If there's one silver lining for Hannah, it's that whatever's in there will be smaller. He's unsure if that means it'll hurt any less, but logically, that follows. He doesn't know enough to make a decent guess.

But he can't help imagining himself in her position. Him, kneeling on the floor or braced against someone's chest. *Him*, breathing through contractions. *Him*, feeling the fetus bearing down between his legs. After all he's done to be a man, something as tiny and routine as a sperm meeting an egg is going to undo it all and leave him pushing something out of his cunt on the floor.

"One more time," Tammy says. "Just push one more time."

"I can't," Hannah pleads.

"Yes, you can."

"We're here," Jess says.

It's born with a splatter of fluid and flurry of movement. Crane doesn't have the line of sight, but he can *feel* it in the way Hannah's body nearly gives out from under her. In the birth video he watched in sophomore year health class, a baby unceremoniously falls out once it hits a certain point.

"Here," Jess says. "Scissors."

It's quiet now. No crying. Just the crinkling of the plastic sheet, Hannah's crying, the rattle of the AC in the living room.

Hannah goes to move, but Crane pins her tight. Don't look.

Silence.

Stillness.

Tammy reaches up to touch Hannah's leg. "Do you want to see it?"

In Crane's arms, Hannah thinks. She sniffles. She wipes her eyes, buries herself deeper into Crane's chest like she can disappear there.

She says, "No."

"Hmm." A plastic bag rustles. Over Hannah's shoulder, he catches a glimpse of Tammy tying a bundle tight with two sharp movements. The same way an old farm woman would tie up kittens meant to be drowned in the river. "Jess, Crane, get this out of my house."

Fourteen

The bag in Crane's hand weighs as much as a ten-dollar grocery run. A package of good cookies, or a discounted tray of nearly expired chicken thighs. On the back porch, he stands as still as he can to feel if the thing inside is moving. The plastic flutters when he breathes, so he stops until his lungs burn.

Nothing. Whatever it was, it was born dead. Not even a twitch or gurgle to show for it.

Jess and Tammy didn't react like anything about it was strange, but. That can't be right. He casts around mentally for an explanation and can only come up with shock, the same way he did on

Aspen and Birdie's porch. It's his go-to. Shock can explain just about anything.

"Um," Jess says, shoulders hunched as Stagger steps out of the shed with a shovel. Crane lowers the bag and loops his fingers through the rabbit-ear handles to hold it normally. "The woods? Away from the house?"

It's late afternoon, balmy with a pleasant breeze smelling like tall grass, the faint scent of the honeysuckle crawling up the rotting back steps. Still holding the bag, because it's hard to forget about the bag, Crane peels a powder-yellow flower from the vine, plucks out the stamen, and places the single bead of nectar on his tongue. Ever since he was a kid, he's had the intense urge to eat the flower whole. He'd never done it, but he got the sense that the petals would crunch and squeak between his teeth like fetal cartilage.

Then, realizing he's been asked a question, he nods. Away from the house. Don't need anybody asking questions, not with a murder weapon buried in the garden.

Jess says, looking at the bag, "Poor thing."

He hears Hannah crying inside, Tammy talking her through passing the placenta. Time to go.

Stagger sticks close as a burr. Even with the gaiter pulled back over his nose, the entirety of his body keeps shifting and readjusting under the skin. His eyes dart between Crane, the bag, Jess, then back again. Crane tries to get his attention, but it won't stay in one place.

Well. They can't be doing anything wrong. If they weren't supposed to be doing this, he's pretty sure Stagger would've stopped them.

Again, Crane one-handed signs, *What?*

"Little one," he says again.

Jess cringes involuntarily at the sound of his worm-chatter voice. "Oh my god."

Unfortunately, it's a nice enough afternoon that people are out. Crane hasn't made a habit of getting to know Washville's few remaining inhabitants. Why would he. The people here are good people, trying to eke out a few more mortgage payments or insurance copays, and Crane is—well, Crane.

Not that it's hard to recognize people. With so few residents, you learn faces eventually. An old man with nine fingers who comes by the gas station every now and again and pays with change; a group of kids from the next town over buying beer every weekend because they've been banned from the local spots. There's a lady at the Dollar General who started smiling at Crane last year and never stopped.

He keeps his distance, though. He's mentally incapable of maintaining two halfway-decent relationships at a time.

A ways down Victory Lane, a woman on her porch raises a hand in greeting.

"Jessie girl," she calls, rough from what must be decades of smoking. "Them boys ain't giving you trouble, are they?"

If it were up to Crane, he'd keep going, but Jess stops, so he stops too—on the side of the road, because there're no sidewalks up here—and Jess breaks into the biggest, most sunbeam-bright smile.

"Hi, Miss Addie!" she says. "No, ma'am, not at all. These are my coworkers. We were just helping Miss Tammy around the house."

Miss Addie pulls down her bifocals to inspect Crane and Stagger, thankfully with enough distance between them that Crane can pull at his shirt and Stagger can duck his head and they won't look *too* wrong.

She seems to at least recognize Crane, because she says, "When did you start working at the gas station?"

"Few months ago. Sean wasn't too happy when I got the job, so Miss Tammy's letting me stay with her is all."

Miss Addie hums. "I ain't seen him around."

"Huh. Not missing much."

Miss Addie says, "You look better for it, sugar, that's all I'll say," and tells the lot of them to get on with their errands then. Jess laughs. It's bright and genuine and sweet.

Sophie smiled too, sure, but she hated to show her teeth. Her favorite pictures of herself caught only a suggestion of her; the back of her head, face obscured by long hair, turned from the camera like a ghost.

Five minutes past the tree line into the woods, Jess stops in front of a tree, looks down into the gap in the roots of an old oak, and says, "Here."

Stagger jams the shovel into the dirt and begins to dig.

Crane, then, is left holding the bag.

He's sat himself in the underbrush because he's tired and his feet hurt. Everything is a goddamn pregnancy symptom these days. Don't get him started on how often he has to piss now, the uterus pushing itself right into his bladder. It doesn't feel right to put the bag on the ground, so it's in his lap.

The bag is translucent, but all he can make out is the off-white dish towel wrapping up the miniature corpse. His long fingers—chewed-on nails with clinging specks of polish, cut-up knuckles—pick at the flimsy knot holding the package closed. The same way they used to pick at his scalp or press nervously against the edge of a knife. Autonomously, without his consent.

He could just *ask* Tammy what it looked like when they get back. Or Jess even, right now. The pregnancy tracker online likes to show a perfect tiny baby, if not uncomfortably spindly, so he has to go to medical photos to get an honest depiction—at this stage, a real baby would be an eerie translucent red with swollen eye sockets and nub-fingers. Unsettling, a growing bird taken out of the egg too soon.

Stagger jams the shovel through a root, pries away a rock. Jess asks him, "So do you have a name, or?" and he doesn't reply.

The bag comes undone.

Crane pushes aside the plastic flaps, skimming the dish towel shroud.

There has to be a difference between *babies* and whatever grows inside people like him and Hannah. Whatever the worms could possibly want so badly as to remove Tammy from her duty, to do this to him on purpose, to force into existence the first children any hive has seen in decades.

"No wonder you and Crane get on," Jess says. A talker when she's nervous. "You're so quiet."

Stagger grunts at her, which, much like Crane's own attempts at communication, gets the point across nonetheless.

Crane lifts the dish towel.

It's . . .

A baby.

Tiny and curled in on itself, head the size of a billiard ball, bones the size of toothpicks. Squinched pug face. Skin almost see-through but not quite, thin enough to show the organs under paper-thin flesh. And a distended belly, from which hangs a bizarrely swollen string, stained blue and white; a deep-sea creature clamped to its stomach.

It's not a larva, or a giant maggot.

Just a baby.

It's only one, *one* fucking week older than what's inside him. What he's carrying is a few ounces lighter, the skin closer to transparent than translucent. He leans in, tries to make out the details. All the tiny pieces of it.

Though, what if it's like Stagger? The worms hiding between the tiny organs. Bugs instead of capillaries. Everything is too small to tell with the wrinkly, half-formed skin in the way.

It *can't* be normal. It *can't be.*

Crane reaches into the bag and props up the sad little creature with one hand. It's warm and uncomfortably soft. Floppy, too. If he pressed his fingers into the cartilage that would have eventually solidified into a rib cage, the same way he'd open an orange, it'd just come apart.

He deserves to know what's inside him, doesn't he? It's the least the hive can give him. A goddamn answer.

He gets his second hand in there and nudges apart the puffy eyelids, then its tiny slit-mouth. Nothing surprising. Only gelatinous eyeballs not yet finished forming, and structures that would have become gums.

Fine. He can't see the worms through Stagger's eyes or mouth either. He's putting his thumbs against the itty-bitty breastbone.

The nail pierces the skin.

Jess shrieks *"Crane!"* with the panicked shrill of someone catching their dog with a mauled animal and snatches the bag. Stagger's head snaps up with a snarl. "What the fuck are you *doing*?"

Crane doesn't try to get the bag back, or make a noise in pro-test, or do anything at all. Even if he spoke, every possible response would make him sound deranged. *I was going to open it up and look for worms?* That is involuntary-hold levels of bullshit, even with the hive's sky-high tolerance for deranged behavior. Like, that's the sort of thing Harry would've said before Levi put him down.

But he wants to beg her to give it back. If he opens it up, he can see. He'll know what's waiting for him at the end of this. Who cares, anyway? Hannah doesn't want it, and it can't feel anything. It's dead. It won't care and neither should she.

Jess stares at him. Waiting.

She gets nothing.

Jess says, "Jesus Christ." Her teeth chatter. "I don't—oh my *god*. What is—" She turns to Stagger. "Move. I'll bury it."

Stagger steps away, almost gratefully abandoning the project to return to Crane's side. Jess doesn't take the shovel. She gets to her knees in the rotting underbrush and places the bag in between the roots of the tree and scoops the soil back in with her hands. Mud from the rain and smears of dirt cake under her nails.

"I know you don't like me," she says.

Stagger puts a hand into the overgrown hair at the back of Crane's neck.

"I'm not stupid. Believe it or not."

Crane glances uncomfortably over his shoulder back to Washville. It sounds like she's going to cry.

The best part about being a mute is that he doesn't have to respond to stuff like this. He could really play up his autist status today too, if he wanted. Just get up and leave.

"And, like, I get it. That's fine. I fucked up that night and—" She packs a handful of dirt around the flimsy bag. The stillborn disappears under bugs and innocent earthworms. "I know I'm a giant baby, and I'm annoying, and I can't take care of myself, I know, believe me. Sean told me all the fucking time. I am *fully* aware of my flaws."

Well. Crane hasn't even been around her enough to make value judgments like that. Sure, she did fuck up, and then she snitched about it, and she's anxious about the register and bad enough at math that he keeps having to recount the cash drawer. But that's not *why* he dislikes her. Not really.

(It should've been her.)

The final handful of dirt goes down. Jess shoves her weight on top of it once, twice, to tamp down the musty earth.

"I don't know." She's sniffling now. "At least I'm grateful, right? Sean's dead. I have my first job. You know this is my first? And when I showed up at your gas station, it was the first time I'd been outside in weeks. I'm not even from here. I'm from *Cleveland*. I thought I was going to die in that stupid fucking cabin. I prayed every night that he'd change his mind and see that what he was doing was wrong and he'd let me out and I could just. I could see the sun again." She gets up. She's unsteady on her feet. "Turns out, after everything, it sucks outside that cabin too."

When she smiles again, it doesn't reach her eyes.

"Why would you care, though. Swear to god, all of you like it here."

Fifteen

Crane can't stomach going back to the apartment. Levi hasn't texted him, hasn't called Tammy demanding his whereabouts, hasn't beat his fist on the door to drag him back. So Crane stays the night like he's seventeen again.

Hannah and Jess sleep in the guest bed that used to be his, curled up facing each other. When Crane wanders past to brush his teeth, because Tammy always keeps a spare toothbrush for him, he hears Jess whispering through a crack under the door. "Are you sure that's what you saw?"

"I don't know," Hannah whimpers. "I thought it moved."

"It was a bad day."

Crane sleeps on the couch. Stagger sits at the end, entranced by the documentary playing on TV, volume turned down to the notch just before mute. It's about filial cannibalism in the animal kingdom. The mother hamster eating her pup to regain the nutrients it stole. A bird destroying its own chicks so it doesn't have to care for them anymore.

Crane tosses a pillow onto Stagger's lap and lies down and watches professors talk about caloric reclamation until his eyes hurt.

His phone buzzes.

Aspen: Hey, Crane.

Aspen: Birdie's asleep, but I just wanted to let you know we're thinking about you.

Crane can't stand to read the texts as they roll in. He jams the screen against the couch and stares at the TV, presses his face into the pillow or Stagger's leg, and waits until his phone stops vibrating and he can read them all at once.

The one class Sophie and Aspen shared for that single overlapping semester was Intro to Art. Honestly, Aspen scared Sophie. Aspen was angry—always bursting into frustrated tears or storming out of class. Looking back, of course they were. Their parents kicked them out of the house for days at a time and the much-older boyfriend whose house they ran to was a massive piece of shit. But they must have made enough of a connection for something to click, right? Because when Aspen reactivated an old social media account to celebrate their second anniversary of HRT, Crane had been brave enough to ask where they'd gone.

That's how it started. With an account Crane was supposed to have deleted, with Crane in the shotgun seat of Birdie's car, driving down to Planned Parenthood with a bruise on the side of Crane's neck that raised one too many questions.

What are they doing? Why do Aspen and Birdie keep doing this to themselves, thinking they can say the right words and fix this?

He can't go back. He won't.

Aspen: If we're pestering you, let us know and we'll lay off. But I know when I was with that motherfucker, people stopped reaching out to me and it was worse than being alone, even when I never knew how to respond to them.

Aspen: So no matter what happens, we're here whenever you want to come back to us.

Aspen: Even if it's with a baby.

There's a baby inside him. Somehow, out of all the things it could've been, a tangle of tapeworms or squirming pile of grubs, this is the worst.

Crane doesn't respond.

In middle school, Sophie was obsessed with childbirth in the same way that kids become obsessed with watching the same scary movie over and over again, the same way she would become obsessed with that dog on the other side of the backyard fence. She liked it because she hated it.

It started with reading the Wikipedia page, because she was an autistic child and that's how autistic children handle situations like this: by consuming as much logical, practical information about the topic as possible. (She memorized the Wikipedia pages for everything else that scared her, too: prion diseases, fatal familial insomnia, computer viruses, and "Timeline of the far future.") She started on the "Childbirth" page and then jumped to "Vaginal delivery," then "Pregnancy" in general, but the "Pregnancy" page wasn't quite as interesting, since she already knew that much sucked. That was terrible; that was a given. But childbirth held a fabled status in the collection of terrible things in Sophie's head.

As much as she wanted to know about it, though, she could never bring herself to actually see it. She absolutely could have seen it if she'd wanted to. There's an industrial complex of family bloggers posting their deliveries on YouTube for views, ranging from tasteful vlogs to snuff-style full frontals, complete with splattering amniotic fluid and shit and all. The videos get cycled around by overeager teenagers running blogs named "I can't wait to be Pregnant," TERF-y mommy forums, and pronatalist internet corners festering with borderline-fetishistic reverence for the act, and then straight-up actual fetishists who at least have the guts to admit that it's a *fetish*, unlike the others, who simperingly pretend to have any other motive. But they were all too much. Sophie couldn't handle any of it.

Then there was the video in biology class—*the* video. Sophie's eighth-grade bio teacher was out sick, and the substitute was visibly hungover, so she found a documentary and stuck it on the screen while she leaned her head back and napped in the corner. The video contained a ten-second clip of a cow pushing out a calf. That's it. Not long at all. It was a regular dairy cow, lying in some straw, while a skinny-limbed creature wrapped in bulbous membranes heaved and shoved its way out of a giant cow vagina.

Sophie replayed the clip in her head for the rest of the school day. In geometry, she thought about the cow's desperate lowing as the calf fell out of her. During a World War II project in social studies, she pictured the gush of brown fluid and the calf's sudden jerking as if it'd realized all at once that it was alive.

That night, she put on her pajamas (Dad's Grateful Dead tee plus fuzzy Hello Kitty bottoms) and lay in bed with her face pressed to the pillow and pretended that she was the cow giving birth. She squeezed her belly as hard as she could because that's probably what contractions felt like. She imagined she could feel the baby slipping through the birth canal with its hooves and long sharp legs. She fantasized about laboring and struggling, and the possibility that the farmer would have to come and grab the calf by the ankles and pull until it all came free.

She sat up, sweating and feeling sick to her stomach. Her hair and clothes were cemented to her skin.

Downstairs, Dad was already in bed, but Mom was half-asleep on the couch in their fancy vaulted living room, watching a ghost hunter show. Sophie didn't say anything. Just slumped into the gap left between her mother's legs and the cushions, where it was warm and safe.

"It's late," Mom said, squeezing the closest part of her daughter she could find. "You okay?"

"Bad dream," Sophie murmured. "Sorry."

"You want a glass of milk?"

Absolutely not.

When Levi does finally show, it's god-awful early, and Hannah and Crane are half-dressed in the kitchen.

Since it's not polite to walk around with your tits out in someone else's house, Crane slept in his sports bra, showing the constellation of uneven black-ink tattoos. The two-headed lamb, the jaw, the centipede. Hannah, in her case, hadn't managed to put on clothes again after the whole thing last afternoon. When she wanders into the kitchen before the sun can even think about rising, Crane's already awake and, well, it's nothing he hasn't already seen. A postpartum pad under a pair of loose linen shorts and nothing else.

He hears her rustling around in the cabinets. The TV is still on, the current show following a game warden in Alaska. Stagger has fallen asleep, head lolled to the side. The worms under his skin pulse rhythmically like they're breathing too.

Crane drags himself into the kitchen, pushing bedhead out of his eyes. Hannah barely looks at him. She's all knotted hair and delicate ankles and faint stretch lines cradling her still-bloated belly.

It's not like he thought the stomach *deflated* after birth. But it never occurred to him that it wouldn't simply go back to normal after a decent night's sleep.

"Who's that?" Hannah says. "On the couch?"

Crane has no way of answering, besides gesturing vaguely and eventually signing, *Mine*, which is true on a technicality.

He thought it was an obvious sign, a pretty self-explanatory one, but she maintains bizarre, unwavering eye contact—maybe that wasn't the answer she was looking for—before turning back to the cabinets. Thank god. He hates eye contact.

"I want a cup," she says.

Crane fetches one from the cabinet over the sink and a bottle of water from the crate beside the fridge. She's from McDowell, so he figures she'll get the hint not to drink the well water. She does.

What she doesn't do is ask what he and Jess had done with what had been inside her. She doesn't get dressed or apologize for the crinkling sound the postpartum pad makes when she moves.

She says, "It's weird. When Levi talked about you, it sounded like he loved you."

Calling their shit *love* feels like an insult to someone who actually knows how to love. Like Aspen and Birdie, or his parents.

"Don't make that face," Hannah says. "I'm serious." She turns away, the strands of her long hair sticking to the sweat on her back. "Whatever. I hope you're a piece of shit, so I don't have to feel bad for you."

Then there're three hard knocks on the door, and it's over. Hannah slips into the guest room. Stagger snaps awake.

When Crane answers the door, Levi is on the porch. He is a crepuscular animal; not nocturnal or diurnal, but something in the middle instead.

In lieu of hello, Levi—barely dressed, basketball shorts and a zip-up hoodie, presumably because it hurts too much to put on an actual shirt with his shoulder fucked-up—presents a cold package wrapped in butcher paper. It's heavy.

"For your buddy," Levi mutters. The way he says *buddy* is not very buddy at all, though a marked improvement from yesterday morning. "Thought he might be hungry."

Stagger stalks over and unwraps a hunk of ugly organ meat. Some kind of liver, by the looks of it.

Crane raises an eyebrow in the shape of a question.

"Roadkill," Levi offers. The closest thing either of them is going to get to an apology. "Thought we could get it broken down, but not much salvageable. Only decent part left."

Stagger disappears into the kitchen to devour the organ over the kitchen sink. Out the open door, the outskirts of Washville are silent. Only a few late-night crickets, a few too-early birds.

Levi holds out the GPS on his phone. "Pick somewhere to eat."

A second's hesitation.

"Anywhere," Levi huffs, annoyed he's having to explain whatever kind gesture this is supposed to be. "I don't give a shit. Pick and tell Tammy you're headed out."

It really sounded like he loved you. Fuck off.

The closest Taco Bell is a half-hour drive over the Maryland border, to the north; staying in West Virginia means going forty miles in the opposite direction, the ass end of the next county over. Levi had been visibly surprised by Crane's choice. Not by the drive time, which he must have expected because there isn't shit in Wash County, but by the selection itself.

"Didn't think you liked that place," Levi admits on the drive.

Crane grunts. The idea that Levi has retained any of his likes or dislikes borders on laughable, but it is a fair assessment. Food is a nightmare. He'd eat the same thing every day if he could get away with it. But it's almost five in the morning, early enough that the twenty-four-hour restaurant hasn't bothered to switch over to the breakfast menu, and the air doesn't smell like afterbirth anymore, and Crane would be willing to commit a handful of petty crimes for a bag of shitty tacos.

Being pregnant—ugh, that fucking *word*, it has too many guttural sounds in it and the consonants are too deep in the throat—is just being hungry and nauseated simultaneously, all the time, constantly.

"Right." When they arrive and step inside, Levi grabs his wallet as Stagger very clearly ignores the NO HOOD, NO FACE COVERING, WE HAVE THE RIGHT TO REFUSE SERVICE sign on the door. "What do you want."

Crane snorts, *give me a second*, and leans on Levi's arm to get a better look at the menu, like he's slumping against Levi's chest the way he used to after a long shift. Behind the register, the trans girl with a bleached-burned pink ponytail and a Gundam tattoo on her wrist picks at her nails to avoid acknowledging them. Probably so she doesn't have to enforce the sign. Her name tag has been covered with packing tape and now reads "Maude."

Crane types his order into the Notes app, and Levi pays using the hard-earned money that the hive scams out of people up and down the mountain, and the three of them take over a booth in the back corner as the sun rises. Stagger gets a single plain taco to pick at—no chance he'll actually eat it, but that's fine. Crane doesn't care. He has way too many tacos, and fruit punch, and the palate of a child.

He tears into his first bite and nearly swallows part of the wrapper in the process.

Crane and Levi used to do stuff like this all the time. Levi would come back from a hunt exhausted, or he'd be smoking in the manager's office while Crane cleaned up the blood trail. All Levi had to do was drawl "Dinner?" and they'd end up in a cheap diner or sticky fast-food joint with as much grub as they could rustle up for twenty dollars, plus whatever quarters Crane could dig out of the cupholders.

It's not like they had a lot to spare, the hive's allowance covers rent and barely anything else, and Levi never tipped—if they went to Denny's, Crane always had to fish around for a five-dollar bill to make up for it. But it was nice. Levi drank his coffee black. Crane put too much ranch on everything. They'd take turns drawing unflattering caricatures on napkins of other patrons there at three a.m., and make bets on Mike and Harry's bullshit, wagering spare change or oral sex. One time an errant text had proved Crane right immediately, and Levi ate him out in the back seat of the truck fifteen minutes later.

They hadn't loved each other. They'd been rough and thoughtless. Levi was a piece of shit who wouldn't listen to a *no* if Crane had ever bothered to say it, and Crane had refused to make a decision about anything besides a tattoo in three years (and sometimes not even then; sometimes he let the artist pick). But it had been nice, almost.

"You're twenty weeks now, right?" Levi says.

Crane shakes his head. Holds up ten fingers, then puts down a thumb for nine. Do the math.

"Close enough," Levi admits, then, "Halfway there. And you're okay?"

Still breathing. The best they're going to get out of him.

"Hive asked how you were doing. I said being a fucking handful, but alive." Levi snorts. Must've gone for a chat while Crane was at Tammy's. "Not due to a lack of trying on your part."

Crane glares. Stagger keeps an eye on them both but continues to pick at his taco; peeling lettuce and cheese from the meat, crunching the hard shell to give his hands something to do.

There's no way Levi actually wants this. Levi with his injured shoulder making it hard for him to lean back in the booth, wincing when he moves, surviving off violence the same way as a carnivorous animal. Levi, the guy who looks like an extra from *American Sniper* or *Zero Dark Thirty*, who hasn't said a kind word to a child the entire time he's lived. He'd make a terrible father too. He'd have to forcibly keep Crane alive every second of every day or let him go and take care of the baby himself. He'd be miserable. The son of a bitch is already miserable now.

Across the booth, Levi rubs the bite mark on his wrist as he chews, and Crane has been spending too much time around Stagger, because the muscle in Levi's jaw looks so much like a worm.

Crane pulls a napkin from the tray and mimes the act of writing.

Levi pats his pockets and comes up with the grease pencil he uses on the map he keeps in his truck—marking his hunting grounds to make sure he doesn't bleed an area too dry, draw too much attention from the cops with too many missing person reports.

"Not accusing me of fucking anyone else, are you?" Levi says.

Crane flattens out the napkin and tries his best to draw.

The caricatures in the back of the Burger King or Denny's were never *good*. Sophie liked to consider herself an artist, spent her younger years filling notebook after notebook with doodles, but by high school she was too exhausted by advanced classes and community service clubs and college applications to keep up with it beyond the odd art elective. Her main weakness had been line confidence, and it shows. Crane's drawing is sketchy and a bit of a mess. He blames it on the lackluster medium.

Still, it does the job. He nails Hannah's braid, her tiny shoulders, the upturned nose that makes her look a bit like a pixie. After a spot of hesitation, sure, he adds the swell of her belly and exaggerates it to get the point across.

He slides it across the table.

Levi narrows his eyes, pulls the napkin closer. "Is that—huh. Hannah Baskin, McDowell hive. Right?"

Then, "She's pregnant too?"

Crane starts to nod, then stops. Sucks on his teeth. Shrugs. She's not anymore, if that's what he's asking.

"Christ."

There it is again. The tic in his jaw. Looking like something is crawling underneath him, working its way into the spaces between the skin and the muscle and the bone where it doesn't belong. Crane can imagine what the hive said to Levi when he walked into the gas station at some point during the past few hours—the ex-soldier furious and seething, stumbling into the office of his superior officer, fired up and needing a direction in which to explode, only to be told to be calm and quiet and still.

You touch the carrier of our little one, they must have said, ***and we will devour you alive.***

If Levi actually intended on apologizing, he'd give Crane what he wants. Fuck pregnancy cravings and half-hearted restitution, whatever this trip was. Push him hard into the wall. Shove fingers down his throat until he gags. Buckle a belt around his neck and fasten it way too tight. Let him be a man and take something. He doesn't care what. Just let him take it.

But he's no different from Hannah, is he.

They finish their food in silence. Crane is somehow angrier than he'd been twenty-four hours ago, and a hundred times more exhausted.

Sixteen

The tail end of the graveyard shift rush—or the closest thing this gas station ever gets to a rush—isn't the best time to clean out a pair of wallets stolen out of the pockets of corpses, but pausing to take a breather isn't an option. If Crane keeps moving, keeps working until exhaustion numbs his hands and leaves him unsteady, he won't think about what Tammy said, or what Jess said, or what Levi said, or what the hive said, or anything at all.

Eleven thirty p.m. The floor has been swept, coffee refreshed, register double-checked, expired food on the shelves removed. Stagger sits behind the counter with his eyes barely open as Crane peels open the Velcro on the first wallet.

Driver's license (organ donor, fitting). Social Security card (good for opening fraudulent lines of credit). Two credit cards (equally good for running up before someone at the bank catches it). Fifty dollars in bills. A phone number written on the back of a mechanic's receipt. An expired coupon for a Butterball turkey.

Crane nicks the cash—score—and sorts the rest into zippered folders for Tammy to pick up later.

So. As far as he could tell, Hannah's baby was normal.

Did he think that the poor girl was going to give birth to the Eraserhead baby? No, of course not. (Kind of.) (Turns out twenty-week fetuses do actually kind of look like the Eraserhead baby if you squint, tilt your head, and are a horrible person.) But a monster would at least make sense. A baby doesn't even have the decency to mean anything. It's a baby. When it comes down to it, a baby is a chemical reaction that's gotten out of control.

He's thinking again. Not good. He goes for the second wallet, a nice leather one with initials stamped into the corner. Another driver's license, a nickel, a photo of a preteen boy on a swing, a Maryland EBT card. Boring.

What does the hive want with a baby? That's the thing he can't get over—as if he can get over any of it, as if he hasn't been ruminating over every loose end he's stumbled across for the past few months, driving himself crazy rehashing every last detail he can remember, over and over and over like suddenly it'll make sense once he finds the right connection. He doesn't *want* to be doing this. The last time he thought too hard he tried to set himself on fire.

If there was any kind god in the universe, Crane would've been born in the fifties, when he would have spent his life after eighteen blitzed out of his mind on tranquilizers like a good housewife, or have his brain scrambled by a lobotomy, and okay, he doesn't *want that*, he doesn't, he swears, it's—it'd be easier, though, wouldn't it? Fuck the cerebral cortex. Animals don't have meltdowns about doing their reproductive duty. Animals get fucked and eat the babies if they decide they don't want them after the fact.

He's being mentally ill about this. He shoves the wallet under the counter and sets aside a carton of Marlboro Reds, since Levi will want it when he swings by, but rips open the side and digs out a pack and produces a single cigarette.

He only ever smokes when Levi does, and sometimes not even then. It tastes awful and the nicotine buzz makes him feel funny—he doesn't even like being tipsy, only ever drank the one time in the back of the car after graduation and never looked at a bottle again. The only thing smoking has going for it is the way Levi looks at him when he lights the cigarette.

Still, something he'll hate sounds perfect right now. Crane grabs a purple Bic from the display beside the leave-a-penny, puts the cigarette into his mouth the way Levi does, and frustratedly attempts to get the lighter to light.

Maybe he needs to go back out to the woods in the dark. Dig up the corpse. Open the bag and see if the worms on the inside have chewed their way out.

The bell above the door rings.

Shit. The cigarette tumbles out of his mouth. He tries to catch it, but it ends up on the counter.

"Oh," says the lady from the Dollar General as she comes in with an apologetic smile. "Ain't nobody told you those're bad for the baby?"

Great—he's at the part of pregnancy where strangers start commenting on it. What happened to *not talking to the mute behind the counter*? Perhaps that piece of common Washville knowledge is being overwritten by the insurmountable human urge to make weird remarks the moment they clock someone's belly.

"Don't matter how small that thing ends up being," the woman says. She plucks a cup from the self-serve coffee station and peers at the available pots, sitting steaming in their nooks—regular and decaf, no dark roast or anything fancy. "Still gonna hurt coming out."

Crane is extremely aware that it will hurt.

The woman offers a smile over her shoulder as she pours the coffee. She's middle-aged, distinctly West Virginian with the Realtree camo jacket over her Dollar General uniform, a plain wedding ring on her left hand.

"I'm playing with you, you know." She sets the pot down, grabs a pack of sugar. "I'm the last person to talk. Smoked through both my pregnancies; swear to the Lord above it's the only thing that got me through." A pump of vanilla creamer, then a tentative sip. "Damn, y'all keep this hot."

Crane makes a low noise in the back of his throat: *Sorry, I guess?* He is also increasingly unsure of how every mother in the history of the world hasn't gone postal at least once.

The woman—he's never caught her name, since she doesn't wear her badge at work—comes over to the counter, fishing out her wallet. "Three fifty-five, I know, give me a second." She tries her damnedest to catch Crane's gaze. He keeps avoiding it. "I'm happy for you, you know. I've had my eye on you since you first moved here, and I'll admit I've been worried—everything you've been doing to your body. No offense. It just breaks my heart what some young girls do to themselves these days."

Crane freezes, finger jam-stuck above the *small coffee* button on the register touchscreen.

"I thought, you know, if she ever changes her mind, ever realizes what she's really doing to herself, it's going to be so hard to undo all the damage those doctors have done to her." She finds the money, but stops after counting it out, holds the transaction hostage. "And if she ever realizes she wants a baby? It'll be so difficult, my lord, I hope she doesn't cut off her breasts. There's no reason for any of that."

He is aware, vaguely, that he could end this conversation right now. Take the coffee, dump it out, point her to the door, and make Stagger escort her out if she won't listen. Stagger is even looking up at him right now, dull eyes focusing behind the hood and mask. Trying to sort out the situation, figure out what's happening and why Crane's pulse is hammering *thump-thump-thump* so hard in his chest.

Crane does not do that.

"So I wanted to let you know I've been praying for you," the woman says. "I know being a girl is so difficult, but you don't have to run from it. Motherhood is wonderful."

She hands over exact change and puts a few extra pennies into the tray as her kind deed for the night.

"Have a good rest of your evening. I'll keep you in my heart."

The bell above the door rings again when she leaves.

And Crane feels something in his stomach.

It confuses him more than anything; almost reminds him of a period cramp, but it's too gentle for that. Too quick. A muscle spasm, then, or the anxiety-nausea that's one of the few emotions he knows how to identify.

Or the warning signs of a chestburster.

A long time ago—ancient Greece or something like that, back when nobody knew jackshit about how pregnancy works because they all thought the uterus could detach from the vagina and wander about, wreaking havoc between organs until her husband knocked her up to anchor it back into place—apparently the first time the baby moved was the moment it became a human. *Quickening*, Tammy called it. The moment it could finally be deemed alive, when it swallowed a soul and turned into a person.

Crane doesn't believe that. If asked when a fetus becomes a person, his answer would be incoherent, borderline contradictory. It's what a human is made of; it is always a person, of course it is. It is also a tapeworm, entitled to nothing, not shelter or nutrients or affection.

Whatever the answer, it doesn't matter, because the thing is really actually fucking alive.

He thought it'd be more drastic. A hard knock to the stomach, an elbow jammed into his ribs. It's not. It's the jerk of a soft-boned, butterfly-skinned limb.

It's hard to stand, suddenly. He braces himself on the counter. Fingertips against the handwritten notes laminated with yellowed packing tape, LIMIT TWO CIGARETTE CARTONS PER CUSTOMER and MUST SHOW ID NO EXCEPTIONS. Stagger whines, gets up to help, but Crane shows his teeth. Don't touch. Don't, *don't*. Wait.

Wait.

For a bit, nothing. The hum of the drink coolers, the tinny voices of the radio set to the country station. It's the end of Throwback Thursday and Crane hates Throwback Thursday, would willingly listen to all the awful post-9/11 bro country in the world if it means he doesn't have to sit through another Kenny Rogers song.

There it is again. A jolt. So faint and gentle, but completely unmistakable.

A shaky breath hisses out from between his teeth, catching in his throat. He bites down on his lip ring hard enough he thinks he might bend it or rip it right out of the skin.

"Okay?" Stagger asks.

Crane doesn't answer. Doesn't sign *OK*, doesn't reach for Stagger's hand to feel the worms to calm himself.

Hannah is such a lucky bitch.

He turns off the OPEN sign, shuts down everything except the emergency light, snatches the hive key from the register, and steps into the manager's office without a sound. Stagger follows grumbling, the dog he is. The hive is buzzing. A single fly darts across the padlock. He fumbles the key once. Twice.

He can hear the hive already.

Blessed child of ours, what brings you to us?

The lock clicks.

How is our little one?

The chain falls and Crane barrels into the hive's room, its sanctuary, and lunges for the first worm he can see.

Nobody knows a thing about the hive. That's the truth of it. Nobody knows if they're aliens or demons or some horrible natural thing that's crawled up from the earth's crust a few decades ago. If they came from space or another world or the dirt.

Of course, that's not to say stories haven't been passed down through the years. An enforcer from Tennessee came through a year or two ago and said that, according to her hive mother, the worms and flies didn't always look like worms and flies. They came down from the sky in the shape of something else, a long time ago. It's only through the decades that they've come to be something recognizable. Levi mentioned that, to the north, hives boast giant horseflies instead of flesh flies; once, visiting a hive in South Carolina, he found a swarm of botflies that attempted to nest their eggs in the tender skin between his fingers. The worms themselves are always the same, though. Some bizarre thing Crane hasn't been able to find on Wikipedia, somewhere between a nightcrawler and a Bobbit worm, wet and slimy and chittering with teeth.

Whatever they are, they mold themselves to their surroundings. Nestle into the gaps. Make themselves a part of the natural world.

And they squirm and panic and shriek *like everything else.*

Crane misses the first one he goes for. It squelches back into the hive of hardened calcium. Shit, shit. He stumbles to the floor. Drags himself closer on his hands and knees.

The swarm explodes into a storm of wings and whining.

CHILD.

They did this. This is *their fault.*

The next one, he gets. By the tail. He hasn't touched a worm since his bite three years ago, and it's warm and wet and slimy, impossible to get a decent hold on. The hive roils and shrieks and snaps its thousand jaws. The worm's head thrashes. He can see all its teeth.

UNGRATEFUL FUCKING HOMINID, WHAT ARE YOU DOING?

It's rancid in this room. The worms are in a panic. They understand their people and they can taste the rage boiling over on his tongue, can smell the fear and hatred. The swarm turns the air into a shimmering roar.

He's going to yank one of these things from its protective shell and hold it tight, head grasped between his fingers like the Crocodile Hunter holding a viper. And then he is going to put every ounce of pressure on that head until it's about to pop.

AND YOU USELESS REJECT, YOU PILE OF DISGUSTING EXILES. ARE YOU JUST STANDING THERE? DO SOMETHING.

All the hive has to do is admit it was wrong. Let him get rid of the baby and he'll stop. He'll agree to anything in return. He'll rat out

Hannah. He'll make sure Jess is the one to carry the baby. If Levi has to be the father, he'll look the other way. And he knows that twenty-week abortions are illegal everywhere in the fucking country, but he'll figure it out. He can bring Tammy to the hive, have them tell her it's okay, they can do whatever they need to do in a chair in her kitchen. No painkillers, no alcohol, no nothing. He'll take it like a man.

All they have to do is agree, and he won't—

Crane almost manages it. Almost unravels the creature from its tunnels.

But Stagger comes up behind him. Always Stagger.

A gloved hand slides under his chin. Another presses hard on his collarbones. Together those hands drag him back, fighting him every centimeter until he's pinned against Stagger's thigh.

The worm slips through Crane's fingers.

Crane thrashes. Fucking dog, fucking half corpse, don't *touch me*. The touch hurts. His skin burns. Every movement, every brush of clothing on flesh feels like a grater ripping him up.

"Shh."

WE GIVE YOU SO MUCH AND THIS IS HOW YOU TREAT US?

Fuck you. *Fuck you.* He tries to dig his nails in. Tries to bite. Why won't they listen? They're supposed to listen. They're supposed to understand, it's not supposed to *be like this*.

"Stop," Stagger rasps.

The last time someone tried to crack open the hive and get their hands on a worm, Levi put the Mossberg to the side of Harry's head and pulled the trigger.

WE HAVE GIVEN YOU EVERYTHING YOU HAVE ASKED FOR, EVERYTHING YOU HAVE EVER WANTED.

He doesn't want this make it stop make it stop he'll do anything *he'll take the shotgun he'll take it he will—*

BUT PERHAPS WE HAVE THOUGHT TOO HIGHLY OF YOU. PERHAPS OUR CHILD NEEDS A FIRMER FUCKING HAND.

Crane tries to fight but can't. Stagger is too strong. Crane is too tired. He's been so tired for so long. With one final moan, he slumps back, falls, helpless.

The hive takes a deep, calming breath.

We did our best for you, they say. *We would like for you to know that. Your mate will come collect you.*

We will discuss the matter then.

The swarm congeals, finally making one shimmering mass in the air, before twisting through the open door.

On the floor of the manager's office.

Sobbing.

You have the sun, the hive growls. *You have the sky, you have the world, and yet you act like this. Would you rather be trapped in here with us? Is that what it would take for you to understand, child?*

One arm sits tight across his belly. Crane knows that waiting to feel another flutter of movement is some form of mental self-harm, but he can't help it. It's better than what his brain is screaming at him to do: to bust his chin open on the concrete office floor, dig his fingers into the wound, and pull pull pull until all the skin on his face comes off in a sheet.

On the floor with him, Stagger hums. There's no tune. Only a low, imperfect frequency, a dying cat still attempting to comfort. It's so gentle. Stagger has always been so gentle and for *what*? He's a prison warden just like Levi. He's the same as the rest of them.

Staggers says, ***"Hurt."***

Crane coughs. Shut up. Shut the fuck up.

"Hurts."

Yes, it hurts. His head hurts from crying, his stomach hurts because there is something inside him, his skin hurts every time he moves. Every nerve ending is raw.

Stagger attempts to say something else, but it's too difficult. He can't get his mouth to cooperate. The worms shift and move and squirm under the skin and all he can do is croak out some syllable or another.

Crane watches, borderline vindicated. It's frustrating, isn't it? To be unable to communicate no matter how hard you try. To have the right words slip through your fingers every time. Hell, you can have all the words in the world, but if none of them can help you, if you can't put them together in an order that will save you or even get them past your lips, what's the point? It's so difficult that eventually you give up.

But Stagger doesn't stop. He takes Crane's hand, repositions every individual finger until it's as close to the letter *Y* as he can manage— and holds it up between the two of them. Makes a mirroring sign with his own. Pushes toward Crane, then himself.

The motion for similar. The same.

And then, the sign for sorry. On his chest first, and then on Crane's. He's sorry. Stagger is sorry, is sorry, is sorry.

You useless reject, you pile of disgusting exiles.

Crane, sniffling, wiping his eyes, crawls forward until he's in Stagger's lap. He reaches under Stagger's jacket, under his shirt, and places a hand on his stomach and feels the worms like the kicking baby inside his own.

The swarm eventually returns, with Levi. The bell over the door rings and Crane curls up with his face in Stagger's neck, doesn't look up, refuses, even when Levi's heavy footsteps clomp past on the hardwood and the drone of the flies gets so loud.

"Fuck," Levi says. "Get off the floor."

Protector.

Levi snaps up. Stands tall, forever a military man.

The end of our patience has been reached. Something must be done.

Levi says, "I'll handle it."

Seventeen

G et up." Levi grabs Crane by the back of the shirt and drags him onto his feet. "Start walking." He nudges the shotgun toward Stagger. "And you too."

Outside, Levi waits impatiently while Crane locks up the gas station—"Jesus," he mutters because Crane can't find the right key with his hands shaking so bad, his vision so blurred with tears—then pushes him toward the truck. Crane stumbles.

Stagger growls.

"You want to fucking start?" Levi yanks the pump action. The

Mossberg makes an animalistic *chuck-chuck* as it cycles a round into the chamber. "We can do this right here."

Crane catches Stagger's gaze. Shakes his head ever so slightly. *Don't. Not now.*

Stagger's nostrils flare, but he acquiesces. Ducks his head in understanding.

"S'what I thought." He yanks open the F-150's passenger door and shoves Crane against the seat, standing to block the only way out. In the dim light from the gas station pumps, sweat gleams across his flushed throat. Muscles stand out hard on the side of his neck. "Give me your phone."

His phone? His phone. That has all the texts from Aspen and Birdie on it.

Levi snaps twice. *"Phone."*

It's fine, Crane tells himself. Levi doesn't know the passcode. There's no reason for Levi to think there's anyone else involved.

He fumbles it out of his pocket and hands it over.

"Good." Levi nudges Crane into the seat, slams the door, and comes around to the driver's side. Stagger takes the back. Crane turns to see him, resists the urge to reach between the seats to hold his wrist and feel the worms, the closest thing Stagger has to a pulse. Or, actually, he doesn't know if Stagger has a pulse. He's never felt it. He should have checked on the floor of the office, should have pressed his ear to his chest to see if that heart is still beating under there. If he is a puppeteered corpse or something else entirely.

The apartment is too dark and too warm. Nothing's been cleaned in weeks because Crane is the only one who bothers and he's barely been able to put food in the microwave these days, let alone do dishes or wash the sink or pick up literally anything. The upstairs neighbors, the only neighbors they have since the family in 202 got an eviction notice last month, play music loud enough that Crane can make out the lyrics.

Levi bolts the front door.

"Sit," he says.

Sitting makes Crane nervous. His limbs don't want to work. He makes it to the couch anyway and his knees give out.

Stagger stands beside him, a big gloved hand opening, closing, opening, closing.

"New ground rules," Levi says, twisting a combination into the big black gun safe next to the door. "These have already been discussed and approved, so there will be no debate. Show me you understand."

Through the haze, Crane nods.

"First one is for you." Levi juts his chin at Stagger as he puts the shotgun up and bangs the safe closed. "Your job is to enforce these rules. If at any point I decide you're not useful enough, I have full clearance to let the hive know, and then I'll be able to do *my* job."

Stagger does not respond. His hand just keeps opening, closing. Crane tries not to think about the muzzle of the gun touching the side of Harry's head, the half second of silence as Harry realized what was happening, the deafening boom and the hiss of blood and brain matter hitting the ground before the body did. Crane spent enough time cleaning that up. He's not sure he could handle it if it was Stagger all over the floor, all the severed worm pieces he'd have to scrape out of the pits in the concrete.

"Then," Levi continues, "you." Looking at Crane now. "You are no longer allowed to leave the apartment without explicit permission from me, and you must be under direct supervision twenty-four seven. This includes the gas station. You're being relieved of all shifts."

Crane can't feel his hands. What? No. Levi can't trap him here like this, he can't—

"We'll be reducing hours, day shift only. The girls can handle it. No more difficult than what you've been doing for the past few months." Levi sniffs. "You need anything, I'll get it for you. You feel anything change with the baby, you let me know immediately. Tammy will be coming down twice a week now. Again, show me you understand."

Another nod.

"Good."

Levi comes over, pushes aside a bottle on the coffee table so he can sit, and leans on his knees so they're about even.

"You get one slipup," he says. "Okay? One. I'm only giving you this because I know you're stubborn and slow, which is a bad combination. And after that first slipup—"

He puts a hand on Crane's shin.

"Every mistake after that is a broken bone."

A bone. A finger, an arm, an ankle, a leg.

Crane recoils, tucking his hands to his chest. Can already feel the creak and the snap of a metacarpal.

"Any questions?"

Yes, actually. He goes for his phone to type it out in his Notes, but Levi took it. His mind stalls. Can't think further than that, can't put together the pieces it takes to find a piece of paper and a pen. His hands flap helplessly, then beat together.

"What?" Levi says. "Shit." He casts around the living room and comes up with the instruction manual for a DVD player they've never used. "Spell it."

A single trembling finger, a tiny speck of black polish still settled near the nailbed, fumbles for three letters: *W, H, Y.*

If this is what's going to happen, he deserves an answer. He deserves to understand. And yes, there are so many things that one-word question could be asking, but he'd take any of the responses, no matter what. Why did the hive choose him. Why does it want this baby so bad. Why is Levi doing this to him.

He'd never thought that the two of them loved each other, but he didn't think Levi hated him enough to do this.

All Levi does is snort. "Why? That ain't my business, and it certainly ain't yours."

There's a cluster of Sharpie tally marks counting weeks on the wall beside the gun safe. When Tammy saw it for the first time, she mumbled, "Lord above." Crane stood apart from her awkwardly. Her visits to the apartment used to be a moment of peace, a chance to lean his head against her, her hair and skin smelling like lavender shampoo and baby powder. These days he can barely look at her. "Twenty already."

Now it's twenty-two. Almost twenty-three. The end of September means the weather is halfway decent and the HVAC failures aren't as noticeable as they used to be. It never rains and the days are long. They drag on. Crane sleeps, checks Stagger's faint but present pulse, eats the same thing every day, watches reruns of the Discovery Channel. He asks Levi for a book of crossword puzzles from the grocery store, then a blank notepad. He tries to teach himself to draw again, but the only things he remembers how to draw are dragons and horses. All his people come out looking stupid.

According to the calendar, if Crane remembers correctly, today is Luna's fourth birthday.

Without his phone, he tries to imagine the kind of photos Birdie is posting on social media, the sorts of things she's posted before.

Pancakes with whipped-cream smiles; a trip to the local bookstore to wander through the picture books and plushies. In each one, Luna's face will be artfully obscured from the camera lens, every identifying mark of the neighborhood scrubbed. The heart emoji covering the house number will look cute instead of rightfully paranoid.

The caption will be plain, *my little girl*, with an unironic *#blessed* because she is. And the photo will have a lot of likes. They always do. Crane has no idea who those people are, if they're Birdie's actual friends, if she knows them, or if there're just a few hundred queers latching on to a trans woman in some version of domestic happiness.

That sort of thing always pissed him off. Those random people don't know her like he does. They haven't helped her make dinner or put Luna down to bed. They haven't showed up on her doorstep, slept in her bed, played cards with her spouse. Not like him.

What gives him the right to be so upset about any of it, though? There aren't even any pictures for him to look at—maybe she didn't post anything at all this year. And it's not like he was ever supposed to be a part of their life, not really.

When Tammy knocks for the second of her twice-weekly check-ins, Crane doesn't get up from the couch and Levi isn't home, so Stagger opens the door to let her inside.

Jess comes in too. Apparently, she's also here.

"Right," Tammy mutters, stepping around Stagger so she doesn't have to get too close. "Sweetheart, when's the last time you took the trash out?"

"I can wait in the car," Jess says.

"Nope. Find the garbage bags and go take everything out to the dumpster."

Jess, still in her summer hand-me-downs supplemented with more seasonally appropriate thrift store finds, wrinkles her nose but does as she's told, disappearing into the kitchen and thumping around in the cabinets. Stagger keeps an eye on her—she even puts her hair the way Sophie used to, twisted up and pinned to the head with that claw clip—while Tammy comes over to the couch, sits stiffly, slaps her arthritic hands in her lap.

"Belly," she says. "Let's see it."

Crane uncurls.

His tits are fatter and heavier, crammed into the same shitty sports bra he's been wearing for years, and his stomach is impossible to ignore now. It encroaches into his lap, demands ever more space from his bladder and lungs, stretches the skin until lines dig across his hips. It doesn't feel like his body anymore.

In the kitchen, Jess finds a trash bag and shakes it out. Stagger grumbles at the noise.

"Getting bigger," Tammy muses, pressing her hands against the bump. "You feel her yet?"

Crane looks up. Her?

"You're carrying high. Just a guess."

Well, stop guessing. Crane is going to continue to use *it*, thank you very much.

As for movement, he shrugs. It isn't very active. Just a jostle every now and then, brushing against the inside of his body. It makes him think he's swallowed a fly and it's crawling its way through his intestines.

Jess fetches the trash from the bathroom, the bedroom, dumps it all into a bag, and hauls it out the door without a word.

Tammy asks her usual questions—has he been drinking enough water, has he been smoking, any pain that he's concerned about. And then there are new ones—how rough is Levi during sex. (They haven't been having sex at all, and Crane vacillates wildly between *fucking*

ANDREW JOSEPH WHITE

touch me and *don't even look at me*.) Is Stagger being gentle. (Always.) Is he safe. (No response.)

Jess comes back, the heavy metal door shutting too heavily like it always does.

"Are you okay?" Tammy asks.

What the fuck is Crane supposed to say to that?

"Saw someone out there trolling for parking stickers," Jess cuts in, saving him. "Should probably head out soon if we don't want to get towed."

Tammy groans and forces herself to her feet. "Goddamn tow trucks. Let me go to the bathroom and I'll be right back."

Tammy shuffles off, and Jess crosses her arms by the front door.

Jess has put on muscle since she started working for the hive. Or maybe she was way too skinny before, and she's finally getting meat back on her bones. She's been helping Tammy in the yard all summer, lugging boxes of drinks and overflowing bags of garbage through the gas station, dragging bodies to the hive. She doesn't flinch away from Stagger anymore, either.

"Levi out?" Jess says, presumably to either of them.

Crane nods.

"He gonna be out for a while? Few days, or?"

Crane thinks for a moment about the specifics, then shrugs. There's an enforcer from South Carolina who's just come down. She's new to the job and swung by to learn the ropes. Crashing in Sean's old house for the week, actually. Levi's been in and out. Why, what does she care?

Jess seems as if she's preparing to say something else but stops herself. Her jaw is taut. Her knuckles are white. She looks at this entire place with unrestrained disgust—but especially him. Of course it's him. With his too-long hair and bloated stomach like a festering corpse and complete inability to get off the couch anymore. A miserable creature rotting in the corner of a cheap apartment.

Tammy comes out of the bathroom and presses a kiss to the top of Crane's head. "'Night, baby." And then she steps out into the ugly concrete hall, crinkling one of the neighbor's windswept chip bags as she goes.

Again, Jess hesitates. Still in the doorway. Jaw moving, her teeth grinding.

"Whatever," she says, and follows.

Eighteen

Without a phone, Crane and Stagger's *learning rudimentary ASL* project has disintegrated into an exercise in frustration and guesswork. The two of them sit at the folding table that makes up the entirety of their dining room, Stagger with his chin in his hand as Crane's pregnancy brain refuses to let him recall the sign for *P* or *Q*.

Stagger taps the notepad between them. The motion to give up and ask for help. Crane refuses.

Wash County does have a library—it's a tiny building with terrible hours and a struggling selection of materials—but Crane is not about to ask Levi to swing by and check if they have an ASL textbook. He could ask Tammy the next time she comes around, but the more he thinks about it, the more he doesn't want her to do that either. If Levi or Tammy knew he was working on this, there's the chance they'll insist on getting involved, or his refusal to communicate will become a directed insult. *Yes, I'm finding ways to communicate—but not with YOU.*

Crane racks his brain for the shape of the letters and comes up with nothing. Lacking a way to look up new words, they'll have to rely on finger spelling, and that's going to be difficult when he can't recall a bunch of signs on a *good* day.

He writes *P, Q* on the notepad. Stagger shows him how to hold his hands. Crane is pissed Stagger has a better memory than he does.

Levi comes home with dinner, consisting of two pizza boxes balanced on one arm, and a stranger.

The stranger's name is Irene. She's a round-faced woman with broad shoulders and heavy boots, a drawl to her words somewhere between deep Southern and high northern Appalachian that he discovers when she laughs and says, "Your place looks like shit."

Crane turns over the notepad he and Stagger have been using. Stagger pulls the neck gaiter over his nose.

"Tell me about it," Levi mutters, depositing the pizza onto the coffee table. The boxes are generic, no brand name on them, which means they're from the run-down restaurant on Main Street with no concept of portion control. Crane loves the place but refuses to go. Too close to the apartment, too many people who might strike up a conversation.

Levi says, "You want a beer or what? Crane, come eat."

As hungry as he is, and as good as that food smells, Crane does not want to—because hey, who is this person and why the fuck is she in his house; it's setting off his nervous system and making him jittery. But he's not about to argue with Levi. Irene regards Crane curiously as he plods to the living room and opens the box of plain cheese clearly intended for him.

If Levi was a better partner, he'd have known to ask for light sauce, but if he was a better partner they wouldn't be here, so Crane can't have everything. He puts two slices onto a paper plate and sulks back to the folding table.

"And who are you?" Irene calls after him.

Levi returns from the kitchen with two beers between his fingers. "That's Crane. Told you about him."

Irene accepts her bottle with a grin and opens her bottle on the side of the coffee table, lid pinging. The bite on her wrist is still irritated.

"He can't answer me himself?" she says.

"He's a mute."

"Huh." She takes a drink, considering this. Her eyes burn the back of Crane's neck. "Didn't take you for gay."

"Pussy is pussy."

Irene laughs. It doesn't put Crane off his food, he's too hungry for that, but it almost does the trick. He forces himself to take a bite, then peels off the cheese to scrape off the sauce with a napkin. There's tomato chunks. Unacceptable.

Levi and Irene shoot the shit as Crane muddles through his food. Apparently, Irene is an ex-con who recently got out of prison for second-degree murder. She stepped out of state custody to find that her family had moved away; her personal effects, when returned to her by the guards, consisted of two hundred dollars, a bus ticket to a city she'd never been to, and an outfit that didn't fit her anymore. She's good with computers, she explains, better than good, but it's not like she could get a job anywhere with her record, not on such short notice and with no good clothes for an interview. She was angry. She thought she might kill someone else, and on purpose this time. She was good at it. She wanted to. She almost did.

Thank god for the swarm, right. For the hive that took her in. She was wound up and finally had a direction in which to pounce.

"Where'd you end up?" Levi asks.

"Cross Keys. Quiet. Not much going for it. We're holed up in a garage, though, which I don't hate." Irene leans across the coffee table to grab a slice of the other pizza, which is laden with mushrooms and peppers and onion and a bunch of other unpalatable extras. "Jed's showing me the basics. It's no coding boot camp, but I think I'm figuring it out fine."

"Better than a gas station."

"No kidding." She takes a bite and says around said bite, "Where are y'all hiding your workshop?"

Levi grunts like he does when he's confused but doesn't want to come off that way. "Workshop?"

"Yeah. The—" Crane imagines she's making some gesture with her hands. "Don't think it's called a workshop. Hive mother just says it's their room. But where you do all your, you know, cuttin' up and sewin' together."

Crane has no idea what she's talking about, but Stagger can't take his eyes off this woman.

"Oh, that shit? Yeah, no, we don't got one of those. Closest one's in McDowell."

Crane signs, *You okay?*

Stagger nods. It's not convincing.

Irene says, "You ever hear all that mess about the sun?"

"Every damn day."

"What are they on about?"

"Don't matter."

They finish their dinner, getting drunker than they should, Irene poking fun at Levi's terrible taste in alcohol and dropping the word *faggot* too hard. Levi doesn't find it funny. Crane can see it on his face—he can't wait for her to get the fuck out of town. Still, when she leaves, Levi leaves with her anyway.

Nineteen

The next morning: banging on the door. Hard. Loud.

It wakes Crane with a jolt, or maybe that's Stagger shaking his shoulder. He sits up, gasping.

The alarm clock on Levi's side of the bed glares at him with a bright green 4:52 a.m. It's dark out. No slips of sunlight creep past the blackout curtains, and Levi's not in bed beside him. Figures. For the past few days, all this shit with Irene, Crane never knew if he was going to fall asleep beside Levi or not, wake up to find the bed empty or not, and it's left him frazzled.

It's not that he wants Levi right now. And Levi certainly doesn't want him, either; sometimes he finds Levi sleeping on the couch. (At least Crane gets the bed. Apparently putting Crane on the couch while this pregnant is too far, even for Levi—small mercies.) But the uncertainty of his daily routine recently has been unmooring.

Another flurry of knocking. Stagger grumbles.

Yeah, yeah, he knows. Crane drags himself out of bed—that's been getting harder recently, what with his center of gravity shifted to his belly—and frustratedly wrestles into whatever shirt Stagger pulled from the dirty clothes for him as he makes his way to the door. Stagger follows through the dark apartment, hunched dutifully within arm's reach in case Levi has returned in a mood. Or if Irene has returned at all.

God, did Levi forget his key when he left with her, drunk, last night? That's what he gets.

Crane unlatches the dead bolt, already prepared to find the key somewhere and shove it into Levi's hands so he can go back to sleep. Or watch another documentary when he inevitably can't pass out again. Whatever he has to do to keep from fantasizing about shoving a pen through his orbital socket.

But when he opens the door, it's not Levi or even Irene standing in the dirty hallway.

It's Jess.

Visibly ill. Reeking of cheap liquor and metal and sweat.

"There you are," she slurs with the same barely contained disgust from her previous visit—as if to say how dare Crane, this ugly unwashed creature, not be expecting her this god-awful early. She shoves forward, tries to get past him into the apartment, and succeeds only in fumbling over the threshold. Her hair sticks in clumps to her clammy face.

She says, "Wondered if you'd finally gotten your shit together and killed yourself."

That wakes him the fuck up.

The heavy door slams shut. Crane catches her by the upper arms. Tries to get her attention and get her to breathe. Not because he likes her, which he doesn't, but because when you panic you get stupid, and when you get stupid you get hurt. And she's already getting stupid if she's running her mouth. How gone is she? How did she get here? Did she *drive*?

"But you didn't," she says. Thick and phlegmy. She's smiling with too many teeth and she's not breathing steady. "God. That's pathetic."

Her eyes focus just long enough to catch sight of Stagger in the dark.

She startles. Full-body flinches. Tears herself out of Crane's grip and hits the armchair.

"Fuck," she says. "Fuck you."

It's Stagger that gathers her up this time, keeps her from eating shit on the hardwood. She's sweating and gasping for air. Throat twitching with her pulse. Alcohol poisoning, maybe? Did she take too many pills?

"Fuck you," Jess insists, louder. "You're pathetic."

Crane doesn't have a phone anymore. He makes the stereotypical gesture for *phone*, then *give it*. If Jess drove, took the only car at 636 Victory Lane, then Tammy won't be able to come get her, but at least the old woman should be able to talk her down. Deal with whatever the hell this is. Maybe the part of Harry's brain that gave out that day is giving out here too.

"If you actually wanted that thing out of you," Jess says, "if you actually wanted to die, you would've *done it already*."

This fucking bitch.

She vomits.

Crane jerks back. Jess tries to catch it and only ends up spilling a watery mess all over her hands and shoes.

Shit, okay, okay. Not here, not in the living room. Crane pushes Jess to the back of the apartment. She doesn't fight. Too busy short-circuiting with puke on her hands and the taste in her mouth—she's groaning, making a sick hiccup-laugh noise. Stagger puts himself between her and the wall when a knee nearly gives out. Bathroom, come on.

"You would've done it," she continues. As soon as she's through the door, she stumbles, barely catches herself on the toilet and the edge of the bathtub. "Have you even tried? I don't think so. You know what, I think you like it. That's what this is. The hive was right. You want it."

Shut up, *shut up*. Jess lurches over the tub, yanks on the faucet to get the stomach acid and half-digested remains of what's probably breakfast and burning liquor off her hands. Crane grinds his teeth. Of course he fucking *tried*. He tried to get an abortion, and it was snatched away the moment Stagger tracked him to Aspen and Birdie's. He begged the hive to change their mind, and when they refused, he tried to threaten them into it. Tammy won't help and Levi won't look the other way and now he's here. Jess has no idea what she's on about. She needs to shut up.

Jess thuds to the narrow strip of floor. Smearing water across the tiles. Stagger leans over her to turn off the tub.

"I'm not you, though," she says.

Her fingers slip over and over in an attempt to unbutton her jeans.

"I was going to die in that room." Her movements are sluggish, every syllable hard-won. "Sean was going to keep me there until I rotted, but then the flies came and said I'd never have to feel like that again. So I'm not. I'm not some—some dog that does whatever it's told." Saliva bubbles up when she speaks. "I'm not gonna lie here and spread my legs and take it like you."

In all the venom and spittle, there's something that's almost a sob. A piece of broken, painful glass in her throat.

"It's just. You're the only person I could think of."

She gets the button only to struggle with the zipper.

"I'm pregnant," she says, "and it's Levi's and I thought I could fix it, but I messed up."

That moment in the manager's office: Levi ducking his head to Jess's ear, Jess pulling away and shaking her head *no*. Every second she looked too much like Crane in the mirror, messy dark hair and thin pink lips and the same sharp collarbones. Every time he glared across the car or the room or the apartment and hated her for it, every time he laughed along with jokes at her expense, every time he wished the hive had done this to her instead of him.

All of that, the whole time, and this happened right under his nose. It feels like a blood vessel in his brain is about to burst.

He wouldn't have wanted it to happen if he knew it actually *would*.

And yeah—some childish part of him wishes with all its might for him to be surprised by this. To be surprised that Levi would do this. But he isn't, because of course Levi would. Obviously.

Jess gets the zipper and yanks her pants down.

There's blood everywhere.

Across her thighs, smearing her cheap blue underwear. Not quite soaking all the way through the seat of her jeans, but about to. A pile of menstrual pads and tissues and a washcloth crammed inside her underwear to stymie the flow that hasn't worked nearly as well as it should've, not with the extent of the hemorrhage.

Jess pulls out a pad and drops it into the trash can. It's all soaked, a dripping red bolus. Her pubic hair is matted.

She must have found Tammy's DIY abortion kit, the one the hive forbid them from using, and grabbed the curette like it was an antidote. Or googled what should theoretically go into a kit and decided any long, sharp object would do. She did what Crane couldn't bring himself to do, but she did it wrong. She hit something bad.

"He didn't force me," Jess snivels, as if this isn't the most blood Crane has seen come out of a living person ever, as if he'd be upset with her. She tries to shimmy out of her pants but she's too weak, resorts to digging between her legs and unravelling deteriorating wads of paper towels from inside her. "Or. I don't, I don't know. I don't think he did. He makes you feel crazy."

Crane touches her legs, permission to get her pants for her. She lets him and he drags them down to her knees. Underwear too. She reeks of copper, and it brings back a high school memory like a slap: waking up to find he'd started his period, groggily coming to in a pool of metallic mess. It's an unmistakable smell. Even if he never has another menstrual cycle again, it's going to follow him for the rest of his life.

Crane clicks his tongue to get Stagger's attention, signs *plastic*, and Stagger steps out to fetch it.

Jess reaches in and pulls out the washcloth. It looks like what Levi tried to use to clean up his back the night he got shot. Crane takes it from her and puts it into the trash can too.

"Sorry," Jess says, spluttering. "I'm sorry."

What is she apologizing for? Losing her shit in the living room, swearing at him, ruining the floor? Letting Levi do this to her?

Stagger comes back with the plastic sheet. Shifting Jess's weight to get it under her makes her sob, but Stagger holds her hand and makes shushing noises and Crane squeezes her knee and she takes deep breaths.

Crane is bad at estimating, but if she hasn't already lost enough blood to classify this as a medical emergency, it's going to turn into an emergency real soon. If she just nicked something, then pressure would've worked. Or maybe it just hasn't had time to clot. He grabs the towel from the sink and gives it to her and she crams it in, his hand on her wrist to tell her to keep it there, press it in, it hurts but she has to. He doesn't know enough about how this works. Maybe it's too deep to get pressure on it at all. You can't exactly put weight on a wound on the other side of the cervix.

They can't tell Tammy. Tammy's pretty much proved she's more loyal to the hive than her people, and who knows what she'll tell the worms if they ask. Can't call 911, either—even if they pick up, which they might not, Crane has heard the townsfolk talk. It'll take the ambulance an hour to get here on a good day.

"It feels bad," she says. "Is it bad?"

Crane doesn't know how to respond to that. The only honest answer is nodding. He nods.

In response, Jess tries to smile. He's glad that his honesty is appreciated—it usually isn't. The way he sees it, it's good to be told the truth. He's spent so much time freaking out over things people considered minuscule that it'd be a blessing to be told yes, it's just as bad as you think it is. You're not overreacting.

She says, "Okay."

Stagger takes a handful of toilet paper and dabs Jess's throat, then wipes the spittle from the corners of her mouth. Crane watches. There's a flicker of something alive in Stagger's lopsided eyes, worry pinching his pallid forehead.

"It's cold," she says.

Crane nods again. Yep, blood loss makes you cold. He's already working through what he'll write out for her once this stops. Drink lots of water, eat iron-rich foods, don't push yourself too hard. It's his responsibility. Levi did this, this is Levi's fault, so Crane has to clean up the mess. When Jess's eyes droop, he shakes his head, pats her cheek, snaps in front of her face. Nope. Awake.

Jess mumbles, "I don't think it's stopping."

It has to clot *eventually*, doesn't it? Crane glances up to Stagger as if for reassurance, but Stagger looks as lost as Crane is. Shit. Crane is good at packing bullet wounds and stitching up lacerations, not fixing, what is this, uterine hemorrhage? And, right, Jess was drinking. That makes the blood thin. Dumps it full of alcohol, stops it from coagulating.

Waiting will kill her as quick as anything else.

Jess pulls out the towel, and so much comes out with it . . . And that's it. She is not going to bleed to death on his watch. Crane dives into her pocket for her phone. Pushes it into her hands for the passcode. Her hands tremble as she punches it in and he opens the GPS, searches *hospital*, tries not to despair at the reality of living in a rural area.

Closest ER is forty minutes out. Better than an hour waiting for an ambulance.

He types in the Notes, *HOSPITAL. GIVE KEYS*.

Jess says numbly, "Can we afford that?"

No, they can't. But if you give the ER a false name, they can't pin you for the charges, and they're still legally required to stabilize you.

Instead of taking the time to explain, he nods one more time. He receives the keys from her back pocket.

Crane nabs a handful of washcloths from under the sink, packs her underwear to keep all the blood in one place, gets Stagger to pull up her pants no matter how much it hurts. Jess holds Stagger's hand tight.

He's not supposed to leave, but Levi gave him one slipup. Seems like a good time to use it.

Together, they help Jess to her feet and lead her across the apartment. Jess whimpers. He knows, he knows it sucks. Just a drive and it'll be fine. Stagger opens the door for them, ushers them through, snatches his neck gaiter, and yanks it on before following them into the dim light of the apartment hallway.

Nobody's out at this hour. There's barely anyone left in this building anyway. The upstairs neighbor who plays music too loud. An old woman on the third floor who needs her son to help her down the stairs since there aren't elevators. That's it.

Through the glass front of the entryway, Crane spots Tammy's car, the ugly gray Accord on the other side of the lot. It's about time to wake up and get ready for work. Tammy's going to notice something's wrong, soon. Fine. Crane will take the consequences.

Seven stairs down to the landing.

If you actually wanted that thing out of you, Jess said.

Come on, easy now, that's it.

If you actually wanted to die, you would've done it by now.

He tries not to imagine Jess dragging herself up the steps only a few minutes ago. How much pain she was in. How much pain she's in now.

You want it.

That's not right. He doesn't want *this*. He wants—no, he needs the hive. He needs somebody to pull his leash, point him in a direction, tell him what to do. He can't make his own decisions. When he thinks for himself, all it does is hurt him. Of course he can't do anything without the hive. Without the hive, he's nothing.

It's just that the hive wasn't supposed to do this to him, and he can't stop them. He can't stop any of it. He doesn't know how.

On the last step, Crane freezes.

Stagger goes still.

Jess whispers, "No."

Flanked by Irene, Levi opens the door to the landing—ten square feet of tile covered in muddy boot-marks and dirt and cast-off beer-bottle caps—and leans against the threshold.

This son of a bitch. With his dog tags and the angry tic in his jaw. Fuck him. *Fuck him.*

"Would you look at that," Levi says. He pulls a cigarette out of his shirt pocket and shoots a glance to Irene, whose expression is so smug it almost sends Crane reeling. "Even came out to meet us."

Levi is smiling.

Twenty

In the truck, parked in the grass in front of Tammy's house, Levi holds Crane by the arm. "Stay."

Irene walks Jess up to the porch and bangs on Tammy's door. The gray Accord grumbles in the driveway. Jess's jeans are stained red.

Through the windshield, Crane watches. He watches Tammy yank open the door. The horror dawning on her face. Irene shoving the car keys into her hands.

Stagger isn't here. That's not to say he hadn't tried to follow; he had. He'd grabbed Levi by the shirt and slammed him into the door, but unfortunately Levi isn't the one with worms in his brain. Levi said he wouldn't tell the hive that Stagger let Crane leave the apartment if he backed up, right now. And Crane took Stagger's hand and pulled him and pulled him until he listened. *I'll be fine, I'll be okay, I get one mistake and you don't, you don't get to fucking die and leave me alone. I won't let you.*

So he stayed because Crane asked, and now Crane is alone.

At least Levi gives him one of the cigarettes. Crane is shivering like he's fighting off cold chills, his back tense from muscle contractions. He has trouble lighting it and Levi refuses to do it for him. When it finally catches and he breathes out, smoke trickles out from between grit teeth.

Is Levi the one who knocked up Hannah?

Did the hive *tell* him to?

That can't be correct. If they did, then Hannah and Jess would've been struggling with the same draconian bullshit Crane's been cracking under for months. The hive doesn't leave things up to chance. The hive doesn't take risks like that.

The hive tells Tammy to stop checking on their girls, and this is what happens.

As Tammy raises her voice at Irene, *"Why the fuck didn't you leave her in the goddamn car,"* Levi starts the truck up again and pulls out onto the gravel road. Wind whistles through the crack in the window meant to let out the smoke. The sun won't rise for another hour now.

Levi gave him one slipup. It's going to be okay.

Without taking his eyes off the road, Levi produces Crane's phone and sticks it into the center console's cupholder.

He says, "Your taste in porn is bizarre."

Crane does not respond, not like he usually would—no grunt of acknowledgment, no snort of annoyance. He's running on autopilot, breathing and blinking and not much else. Most of all, he has no idea what Levi is talking about, or why he would bring this up.

"Sure, the weird BDSM stuff I get," Levi says. "I know what you're like. But . . ." Crane runs through what's in his search history—the entirety of the gangbang and anal tags on XVideos; sadism scenes that always left him feeling gross even though he wanted to be the girl in those videos, not the sadist. Levi changes his mind and plucks the cigarette from Crane's mouth because Crane must be paying too much attention to something that isn't him. "That AI-generated dog-fucker stuff is next level. I knew you had issues, but Jesus."

It's not often that Crane hates being autistic, but he does now. His brain feels like a tire spinning in the mud.

Levi frustratedly flicks the cigarette out the open window as they pull onto Corridor H. "Irene knows how to crack phones. She's got a whole program for it and everything."

No.

Crane snatches up his phone. He ignores his search history and his Notes and his photos, every other embarrassing or incriminating thing, and fumbles into his messages.

Levi couldn't have, he wouldn't, he said in the parking lot that he'd look the other way, that it was water under the bridge—

"We spent some time asking around," he continues, "but we never did manage to track down any friends named Aspen or Birdie. They ain't with a hive, are they?" They both already know the answer. "They've got a kid and everything. I knew you were slow, and that's fine, I don't got a problem with that, but I didn't think you were *stupid*."

The messages load. The latest one is from earlier this morning, three a.m.

Levi did a good job—the texts sent from Crane's phone read almost like Crane himself. Not perfect, of course, but close enough in cadence and grammar that Aspen and Birdie wouldn't be able to tell the difference.

Crane, but not really, not actually him: sorry

Crane: sorry, I'm sorry

Aspen: Crane?

A missed video call notification, then another. He can't believe they were up. That they were awake to see the message come in.

Birdie: weve been so worried oh my god we were so scared

Birdie: is everything okay???

Crane: I need to get out I need to leave. Please

And then the address of the abandoned livestock exchange.

His vision blurs. The tiny words on the screen smear into near illegibility. Levi mimicked Crane's panic and desperation as he begged them to come, said he'd be hiding inside, he'll be ready at six a.m. and he's sorry he scared them so much, he's so sorry.

Crane has never been colder in his life. Not when he plunged himself into an ice bath in high school to keep from panicking over his AP tests. Not when he saw the second line on that pregnancy test. Not when he crawled out of the trunk of Mike's car covered in vomit and collapsed into the cool grass.

Aspen and Birdie are on their way. The truck's clock says 5:40. The livestock auction is ten minutes out.

The shotgun is in the truck, the box of bright red shells crammed under the seat.

Crane: don't—

Levi snatches the phone and sends it after the cigarette. They're moving fast enough that Crane doesn't get the chance to watch the off-brand smartphone shatter on the concrete road.

Crane's hands are held awkwardly, like the phone is still between his fingers. Everything's shut down, complete disconnection between his head and his hands, his brain and the rest of him.

"First strike was leaving the apartment," Levi says. "But the second was this."

The abandoned auction building, the ugly brick thing at the end of a weed-infested concrete lot, is called the Farmers Livestock Exchange Inc., Washville WV, Auction Every Monday, and yes that is the full legal name on all official government documents and nailed in big letters above the entrance. It's never once run the entire time Crane has been in Wash County. No cars in the lot and no cows in the pens. Just busted-out windows and a front door covered in papers informing trespassers that this is private property, and also deeply unfit for human habitation or use.

Levi holds the shotgun in one hand and the back of Crane's neck in the other as he leads him into the building. The front door is locked, so he has to yank open the cattle gate, push Crane through, shove him under a metal roll-up door stuck partway open. The place has been abandoned so long it doesn't smell like animals anymore. It's all dirt and the residual heat from the end of summer.

The only reason Crane isn't crying is because everything has gone offline. A computer closing every noncritical function to keep from destroying its processors.

Jess was right. Levi makes you feel crazy. Wears you down until you're too confused or scared or dead to fight back.

"Considering how shit you are with people," Levi says as he marches Crane through the maze of dirt floors, concrete and tall ceilings, and wooden supports, "I'm shocked you managed to trick two other people into fucking you."

Crane's never slept with Aspen or Birdie. That's not to say he hadn't thought about it, or wanted to, or tried. He dreamed of it: letting both of them use him however they wanted. Hell, they're literally in an open marriage. It's just that the one time he asked, the one time he typed it into his AAC app, they'd looked at each other and had a moment of long-term-relationship telepathy that must've consisted of *absolutely not.*

On moral grounds, apparently. They didn't want to take advantage of him, and Crane didn't have the heart to type, *But that's what I want.*

"Guess it's only fair, though. Shocked you figured out the thing with me and Jess."

They're not walking where the farmers would follow the cattle to the inside holding pens and auction rooms. Instead, they're down where the livestock would trundle to sale. A bird flutters through the rafters.

Levi's still smiling. It's cracking at the corners.

"If you'd had the brain cells to fuck somebody from McDowell—or hell, even the Ivanhoe hive—we wouldn't have to do all this. But here we are. We've always gotta do things the hard way with you."

And, of course. The one time Crane wants to break his silence, wants to beg—*don't hurt them, please don't hurt them.* On his hands and knees, plead for him not to take Aspen and Birdie away from Luna, to not involve them, to punish him and not them, not them please.

The one time he wants to speak, he opens his mouth and only croaks.

The door to the main showroom is open. Together, they step into the sunken pit, shoes crunching in the ancient wood chips and sawdust bedding. They're flanked by towering fences, the auctioneer's box, the concrete bleachers and old chairs and advertisements for companies that haven't been in Washville for years. Anything interesting or useful has been picked clean. No computers left in the box, no speakers still anchored to the walls.

"In the interest of clarity," Levi continues, "I did some research. And as it turns out, they are both—"

He double-checks the slug in the chamber of the shotgun.

"—decently known and well-liked members of their community. A journalist and a teacher. They'd be deeply missed, grieved, all that annoying shit."

Crane absolutely does not correct him that Aspen is only an assistant at the news outlet and Birdie is just IT for the school system, who helps out with computer classes sometimes.

The safety comes off.

"It's nothing we can't handle, but you're enough as it is. I don't *want* to deal with cleaning up the mess their deaths will make. Especially with a kid involved."

Levi hands over the key to Aspen and Birdie's house.

"So I'm giving you a chance to fix the situation before I do."

This motherfucker. This awful, cruel, unfathomable monster of a man. Crane wishes he could have beaten him to death with that pipe months ago. It wouldn't have done anything about the pregnancy, but then Crane would have gotten to see Levi's face bashed in and bleeding out into the gravel, and it would have been beautiful.

Crane hears Aspen and Birdie before he sees them.

They're calling his name. Or, Birdie is. Her voice echoes through the bones of the abandoned building, bouncing off tall ceilings and soft beams of rotting wood.

He knew, before hearing her, that he was actually *in* this situation, that this was in fact happening. But the tiny slivers of hope that'd managed to lodge in his chest, whispering maybe it wasn't going to happen the way it inevitably would—that their car would catch a flat halfway up the mountain, that they'd realized it was a trap and turned back—finally dissolves.

"Crane?"

Levi takes it as his cue, climbing out of the pit and into the pitch-black stands. No light touches him at all. Crane can find only the outline of him because he knows Levi is there, settling himself into a plastic chair with the Mossberg across his lap. Those things are good for fifty yards minimum, and Crane finds himself wondering about the ammunition. The spread situation, mainly. With buckshot it's, what is it, an inch every three feet, he thinks. If this goes south, if there's buckshot in that gun instead of a slug, could Levi put lead in them both?

Crane forces himself to breathe. His lungs are operating manually.

And, god, there they are.

Birdie, using her phone as a flashlight, probably because her therapist and anxiety meds *just* convinced her it was okay to disassemble her own bugout bag, steps awkwardly into the showroom pit. Aspen follows, backpack hoisted over one shoulder. Birdie's flashlight sears into Crane's vision. He raises a hand to block it, blinking against the beam digging into his corneas. It obliterates his night vision. He loses track of Levi immediately.

"Oh," Birdie says, "shit."

She points the light at the ground. Aspen stops in the middle of the dusty wood chips, attention locked on Crane's distended belly. It reminds Crane of the way you'd look at a friend's amputated leg or gunshot wound for the first time: recalibrating your mental image of their body, permanently altered.

"We were calling for you," Birdie says, maniacally nervous. The spot of light on the ground jitters. She takes a step forward, then another. "Did you not hear us? The car's right outside. Let's go."

In the corner of Crane's eye, the darkness shifts. The shotgun.

Crane takes a step back.

Birdie stops mid-stride, face suddenly stricken with some emotion or another, Crane's always been bad at this, don't ask him to translate those minute muscle adjustments *now*.

"Okay," Aspen says, putting out a reassuring hand. "Okay."

They both look different. That makes sense, as people tend to change over the course of a couple months. Aspen has an honest-to-god beard now, far more filled out than Crane's awkward patches, and a new tattoo covering up the remnants of their third and final childhood attempt. And Birdie's hair has grown out longer. It's currently tied back in the plain ponytail of every tired mom. Motherhood suits her, but that's not new. It always has.

Crane misses them so much. Everything he hasn't let himself feel to stay sane collides into his brain at once. It hurts. Aspen's soft hands and Birdie's gentle smile. The way Birdie tears up when she laughs, how Aspen talks to Luna like she's a grown woman instead of a toddler. The time Crane awoke on the couch to find the two of them slow-dancing to a commercial on the radio. Their love for each other spilling over into their daughter and into him too.

It's not fair that this is how it ends, it's not *fair*.

But this is what happens when he makes his own decisions.

Aspen finds a new angle. "Crane," they say, "what's going on?"

It's been so long since Crane strung a sentence together out loud that it fails him. The part of his brain in charge of this has been disconnected, or fried, or hacked away.

Another attempt: "Whatever's going on, we can figure it out. Do you have a bag with you? It's fine if you don't. I brought clothes, and we can pick up anything else. Listen to Birdie." Birdie blinks nervously, staring into the dark. "The car's right outside. We can be gone before your boyfriend has any idea."

Crane can almost hear Levi smiling in the stands. The son of a bitch could be looking directly at Birdie, showing her all his teeth in the dark, and she'd have no idea.

He wants to lose it but he doesn't. Once they're gone, Crane can lose it all he wants. Levi can drag him to the gas station and run the bathroom sink and shove his head underwater, shut him in with the hive until his meltdown is done, ignore him and walk away—whatever. It doesn't matter. Crane doesn't care. Aspen and Birdie and Luna will be safe.

Birdie is panting now, one of her usual tactics for trying to get enough oxygen into her blood, or maybe getting enough carbon dioxide out of her lungs.

"Babe?" she says as if her throat is constricted. "I think—"

Crane holds up the key to the townhouse.

"Okay," Aspen says again, fixed on the key's dull metal. "I think we're in crisis mode. Am I right? You're scared. Probably having trouble thinking straight. That's all the adrenaline in your brain; makes it tough to figure out what to do. That's okay. I get it."

Aspen sounds like their fucking shrink. Who gives a shit about therapy-speak. There's a gun in this room and it's trained at their center mass.

It's not enough to make them leave, is it. If they just leave, there's always the chance they'll come back, there's always the chance Levi will deem it all a failure and swing down from the stands and do it himself. Cut out their livers and kidneys for Stagger, feed the rest to the hive, take their wedding bands as trophies, and put them on Crane's nightstand.

Crane jabs the key.

"You're giving it back," Aspen says plainly, double-checking they understand.

To Crane's surprise, it's Birdie who snaps.

"What the fuck!" she says. Aspen flinches, but she ignores it. "No. *No.* Who's making you do this? Where's that piece of shit boyfriend. This is him. Isn't it?"

"Birdie," Aspen warns.

"No! He didn't—you *didn't* bring us all the way out here for this."

Another shift of the shotgun. Levi lifting it to the shoulder, just inches from looking down the sights.

"Birdie," Aspen says again.

Birdie sucks in air, looking at her spouse. Crane watches them both do the mental math. The glance they share, that telepathic communication.

What are they debating in those heads of theirs? How much they love him versus the danger they're just now realizing they might be in, what with the weight of Crane's *piece of shit boyfriend* suddenly bearing down on them? Reviewing every memory of abusive parents and siblings and spouses left behind, the risk they'd be exposing Luna to, lessons of *you can't help someone who doesn't want to be helped.* Battling the queer urge to light yourself on fire to keep someone else warm, giving everything you have to save a member of your community because you know, you *know* nobody but you will ever help.

Aspen and Birdie don't just need to leave. They need to hate him.

Birdie's already showing her dainty little teeth.

Aspen steps forward and takes the key.

And there's a moment when it looks like they're readying themself to say something stern—not just as a friend or a fellow queer, but as a journalist. Moments away from laying out the facts and dragging someone over to their side by force.

Okay, so.

Levi taught Crane how to throw a good punch. For what it's worth, Crane doesn't do that. His feet aren't positioned properly, his body is permanently off-balance, he doesn't follow through the way he should. It's sloppy and weak. Crane tells himself he did it on purpose, because he doesn't *really* want to hurt them, which is better than accepting that this is the best he can do now.

Aspen's still not prepared for it, though. Whatever they lived through before, whatever shit they've hid, it didn't teach them to take a hit.

Crane's fist collides with their jaw and sends them reeling, thumping mutedly into Birdie, who barely manages to keep them upright.

Birdie's watery eyes flash with rage.

And then she's screaming, *"Fuck you!"*

He's never seen her like this. He didn't think she was capable of it.

"Fuck you, Crane!" Birdie says. "Fine! You want to do this to yourself so bad, go ahead—I'm not about to drag you kicking and screaming—" Aspen straightens up, puts a hand to their jaw, opens their mouth, and closes it experimentally to check that nothing's been knocked out of place. "Kicking and screaming, when you're just going to go back to him like you *always do*."

It hurts, but it should. He deserves it.

"Are you okay?" Birdie murmurs to Aspen.

"Yeah," Aspen says cautiously. Holding the key, eyeing Crane like he's a wild animal. Aspen and Birdie have never looked at him that way before. "Think so."

"Okay." Those pale eyes go back to Crane. "We're leaving."

Aspen, though, doesn't move until Birdie takes them by the arm and pulls, so gently.

They step out of the auction pit.

Crane can't remember how to breathe. It's getting caught in his throat. His hand throbs where it hit the bone of Aspen's jaw.

A few moments later, in the stands, Levi lowers the shotgun. He's whispering. Counting out the time it takes to leave the auction building, get into the car, drive away.

One, two, three.

They're safe, Crane tells himself. Aspen and Birdie and Luna are safe, and they'll never come back to Washville again.

Fifty-four, fifty-five, fifty-six.

They're alive, and they'll stay that way, far away from him.

Ninety-seven, ninety-eight, ninety-nine—

One hundred.

They're gone.

Levi lowers the shotgun, and Crane crumples onto the dusty, rotting floor.

Twenty-One

L evi says, "There we go."

He climbs down to the showroom floor and crouches beside Crane's slumped body, cradling his temple.

"See how easy that was?" Levi says. "You did the right thing."

It doesn't feel like it. It feels like he wants to die.

"I keep saying, if you just do what we tell you, it's gonna be so much better for all of us."

Crane hiccups.

Sobs.

Jess was right: he's spent all this time waiting for permission. Permission to transition, permission to be silent, permission to make it stop.

"Are you going to keep being good?" Levi asks.

Crane nods.

Levi puts Crane onto his back and shoves calloused hands under his shirt to feel his bulging stomach, then higher; to grope possessively at his tits, pinch his darkened nipples. They ache but Crane doesn't push him away. Crane likes when it hurts.

"That's what I thought."

Levi is breathing hard now. Tugging Crane's shirt up to expose his swollen breasts to the warm air. Strips Crane of his shoes, his jeans, his boxers. Nudges apart his knees to settle between them. The dog tags drag across Crane's skin. The shotgun lies within arm's reach.

Nobody is going to give him permission this time.

Crane tries to remember: What was it he said? Well, not said. Bad choice of words. What was it he thought the night Jess arrived at the gas station, the night he was bent over the manager's desk? The sex is better when he doesn't know if he agreed to it. It's better when it hurts and there's a hand around his throat because it's correct. Because that's where he's supposed to be.

It's different this time.

Levi's taken out his cock and he's nudging it against Crane's cunt, lining it up, groaning that raspy *"fuck"* he does as soon as the tip slips in. And Crane is being good. He spreads his legs so Levi can bury himself inside, even though it stings and he winces. He doesn't pull away. Instead he puts a hand over his belly as if to protect it, as if he's some kind of mother.

"There you go," Levi growls. He's pulling Crane's hips against him so he can get a better angle. The other hand is holding him down by the throat. The heel of his palm presses into the windpipe. Crane didn't realize he was moaning until he suddenly chokes. His lungs struggle to inflate. "Just like that."

Does he want this? The question isn't *does he like it*, the question isn't *is it hot*, it isn't *is he going to cum so hard he'll be weak-kneed and shaky*. That's not what's being asked. None of those are the same question. None of them have anything to do with each other.

The question *is*, would he have said yes? Right now, if Levi would really listen to the answer, would he have said no?

Or would he say please? Because that's the only thing he can think right now. Because Crane can't tell the difference between one question and the other, because this is the only thing that feels right. The boys in the locker room, the dog, the time Levi fucked his throat so hard he vomited.

Levi keeps talking as he thrusts into him, fucks Crane into the dusty floor. About how wet his cunt feels. About how hot Crane sounds when he's choking. He rambles sex-slurred fantasies about what Crane must've looked like fucking Aspen and Birdie and calls him a slut, that the hive chose Crane because he's a slut. He says Crane would've let himself get knocked up by anything that'd have him. He says Crane is perfect for this, Crane has always been a bitch in heat, Crane is being such a good girl.

And Crane can't even be mad because Levi is right. Levi pants like an animal and snarls when he calls Crane a whore, and Crane likes it, of course he likes it. What's the point of having sex with men if you don't get to see the grunting, sweaty beast-thing they turn into when they fuck you? Crane's eyes flutter shut, lips parted, hand fumbling around his stomach for his clit because if this is going to happen he might as well get off too. It feels good, doesn't it? It feels good, it feels good, it feels—

How dare he get off on this. What the fuck is wrong with him. Disgusting motherfucker. Fucking whore.

They don't finish at the same time, but it's close. Levi groans, releases Crane's throat from his grip, slumps over to press his sweaty face to a bruised, blue-veined breast. His hips are still rolling, working through the aftershocks. He's still whispering. God knows what. And Crane shudders. His thighs shake.

"I know," Levi whispers. He takes Crane's left hand, pulls it from his belly, presses it against the floor. Readjusts his grip. Holds two fingers tight. "I know. Let's just get this part over with."

The fingers break easily. The wet crack sounds like a stick snapping in the mud. Crane screams.

He'll do what he's told. He'll be everything the hive wants, give it every single shred of himself. Every piece, every shard. Every damn thing in his womb. He'll be so perfect and so good, and when the baby's finally born and the lockdown lifts and Levi slips for a second, when he's distracted for *just a second*, Crane's going to do it.

All he has to do is make it there. He's not sure how.

Twenty-Two

Twenty-four weeks.

Levi refuses a request to go to urgent care for Crane's broken bones—it's the pointer and middle finger of his nondominant hand, swollen and purple and visibly incorrect—so Tammy sets them in the living room and splints them with popsicle sticks and duct tape from Dollar General.

Jess doesn't come with. Tammy doesn't bring her up.

Twenty-five.

Crane can't remember the last time he showered. His hair is too long. One Sunday he wakes up and realizes he hasn't done his testosterone shot in almost a month. He stares at the vent where he'd hidden the vial of hormones and can't make himself get up to retrieve it.

Twenty-six.

The baby moves regularly now. Turning, stretching, pressing hands or feet into Crane's ribs. Every movement conjures an image: a severed dog head in a Soviet documentary, reacting to stimuli while attached to an ugly machine. Veterinarians rescuing an unborn fawn by cracking open a smeared piece of roadkill.

Still, he catches himself rubbing the places it touches, following its fingers with his own. He hums, too. Not gently or anything; it's just that it seems to calm the baby down when he needs a break. There's no voice for it to get accustomed to, only the specific vibration, or the unique muscular fingerprint of his heartbeat.

Twenty-seven.

Sophie is supposed to be dead.

Crane doesn't hold any particular malice toward Sophie. That flattens the reality of the situation to the point of inaccuracy. She was fucked-up, but she was a sweet kid. She did her best with what she had; half-convinced that if she graduated high school and went to college and got a good job and married a nice boy, she'd be fine, half convinced she wouldn't make it to twenty if she didn't do something drastic soon. The imbalance was eating her alive.

It wasn't that Crane wanted her dead. It was just that she was never going to survive what it took for him to crawl out of her.

So, looking in the mirror now is like catching sight of a zombie.

Sophie isn't alive again. She's been dug up and stolen out of her resting place and propped up between his bones. The grave dirt mixes with the dust from the auction house that Crane still hasn't been able to get rid of, can swear he feels turning into grit on his molars.

All he has to do is make it until the baby is born, but he's not sure he can do that with Sophie peering back from reflective surfaces like Bloody Mary. He's supposed to be good, but he has to thump his chest and rock on his feet to keep from breaking the mirror and using the shards. He has to make it without shattering so completely that he can't do what needs to be done.

The dirt won't go away.

He hopes Aspen and Birdie are okay.

Crane gets the idea while he's leaning against the counter in the kitchen, eyes closed while a pot of water boils on the stove.

Stagger eats chicken gizzards over the sink, and the smell is making Crane ill. Levi is napping on the couch. Also, everything aches, but that's normal at this point. Crane can't believe the human species has made it this far. It's the ass-end of the second trimester and it feels like his spine is going to slip out of alignment. He has to prop his belly up with his hand to take the pressure off.

He read somewhere—Sophie, in her teenage obsession, practically memorized the article—that human evolution has been a back-and-forth struggle between fetus and host. It's the same evolution observed between predator and prey. The fetus attempts to consume as much as possible to ensure its survival, and the host, in turn, is forced to construct more and more complex defenses to keep from being sucked dry. The uterine lining is cruel, expelling every embryo it deems unworthy, because any embryo that sticks will take *everything*. It will manipulate its mother's immune system to keep from being destroyed, and widen blood vessels to suck up oxygen for its massive brain. It's antagonistic. A tapeworm.

Why would anyone make the conscious decision to do this. It's the medical equivalent of sticking your head into a bear trap and hoping it doesn't go off.

The pot of water on the stove bubbles vaguely, but not enough to put the pasta in yet. It's a big pot because obviously, autism, eating the same thing every day, it's easier to just make two boxes of macaroni at once and portion it out. Maybe he'll actually start eating regularly if all he has to do is throw a Tupperware into the microwave. Stagger chews through a piece of cartilage, bloody juice trailing over his chin.

Crane breathes in, holds it for as long as he can, and breathes out.

Being in the same apartment as Levi is making him crazy. It's making him sick. He can't get clean. His skin is disgusting, but the idea of taking a shower is too much, too many steps, he can't string them together anymore. Every few days he manages to pull a washcloth from the linen closet and scrape himself half-clean, smear it with soap, try again.

Slowly, the pot reaches a rolling boil. The vent above the stove churns at a high whir, sucking up clouds of vapor. The electric coils burn red and steam heats up the tiny kitchen, fogging up the windows, making it a little too warm for his sweatshirt.

Crane steps closer to the pot. Peers at it.

He puts his injured hand in the vapor. It's hot. Obviously.

At the sink, Stagger rasps, *"Careful."*

Crane shrugs one shoulder at him.

He has never wanted anything so bad in his life. The steam clogging his mouth and burning his eyes. He wants to swallow boiling water until his tongue swells and scalds, welding itself to the roof of his mouth.

Sophie had the right idea.

He leans in. The heat is suffocating. Steam condenses across his cheeks. The pot is big enough. Hot enough. It would work.

It feels like it would fix everything.

Make the outside match the inside, right?

When he puts his face into the water—before Stagger realizes what's happening, before he can grab Crane by the shirt and rip him free, before Crane can think too hard or too much about what he's finally finally finally able to do—the world goes white with pain.

Third
Trimester

Twenty-Three

It hurts so much.

It's everything Sophie would've wanted.

Twenty-Four

Tammy presses cool washcloths to Crane's face, googling home remedies for scalds. She tells Levi to get hand soap, instructs Stagger to fetch bandages, lets out a shuddering sigh at this complete nightmare of a situation.

"Now, what'd you go and do this for," she murmurs.

Crane whimpers at her touch. He can't open his eyes and he wants to know what he looks like, he wants to know so badly.

"It's okay," she says. "I'm here. We're all here now."

"Nah, I ain't worried," Levi says the next day. Presumably over the phone. Crane didn't hear anyone come into the apartment, and Stagger is sleeping at the foot of the bed. "It's not like he hurt the baby, so. Might as well just let him have it."

Levi sniffs.

"The recovery's consequence enough."

After days spent crusted shut with discharge, Crane's eyes blink open.

It takes a minute for the blurry forms around him, Stagger by the side of the bed and Levi folding laundry, to solidify into recognizable *things*. But there they are, and then the rest of the bedroom too: the nightstand, the alarm clock, the American flag tacked to the wall, the trees beyond the window.

The scalding water, at least, did its job. When Crane makes it to the mirror and he sees not Sophie but himself—the first time he leans into his reflection, bright red burns and yellow crusts and peeling skin splashed across his nose, his cheeks, his mouth—he laughs.

It's so bad.

It's perfect.

It's him.

The outside matches the inside. *Something's wrong here*, it says, *tread with caution, I beg you.*

Crane's stomach has swollen enough that his navel has popped into an outie. The start of stretch marks climb up from his hips to cradle the swell of his belly. Some of them cut through a tattoo, but he doesn't mind. They look like claw marks, and they're deep and scored.

However, he'd forgotten to take out his piercings before pushing his face into the water, and now that the skin is healing in a mess of crusts and pus, they've gotten disgusting. They need to be removed. But they're stuck, melted into the skin, and Crane can't do it himself with two of his fingers still out of commission. Levi has things to do, he says, so Stagger takes Crane into the bathroom and pins him down while he wrestles every piece of metal out of the red, raw skin.

One at a time. Septum, lip stud, a pair of eyebrow rings on the same side. All sitting on a paper towel on the edge of the sink, shiny with blister fluid.

How many weeks pregnant now? Crane stares at the calendar in the kitchen and struggles to do the math.

Thirty-two?

Stagger eases lotion across the stretch marks that have now started to itch and carefully cleans the holes the piercings left behind. The scald has begun to peel, skin sloughing away in layers as it heals badly. His face is new and shiny, uneven. He'll be scarred for the rest of his life. Thank god, thank god.

His fingers are healing badly too. Tammy takes off the splint during one visit and finds she hadn't set the fingers as well as she'd thought. They don't move the way they used to. Crane tries to bend them and can't quite get it.

Tammy tries to ignore it, just counts the baby's movements as she stares at her watch. "You can hear the heartbeat," she says to Levi. "If you get close enough."

Levi doesn't.

And sometimes there are contractions. Tammy says they aren't the real ones, not yet. They're called Braxton-Hicks. Sometimes Crane sits on the edge of the bed, holding his belly, eyes squeezed shut as he waits for it to pass.

Thirty-three marks on the living room wall. It's hard to sleep with a tiny foot in his ribs. He's tired, all the time.

Through the haze of cotton in his head, the fog in his brain, he thinks he hears Tammy yelling at Levi.

"I don't give a shit what he did to his face," she snarls. *"You got him pregnant, you take care of him, you hear me? You HEAR me, boy?"*

Then Tammy is coming into the bedroom, knocking on the doorframe with her gnarled hands. Crane thinks it's kind of funny, that some of his fingers look like hers now. For a moment he feels bad that he hasn't been paying attention to how far along her arthritis was getting, but it's difficult to muster sympathy for her.

She still hasn't said anything about Jess.

"Hey, sweetheart," she says gently, like this isn't partially her fault. She nudges Stagger, sitting on the floor with his back against the bedframe, with her foot. "Give us some privacy, will you."

Stagger looks to Crane.

"I won't let him do nothing," Tammy says.

Crane nods that it's okay, and Stagger leaves.

Tammy crosses the sparse room to throw open the blackout

curtains. Mid-November in Washville ushers in the first real snow-storms of the season, blizzards that bring the county up to that annual one hundred inches of snow. Fat wet flakes drift down be-tween bare branches and the sky is white. It's bright outside. Crane blinks—he isn't used to it.

"Get some light in here," Tammy says, having some difficulty with the window. "And some fresh air."

The latches in this apartment are bullshit. Crane slides out of bed the best he can, steadying himself on the bedframe to do it for her.

As soon as the windows slip open, frigid air eddies into the bed-room. Crane props it ajar with a broken paint stirrer.

Neither of them looks quite right here. Tammy's huddled into a hand-knit sweater that brutally contrasts with the corporate landlord feel of the barely decorated walls. Crane's worst blown-out tattoos have more thoughtful details than this place.

"How much thought have you given it?" Tammy asks. "The baby?"

Crane grunts. *None.*

"You don't got that much time," she chides. He fucking knows that. "Figure we ain't going to a hospital. I was thinking my house. My tub is deeper, if you wanted a water birth. Helps with the—" She motions like she's shooing something out of her stomach. "Makes it hurt a little less, I think. S'what I did."

Tammy doesn't talk about her daughter. If it weren't for the letters in the trash, Crane wouldn't have known. Every time he dug them out from underneath food wrappers and napkins, they were unopened.

"I know you don't want this," Tammy says. "But that baby don't care. It's coming whether you're ready or not."

As if it knows it's being discussed, the baby jams itself right into Crane's lung. He grunts, loses his breath for a second. Sometimes when it does that, he can see the movement under the skin. The chestburster analogy is particularly apt.

Tammy asks, "How are you feeling?"

He feels like he's doing what needs to be done.

It is relatively important to note that, at this point in time, Crane has not had a testosterone injection in three months.

He tried to convince himself that it was just because it was too hard to continue the shots with his belly in the way; no more soft fat above the waistband of his boxers to push the needle into. If he really wanted to, though, he could have easily moved to another injection spot. Taken up a location in the arm or thigh, followed the intramuscular instructions listed on the booklet.

But truly, genuinely, what would be the point? It's not like there's anybody he needs to convince anymore, and it won't be his problem for much longer.

While Levi sleeps one afternoon, Crane plods into the living room and slips Levi's phone from the charger. The passcode is 3232, because Levi can't be assed to think of anything better, and also because what's on there that Crane could care about?

In the cheap armchair across from the couch, Crane finds articles—it's hard to hold a phone with a fucked-up hand, he learns—and reads.

What it looks like to be a pregnant trans man.

My Brother's Pregnancy.

Seahorse Dad: What I wish I knew during my transmasculine pregnancy journey.

They're all old pieces. This is the sort of shit that can't get run in any major publications anymore. And they're infuriating. He understands, on a technical level, the need to provide an image to the public of a good, all-American father who just happens to be the one, you know, having the baby. It was an old survival tactic in the name of recognition and safety. Dreamy photos of fathers with their children in pastel nurseries. The insistence that they just wanted a baby so, so badly.

The articles go in depth with the struggles; everything these men fought for in order to have their children. Pushing back against bigoted doctors and misinformed midwives.

It all makes him want to speed up the whole *killing himself* thing.

The only thing that feels right is the slew of articles from years and years ago, when *Roe v. Wade* fell—shit, when? 2022? He was little then. The forums and micro-press news stories about queers talking abortion. "The dysphoria made me suicidal." "I couldn't carry my rapist's baby." "I was seventeen." "Birth would've killed me." "I can only conceive of pregnancy as forced detransition—and, death before detransition, you know? It was abortion or a noose. Sorry, that's dark. You don't have to print that."

He can't bring himself to watch human childbirth videos, so he pulls up YouTube and searches *dog whelping*, and *cat queening*, and *horse foaling*. Lots of wet membranes and amniotic fluid. Lots of tiny animals with their eyes squinched shut. It doesn't look like it hurts much at all—lucky motherfuckers.

Once his stomach feels too sick to continue, he searches *thirty-three weeks pregnant*. According to an adorable maternity health website, the baby is the size of a pineapple. It can blink, and dream, and make faces. In comparison to that baby horse struggling to its feet within the hour, this thing is practically a slug.

Then he clears the day's search history and puts Levi's phone back up to charge.

The next time Stagger comes into the room to check on him, Crane makes the same fist that Stagger had made months ago. Presses it to his own chest in a shaky circle, and then Stagger's. *I'm sorry.*

Stagger blinks.

"It is—" He tries, so hard, putting a knuckle to Crane's cheek. **"Okay. It is."**

Crane shakes his head. No, he's not talking about his face. That's not what he's apologizing for. But there's no other way to get the point across. He could finger spell the words, but he can't figure out what words to use.

Twenty-Five

The apartment—750 square feet of landlord specials, paint splatters on uneven hardwood, and windows so horribly drafty that any furniture against an external wall is too cold to use four months out of the year—has a dining room, according to the management website. In real life, it's a cramped corner across from the kitchen that can't in good conscience be considered anything other than an awkward extension of the living room. Levi put the folding table there when they moved in, but they eat on the couch anyway, or in the kitchen, standing.

Crane leans in the dirty hallway, wearing Stagger's jacket and supporting his heavy belly with one hand, while Levi drags in a pile of curtains, poles, a torn-up box sporting a faded picture of a crib, and a few other things that all melt together in Crane's head as *baby stuff*.

This is, for all intents and purposes, none of his business. But while Crane knows absolutely fuck-all about raising babies, this doesn't exactly seem like a lot.

Levi must notice the unimpressed vibe, because he snorts and dumps everything on the ground. Stagger, from his place half-awake on the couch, keeps an eye on the situation like a hawk watching a rabbit.

"Your ma was gonna give us a changing table," Levi says, "but it was a cheap piece of shit. Dry-rotted." He pulls out a quilt with the Goodwill tag still on it. "The floor'll work fine."

The folding table gets shoved to the side and Levi sets to work with the measuring tape and a step stool, grease pencil in his mouth, marking out tracks on the ceiling to cordon off a nursery with curtains. Screws lay scattered on the floor.

Crane wants something to do. He drags the busted crib-box to the designated corner and rips it open because it's already in bad-enough shape.

"Screwdriver's in the toolbox," Levi mutters around the grease pencil, fumbling with the tape measure. This is more than Levi has spoken to Crane in weeks. "Allen wrenches too, if you need 'em."

The instruction manual is two pages of actual instructions and three pages of YOUR BABY WILL DIE IF YOU LOOK AT IT FUNNY, which doesn't feel like a great ratio. According to the manufacturer, anything will kill a baby. Pillows, draw cords, plastic bags, the crib itself if you're not careful. Crane is both unsure of how the human species has managed to exist when their offspring spend every waking second attempting to destroy themselves, and also relates to this deeply.

It's nice to actually build something, though. Even if it's slow going, two fingers on the left hand out of commission and all. He lays out the pieces and the hardware and hopes he doesn't have to fetch anything else, because sitting on the floor at thirty-four weeks without a plan on how to get back up is a bad decision he keeps making.

Levi takes the grease pencil out of his mouth, makes another mark on the ceiling, lets the tape measure slide closed with a slap.

"So," he says. "You get what you wanted out of that?"

Crane looks up. Levi points the pencil in the general vicinity of Crane's face.

"That. Is that what all this shit's been about?"

Crane nods as he works a screw into one of the legs of the crib. All the blisters have popped, but the skin is still raw; his lips and eyelids have lost definition. He's discolored and visibly changed.

It's not as much as he used to want—certainly not as bad as Sophie always wanted it to be. But it's enough to last.

"Huh." Levi glares at his work on the ceiling for a moment before deciding it's close enough, then drags the step stool over to plan out the other half. "Should've told me. I would've done it for you a while ago, if you wanted. Feel like it would've saved us some trouble."

Across the apartment, Stagger growls, and Levi shoots back with, "It was a fucking joke," but Crane is thinking about it.

Last year, if Levi had offered to disfigure him, it would have been the kindest thing ever done for him. It would have been a declaration of love. Nobody had ever loved him so much they would do something terrible on his behalf. As Crane mulls over the instructions, trying to figure out how the wooden feet fit onto the crib's leg, he pictures it. Levi laying him down, arms pinned under knees, and a hand in his hair to hold him still, knife poised to open his mouth in massive gashes to his ears. Consensual vitriolage behind the gas station. Levi easing matches from Crane's hand and cradling him, whispering against his temple, "C'mere, baby. Let me do it."

He would've been smitten. He would've been so fucking wet.

These days, though, he feels the dirt every time Levi gets too close. Even when it's almost impossible to brush his teeth, he tries scraping the plaque away with a tissue, or the hem of his shirt if he can't manage standing to fetch one. It never works. It's still there.

At least Levi hasn't touched him since the morning at the auction house. Hasn't tried to put his cock inside him, or fingers.

Sometimes, instead, Crane thinks about fucking Stagger. Signing *please*, signing *can I*, stripping those ripstop pants off his thighs and swallowing whatever he finds down there.

With one leg of the crib done, Crane moves onto the next. Levi extends the tape measure, makes another few marks, then gets off the step stool and backs away to eyeball the whole thing. The baby shifts and Crane hums. *Give me a break, I'm busy.*

"You think it matters if there's a gap?" Levi says. He crosses his arms, gives the measurements another hard stare as if that'll make them shape up. "I figure it's a baby, it won't give a shit."

From what Crane's read, it will *absolutely* give a shit. It's going to be one hundred percent Levi's problem, though. Crane lets out a loud snort, and Levi sighs.

"I'll figure it out," he says. "Or Tammy will."

That's true. Tammy's going to be doing a lot of work around here. There's no way in hell Levi is going to touch a diaper.

Eventually, two sides of the crib come together—it's bigger than Crane thought it would be, there's no way that babies are this big, right?—and Levi screws supports for the curtain rods into the ceiling, which would've forfeited their security deposit if there wasn't already blood irreversibly smeared into the bathtub. (Again, who the absolute fuck *paints* a *bathtub*.) Besides that, there's not much else that got brought home; a quilt that'll go on the floor to act as a changing table, a set of sheets for the crib mattress. One of the bags, which Levi says he got off Facebook Marketplace, was from a mom cleaning out her closet. Most of it seems promising, even if some of the onesies are stained. Levi is convinced the idea of a baby monitor is stupid.

Crane pauses to inspect a onesie. The crabs printed on it look exactly like Luna's squishy crab toy. It's newborn-size. It seems small until he remembers he's going to have to push this thing out.

It was easier to hate the baby when he thought it was a maggot.

He's still managing it.

It's half Levi. No matter what he does, or how much he manages to distract himself, Levi is always inside him. Always feeding off him. Maybe that's the grit on the back of his teeth. Maybe that's the dirt.

He hopes that the son of a bitch, currently taking off his shirt because there's no way to adjust the heat in the apartment—and god, is the HVAC stuck on *high*?—is starting to clock the consequences of his actions, but Crane cannot name a single cis man who's ever had to deal with the *consequences* of having a baby, so.

Though. There's that scar again. Not the one on the shoulder that Crane had stitched up months ago, but the other one, the one he'd almost forgotten about: the raised keloid right on the side of the gut.

The curtains go up. They're gray, and probably could do better at blocking out light, but they're fine. When Levi closes them, it turns this corner of the apartment into a dim cave, quiet and muffled. Stagger doesn't like not being able to see them, or maybe he's intrigued by the new setup. He comes over and fiddles with the fabric.

"It'll work," Levi decides.

The crib is almost done, and Levi sits down beside Crane, picks up some of the extra tools, nudges his way in to finish it up. Their legs touch. Crane doesn't like it, but he doesn't move because he's being good.

Of course, the baby thinks it's a great time to try to roll over. What's probably a head jams right into the spine and what might be a knee or foot paws at the walls of its fleshy prison cell, wriggling until it finds a good spot and, Jesus, where's that photo of an eel ripping out of a heron's stomach, that is exactly what it feels like. Crane glares at his belly and hisses, an odd catlike *tshhh* sound. Fucking *settle*.

Levi snorts. "Is it messing with you?"

No shit.

"If it's anything like you, it's going to be one stubborn motherfucker." He screws on one of the crib walls and shakes it to make sure it's sturdy, which jingles his dog tags. "Frustrating, too."

Crane leans back on his hands. Not if Levi breaks it first.

Levi's gaze narrows in on the belly.

If he's noticed that Crane is wearing Stagger's jacket, he hasn't given any indication, but it's unbuttoned and drapes around the swollen stomach, showing an oversized Metallica tee from Levi's time in Fort Knox. Levi's clothes are the only things he feels comfortable in anymore, with regard to size, even if the smell of him is sickening. Levi looks at Crane's belly the way Stagger looked at Hannah, or Jess—drawn to it, possibly unsure why.

Levi pushes under the shirt to feel it.

Crane does not wince. He lets it happen. Levi presses in just a little bit, tries to locate where exactly the baby might be, as if there's a whole lot of space left for it to go anymore.

The baby responds with a nudge.

Levi recoils, visibly disgusted. "Fuck."

Crane doesn't react, but he wants to take the screwdriver and put it through his eyeball directly into the brain.

Levi does *not* get to do that. Levi doesn't get to act like this is gross to *him*, like this is freaking *him* out or leaving a bad taste in *his* mouth. Not after fucking Crane on the auction house floor while he cried, not after Jess bled over the bathroom floor after shoving a sharp object up her cunt to kill a fetus.

Is it finally clicking for him? Was he asked to do this by the hive and is only now arriving at the reality of the situation, now that it's not just getting off? Is that why he's been sleeping on the couch—because he doesn't want to get too close to what he's done? Fun part's over, huh. Maybe he's realizing that Crane won't be able to take care of a baby with a disability that's currently making it near impossible to bathe, that if anything goes wrong the hive will blame *him*, that it's real and it's happening and there's only six weeks left.

And Levi doesn't even know that Crane's not gonna be there at all. Sorry. Hope he and Tammy can steal enough money to cover formula.

Crane should probably feel guilty that he's leaving the baby with the man sitting across from him, but that would require a level of care that he is psychologically incapable of at the moment.

Levi finishes the crib. It's made of pale oak and seems pretty decent considering that it was probably picked up off the side of the road. The mattress board gets moved up to the highest rung, the green sheets put on the mattress itself, and Levi gets up to push it into place.

That keloid scar is just inches from Crane's nose.

The strange keloid scar. In such an odd place, healing worse than he's seen anything heal on Levi before.

He reaches up to touch it.

Levi grabs his wrist. "Mm-mm. Nope."

Stagger doesn't even have to make a sound before Levi lets go. Just cuts a glance across the tiny nursery. Levi gets the hint.

Twenty-Six

The insomnia is killer. Out of everything, that's what gets him the most. The practice contractions are bad, and the hip pain, which Tammy explained is the result of ligaments loosening so the baby actually has a chance of getting the hell out, is a nightmare. But the insomnia? Fuck that. The only thing that reliably works is forcing himself to stay up as long as possible, sitting too close to the TV or turning on the terrible "big light," until he passes out wherever he happens to be. Not that he ever feels rested upon waking up.

When he does sleep, he dreams of finding a knife hidden in the silverware drawer, a knife that Levi must have missed, and sneaking up on him while he sleeps and opening up that scar. In the dream, Crane reaches inside the wound and grabs what he thinks is a worm, but by the time he's pulled it out, it's just an unraveled jumble of intestine.

There can't be any evolutionary benefit to this shit. It's got to be a mistake, like the whole "human heads are too big to fit through the pelvis properly" thing.

Crane misses sleeping on his stomach. And not getting up every hour to piss.

Levi's alarm clock says 2:16 p.m., and through the crack in the blackout curtains it's snowing again, turning the woods beyond the property into a haze of brown and white. Crane is actively attempting to sleep, and failing, so he's awake when there's a knock on the door.

It spikes his heart rate. After what happened last time, of course it does. His anxiety is on a hair trigger. He reels, struggles upright, has to stop because the world swims and his vision darkens at the corners.

At the foot of the bed, Stagger sits up too.

Through the bedroom door, voices in the living room:

"Jess."

"*Heyyy.* Can I come in? Thanks so much."

Jess? She's here. Jess is here.

The front door whines and bangs shut.

"Does Tammy know you're here?"

"Eh, she thinks I'm picking up a late lunch. Truck came to fill up the gas tanks and it fucked up our morning. I—no, back up. I wanted to see if Crane could chat. Go for a quick walk or something. We won't go far, just right there, you can see it from the living room."

"If he wants fresh air, he can open a window. You should probably go."

"I'll tell the worms what you did to Hannah."

There is a long silence, and then footsteps, and then Jess is nudging her way into the bedroom.

She's *here*. She's got the baggy work pants, tan boots, and a blaze orange winter coat she definitely stole from Tammy's dead husband, snow still stuck in her dark hair. Cheeks flushed red from the cold. In one piece. Alive, smiling apologetically.

"Oh my god," she says. "You look like ass. Come on, let's go outside. Let's go."

When the apartment complex was originally built just outside Washville, however long ago that was, there'd been a few decent amenities—a tiny pool, a playground, a picnic area. Now, during the summer, the playground is a mess of wasp nests. The pool hasn't been operational since he moved in, either; used to be that Crane had to walk over to the ugly pool maintenance building every few weeks to reload the cheap plastic card for the laundry room, since that's where they decided to park the terminal for some reason, and the only water in the pool has ever been shallow puddles stagnating on the tarp. These days, Crane knows the operator code for the washer that runs a load for free (press *light soil* and *normal cycle* at the same time, then *cold temp* twice), so he hasn't checked on it lately.

The complex isn't doing well as a whole. None of the tenants acknowledge each other, and there're more empty units every week, less cars in the parking lot. The dumpsters are overflowing, littered with broken glass, and someone left a couch on the edge of the lot last month to get chewed through by rats. The heat still feels like it's stuck *on*. The bedroom windows stay open no matter how cold it is outside, because that's the only way it's tolerable. He's jotted it down in a notebook even though the leasing agent will never see it.

Now Crane is wearing one of Levi's oversized camo jackets and slogging through the snow toward the picnic area, Jess trying not to laugh at the pregnant waddle.

"It's not *that* noticeable," she assures him. She looks to Stagger. "Right? It's not that bad. Only if you're looking for it."

Stagger grunts, and Crane gives him the finger.

The air is crisp and cold and perfect. It's been a while since he's been outside, let alone in the sun, and Crane has to squint. Stagger clears off a space on a bench for both of them to sit, but Jess stays standing, breath clouding in front of her face, hands jammed into her pockets against the chill.

While it would be technically true to say that Jess looks better than she did, considering the circumstances under which they last saw each other, almost anything would be better than that. She's in one piece. She's alive. She's not drunk or bleeding out on the bathroom floor.

She says, "Tammy kept me updated. Said you messed yourself up, said it was bad, but. Fuck, dude."

Crane just shrugs. He didn't appreciate accidentally welding his eyes closed and nearly giving himself an infection with the piercings, but those were small prices to pay.

"Also . . ." She looks him up and down. "Don't take this the wrong way, but *seriously*, when is the last time you showered."

Crane does not want to talk about that.

Jess waves to get Stagger's attention. "You fix that, okay? I know that piece of shit up there isn't going to help."

And then she hands over her phone, which has been opened to the jankiest text-to-speech app Crane has ever seen in his life. It's riddled with advertisements and the UI is ugly as sin.

She says, "The good ones are like a hundred dollars, but I thought it might work for now?"

Crane frowns.

"Only if you're okay with it, though. Tammy says you don't even like writing notes, so I was worried this might be pushing it."

Crane doesn't respond. He's too busy tapping through the options. It's nothing like the AAC program Aspen and Birdie have on the tablet. No prepared phrases, no autofill, nothing. It seems straightforward enough, though.

It's embarrassing how long he wanted to be silent before the hive finally gave him permission. In kindergarten, Sophie growled and hissed at people until Mom got sick of it and begged her to use her words like a big girl. In middle school, she researched what injuries could damage her voice box until the computer's cyber-nanny kicked in and alerted the teacher. She wanted to stop, but she was so smart and so eloquent that it was never going to happen.

Crane is silent now. He has control.

He takes the phone and types, *"Thank you."* The generated voice is a janky mishmash cobbled together from cut-and-paste syllables.

"Oh god," Jess says, "it sounds so bad."

"That's why it was free."

"Yeah, I hear it now!" Jess leans over Crane's shoulder as if looking at the screen will reveal why the audio quality is utter shit. "I'm sorry, that sucks. We don't have to use this if you don't want."

"It's fine."

"Can I ask? Why you don't talk. If that's too personal, you can tell me to fuck off, but—when we met, you said you could, so I've been curious. Sue me."

Crane mulls over his answer for a bit. *"In high school, I won the statewide public speaking championship."*

Jess gapes. "No way."

"Twice. Was gonna go to school for political comm, PR as backup."

"Political—no. Absolutely not. You're an asshole."

The robotic voice reading out *"Fuck you"* is funny enough that Jess laughs, throwing back her head, vapor trailing into the air. The window to the apartment living room is right above them; Levi could probably see it, if he was keeping an eye on them.

"So, you were headed to school, had big dreams and everything. What happened?"

"Mental illness."

"Oh hey," Jess says. "Same."

Crane raises an eyebrow.

"Probably," she backtracks. "What, you think an okay person ends up here?"

Still, Crane isn't sure it's the same. The hive found Jess locked in a boarded-up room. Nothing even happened to Crane. She has a reason to be like this. He's not sure he does.

They sit and watch the snow for a while. Jess sticks out her tongue to catch a flake. Crane leans against Stagger's arm for warmth, tries breathing out like a dragon the way he used to when he was little. He hadn't realized how much he missed fresh air until he was out here.

Jess says, "Anyway, I wanted to apologize. For, you know, everything I said last time. I was drunk and fucked-up and had definitely lost a lot of blood, but it was still awful."

Crane hates apologies, and explaining that she was, in fact, correct about everything she said would probably take too much time. Holding the phone properly is hard enough as it is. *"I should be apologizing to you."*

"Don't you dare. If you say sorry to me, I'm taking my phone back."

"He does make you feel crazy."

Jess's eyes suddenly go a bit glassy. "Oh. Yeah. He does."

"Did it work?"

Jess sniffles and presses a knuckle into the corner of her eye. "I told myself I wasn't going to get emotional, you motherfucker." She clears her throat to get the hitch out of her voice but it doesn't work, and then she's hugging him.

Crane freezes. It's awkward, Jess kind of half-collapsed onto the bench to get down to his level, but her arms are wrapped tight. She smells like Tammy's cheap body wash and dollar-store hair conditioner, a generic brand of dryer sheets. Like the closest thing Crane's had to home in a long time.

"No," she mumbles against Crane's shoulder, and now she's really crying. "It didn't work. Uh, I really managed to wreck my internal organs, but when we got to the hospital and they stitched it all up, turns out the fetus was still fine. Then one of the nurses slipped me this."

It's a business card. Shoddy and simple, definitely mass-produced in someone's living room, but it gets the point across.

Pregnant? Need help? Call.

"They mailed abortion pills to the house. I miscarried. It's gone."

Crane, for a moment, is flooded with so much rage and regret and helplessness it makes him sick. It's not fair that he didn't realize what had happened until it was too late. It's not fair that the hive dragged him back before Aspen and Birdie could save him. It's not fair that this is how it's ending.

But he is glad for Jess. If anyone deserves to avoid this, it's her.

Once Jess has finished crying, wiping her nose on her sleeve, she clears snow off the edge of the table and hops up to look out into the forest behind the apartment complex, feet swinging.

"Can you be honest with me real quick?" she says.

"I reserve the right to change my mind."

She snorts. "That night in the car. When you told me that if I tried to leave, y'all would kill me. Is that true?"

"Do you plan on finding out?"

Jess doesn't give him anything to go on. She just keeps looking out toward the woods. The big, hibernating trees bending under the weight of wet snow. It's so quiet out here that, without Jess's voice or the droning of the app, if they wait long enough, they can hear a branch snap under the weight of it.

"If you ran," she says, "where would you go?"

Crane is aware that his knee-jerk answer is stupid. Canaan Valley. It's stupid because Canaan is literally fifteen minutes away from Wash-ville, right past the Wash County line, and also because the main draw of the place is a ski resort, which Crane has no interest in. It's just that, last year, a customer at the gas station was talking about the townhouse her family rented for a ski trip, and it had sounded so wonderful that he hasn't been able to get it out of his head since. Rugs on the wooden walls, a spiral staircase, low ceilings, and dark carpets. Crane wouldn't even do anything. He'd lie on the couch, probably do crosswords in a book left behind by the last vacation-renters, sit on the back porch in his coat alone.

But if Jess was right about one thing, so was the hive.

This world was not made for ones like you.

He's made peace with how this is ending, he thinks. He's pretty sure. The idea of running—of getting away, of living—is so impossible to consider that it borders on painful.

Crane types, *"I wouldn't survive out there."*

Jess's expression is tinged with pity, but she says, "I've always wanted to go to California."

That sounds nice, too.

Even if Crane *did* go back to the world, even if he was capable of leaving all this behind, which he's not, what would he even do? He has no legal ID that isn't a fake, no money that actually belongs to him, no place to sleep that wouldn't be the back of the Camry. Aspen and Birdie want nothing to do with him, and returning to his parents would be an act of unimaginable cruelty. They probably accepted Sophie's death years ago. Grieved her properly and moved on, still loving the little girl they lost. He can't do that to them.

When Crane gets back to the apartment, Levi has the TV on. It's the news, the same thing as always. Cost of living rising exponentially, overlapping zoonotic diseases, investigations of the terrorist who drove a truck into a Thanksgiving crowd. Conspiracy theories that Crane doesn't believe, like pasteurized milk turning children trans, and conspiracy theories he *does* believe, like the vice president having a brain-eating amoeba (because why else would he be acting this way). There are people who believe the theory to the point of trying to give themselves amoebas, though. Crane is gone but he's not that far gone.

Twenty-Seven

Levi has to call Tammy in early today.

"Breathe," she says, a hand on Crane's stomach as he leans against the bathroom sink. "There we go."

The baby has snuggled itself against Crane's spine, and swear to god, he can feel its head low in his pelvis—threateningly low, shockingly low. Everyone on the internet who said that Braxton-Hicks contractions aren't painful can go fuck themselves. It feels like he's being squeezed with a vise.

"Are they getting stronger?" Tammy asks.

Crane shakes his head.

"And they're not getting any closer together . . ."

It sure *feels like they are.*

"And your water ain't broke, so." Tammy straightens up. "Not yet. Just breathe, baby, it'll go away."

Not yet? Crane whimpers helplessly. He can't do another month of this. The skin of his hips is paper-thin, with no more room to stretch; the dull red marks have taken on the texture of stringy meat and give the distinct impression that they could open up into a dozen wounds at the slightest provocation. His breasts sport thick, dark nipples that have started leaking, leading him to cramming handfuls of toilet paper and tissues into his bra to keep it from soaking through to his shirt.

His belly reminds him of the hive when it gets excited. When it begins to move and thrum and the swarm starts to shiver.

Tammy says, "I know it's bad, but you can do it." She manages a breathy laugh. "Bodies like ours have been doing this for thousands and thousands of years. It'll manage on its own. All you gotta do is survive it."

Crane would like to correct her on that, but Tammy wouldn't be interested in the death-via-childbirth statistics Sophie memorized in high school.

Tammy has to go. She makes no mention of Jess, which could mean nothing. Levi sees her out, but Crane doesn't leave the bathroom—he's too busy measuring his breathing, waiting until his muscles unclench and he can unstick his jaw. He has to jam fingers in his mouth to pry his teeth apart. He's still shaking, and he wraps an arm around his stomach, runs a hand down the too-thin skin, tries to soothe the thing inside so it stops attempting to puncture his organs. *I don't like that you're in there, either,* he wants to tell it. *I want you out too.*

Looking in the mirror is a bad idea, though. His hair is disgusting. It'd just be easier to shave his head at this point. The last time he managed to wash it was, what, a week ago? Two? And barely even then—he stuck his head into the sink, and he can't remember if he used shampoo.

He's always had hygiene issues. It's a point of contention, to say the least. There's a unique shame attached to hygiene issues, because *bad hygiene* is associated with *autism* with unbelievable ferocity. One time, Crane had gone down to Aspen and Birdie's because he couldn't get himself clean, and while Birdie sat and talked him through the steps, Aspen explained: there're a lot of different reasons this might happen. Did he have trouble with toothpaste growing up, or was the taste strong enough to make him panic, no matter the flavor? There are so many different parts to it, and if his brain is overwhelmed, it becomes impossible to string into anything useful. Let alone how difficult it can be to move from one task to another. The willpower it takes to get up and do any of it—it's suffocating.

Crane had looked at Aspen curiously—*how do you know all this?*—and Birdie supplied that Aspen had googled it because they wanted to help.

So yeah. Sophie lied about brushing her teeth until Mom started checking the brush bristles and smelling her breath before bed. Middle school was spent avoiding showers, until Dad gently informed her that the grease made her hair look wet. She'd gotten her act together by high school, thanks to them both, but was never able to shower *daily* like everyone else seemed to. Every other day was the best she could manage.

It's been a lot longer than that now.

In the doorway, Stagger watches.

"Alright," Levi calls from across the apartment. "I'm headed out too. Keep your shit together."

For some reason, Crane huff-laughs. Another hunt for the hive. As long as Levi doesn't come back with a bullet wound again, he doesn't care.

The moment the door closes and the lock clicks into place, Stagger takes Crane's chin in his hand and lifts it, letting the harsh white light of the bathroom illuminate the healed mess of his face. The too-smooth skin, the melted upper lip. Crane's eyes slide shut.

Stagger's thumb slips into Crane's mouth and works its way between the teeth. He tastes decidedly salty.

Crane finds Stagger attractive the way he found that burned-up fireman attractive at fifteen. He would hesitate to use the word *attractive*, because that doesn't seem right—it's less aesthetics and more a combination of different desires coalescing into a general sense of wanting to fuck him. Though maybe that *is* what the word means. The bizarre middle ground of *you make sense* and *you're like me* and *I want to feel something.*

After they had sex in the back of the truck that first time, Levi had leaned down to kiss him. That had been Crane's first kiss, too.

How different would it be with someone else?

Maybe that's what he wants.

A tiny *click* sounds from the sink, and Stagger retracts his thumb from Crane's mouth. Crane frowns and cracks open an eye.

Stagger is putting toothpaste on Crane's brush, mimicking the very specific steps he's seen—wetting the bristles, massaging in the toothpaste so there's no awful texture when it hits the mouth, and tapping it twice on the sink to shake off any stray drops of water.

"Open."

Crane opens his mouth.

Stagger brushes Crane's teeth. His lopsided face scrunches with concentration, a worm in the crook of his neck moving as the muscles tense. That thumb pushes aside Crane's lips, tilts Crane's head to get the best angle for each tooth. Stagger hums as he works. When he's done, he steps aside to let Crane spit and rinse his mouth in the sink, and then he walks over to the stained tub and turns on the water.

Stagger attempts to help Crane take off his clothes, but Crane pulls away, so Stagger turns off the bathroom lights and suddenly it's okay.

Dim sun trickles in through the tiny window high over the tub. Everything comes off. Levi's shirt, the sports bra with the leak-stains on the inside, pants, boxers, and all of it goes into the dirty clothes pile. Crane has no idea when he last managed to change his underwear. The water in the tub roars. Stagger puts a hand under the stream to check the temperature, lets Crane do the same to double-check, and when it's half-full, he helps Crane in.

The water is warm and perfect, and Crane wants to cry but doesn't. He's felt disgusting for so long. Fighting to get himself into the shower or wipe himself down whenever he could but never managing it. Stagger washes Crane's hair, twice since it doesn't feel clean after the first go. A soft cloth rubs down his face and neck, where funnily enough, some amount of facial hair has managed to survive the scalding water and lack of testosterone; moves across the shoulders and back, maneuvers gently around aching breasts. He lingers on the tattoos, but never for too long.

Eventually, Stagger washes the suds from Crane's shoulders, reaches into the water to wipe down Crane's thighs, and signs, *Good?*

Good, Crane signs back, and the sign is close enough to *thank you* that he decides it means that too.

Stagger pulls the drain.

And then doesn't move. As if doing this has taken all the energy out of him—or as if he'd thrown himself into caring for Crane to distract himself from something. When Stagger breathes, lungs operated like billows by all the worms crawling around inside him, he shudders.

"Hurts."

Crane nods gently. Yes, it hurts. It's going to hurt until it's over. It's going to hurt them both.

That doesn't seem to be the response Stagger wanted, though. He groans. Gives a jerky shake of the head. Fumbles for a bit, tries to find words, can't. He keeps starting sounds but finding himself unable to finish them or form them into anything with real meaning.

Crane signs, *Okay?*

"Want," he says, then frustrated, *"No."*

Crane shows Stagger a big breath, motioning for him to repeat it. *Big* breath. Start over.

Stagger tries again, concentrating so so hard. *"Worms—inside."*

That is also correct, that is in fact where the worms are, but apparently that isn't right either. With a sound bordering on a whimper, Stagger gets up and leaves the bathroom.

The tub finishes draining. It makes that awful sucking sound it does at the end of every bath. Crane hesitates; is he supposed to follow? Stagger didn't tell him to follow. The bathroom is freezing in the winter and he's cold. He slicks his wet hair back from his face and sits up, shivering.

Stagger returns with—what the fuck?

One of Levi's knives. One of the knives he uses to take apart roadkill and/or people, the *nice* one he takes on hunts only half the time because he likes it too much. Crane has always, admittedly, been smitten with it; the slight curve to the black blade, the drab paracord handle distinctly military in a porn-parody sort of way. The fact that Levi keeps his knives perfectly sharp.

Levi also has managed to keep them *in the apartment.* Stagger did not go outside to fetch this. They've been here the whole time. Crane swears he'd searched the place up and down in a fit months ago, looking for a workable blade. Even inside the couch cushions, and the loose slab of drywall under the sink where the cockroaches come in.

Stagger strips his clothing. All of it.

Crane is too tired to pretend he's not staring.

Stagger is heavier than Levi, fatter around the belly. Less hairy, though. All the hair is concentrated below the navel, his flaccid cock resting limply against his thigh, and in the dim light it's just possible to make out the things that don't line up. The pubic hair pattern bisected and rejoined half an inch from where it should be, a puckering scar from the groin to the belly. He is made of skin sitting wrong on the muscle, muscle packed wrong on the bone, worms visible in the forearms and hips and thighs.

What had Irene said? *All that cuttin' up and sewin' together.*

Then Stagger is getting into the tub. Crane snorts, tries to gesture something along the lines of *hey, a little cramped in here,* but that doesn't stop him. Crane has to settle between Stagger's knees, belly resting on his thighs while Stagger lies back. It's weird to be up here, looking down at him. Usually Crane is under someone else.

Stagger pulls the skin of his lower stomach taut.

Crane's attention snaps to the tip of the knife.

Just as it sinks into the soft skin just above the groin.

Crane doesn't flinch. He's been with the hive too long for that. He watches with a sick fascination, the same way he watched those animal birth videos on Levi's phone. Stagger cuts through his skin a small slice at a time, working hide off a deer, an inch and then two. He doesn't make any noise of pain, either, give any indication that it hurts; only breathes out hard through his nose, shudders with the collective movement of subcutaneous creatures shuffling to avoid the sharp point. Stagger bleeds. Crane doesn't know why he's surprised by this.

Three inches. When Stagger breathes, it forces the edges of the wound apart, shows the layers of skin and muscle and the black pit leading to his insides. Blood streams down Stagger's sides, the crook of his thighs. It catches in the gnarled hair above his dick. Crane tries to tell himself that the wound doesn't remind him of a pussy but come on, *look* at it. He wants to touch it. He wants to soak in the heat to ward off the cold, stick his hands in the cut and *feel it*.

Four inches now. Stagger sets the knife aside and takes Crane's hands to warm them between his own. Together, they move toward the wound, and the blood is burning hot.

"Okay," Stagger says, panting.

Two fingers skim the cut. The same way Crane would touch his cunt before finally giving in. The skin bends under the pressure. Stagger holds his wrist tight, assuring him.

Crane slips inside.

Stagger groans, head lolling back against the tile. The split muscles spasm. Something brushes Crane's fingers, and for a moment he thinks it might be intestines, if Stagger still has those anymore. He remembers hearing somewhere that during abdominal surgery, doctors hang the intestines on racks and they wriggle impatiently up there, annoyed to have been removed from their den.

It's not intestines, though. It was never going to be.

Stagger's fingers fumble for the wound and spread it open. Inviting him. Begging.

Crane leans over him in the cramped tub, holding himself up, trying to find purchase on the slick porcelain. He ends up straddling Stagger's thighs instead of sitting between them. There it goes. This is better. A third finger slips into the cut, and then another, all of them—pushing aside layers of flesh, fingers splayed, searching. Stagger gasps, lips curling back from his teeth, uneven eyes fluttering. Crane imagines it's the same expression Stagger would make if Crane leaned down and put that cock in his mouth. He thinks about the night he and Levi figured out how much lube it takes to fit a clenched fist all the way to the cervix. His clit throbs at the memory and now's not the time but maybe it is. He loses control of his breathing. Stagger reaches for Crane's thigh and squeezes.

It's the first time Crane has felt attractive since he started to show. God, it'd be so easy to sign *please*, take that cock in hand until it hardens, lift his hips just a little and guide it in. Stagger would be too gentle, but he's strong, Crane could convince him; he wouldn't be hurting the baby, only him. Just bruises, no broken bones.

In the burning, wretched space of Stagger's belly, a worm slips against Crane's palm. He snatches it. It resists, squirming away, but he's not messing up this time. He wraps it around his fingers and pulls.

Stagger breathes as if he's the one giving birth, grunting pitifully. *Look at you*, Crane wants to tell him, wishes he had the free hands to sign. *You're perfect.*

The worm emerges. Just a part of it at first, a wet, squirming middle trapped in the hand. It's an anatomical pink, the same color as uncooked meat. This close, the details are finally clear. The squishy, ridged body. Lines of nubby tendrils gripping Crane's fingers, trying to make sense of what's grabbed hold of it.

Then it's all out, slipping free from the bizarre cesarean.

It's a small worm. A foot long, a bit thicker than his thumb; it must be young. He's seen them get up to a yard, as wide as his wrist at the thickest parts, and he can't discount the idea that Stagger has one of those big bastards where his large intestine had once been, or maybe nestled in between the curves of it. But this little one dangles from Crane's fingers, waving wildly, searching for the hole it'd come from.

The worst part of the worms is the face. Or what passes for the face. Splayed jaws surrounded by, what, feelers, antennae?

Stagger's throat shines with sweat despite the chill. His belly is slick. All Crane can think to do is take his free hand and run it across Stagger's arm to comfort him.

"In," Stagger moans. Stagger's bloody hand pats his own cheek, his temple, then slides down to the scar where he'd been cut so neatly in half and then put back together wrong. *"In."*

Crane touches the scar too. Was he alive when it happened? Was he awake? Is he alive or awake now?

He remembers, months ago, Levi talking to Stagger on the other side of the bedroom door. *You still in there or what?* Levi knew who Stagger had been, then. Maybe Stagger had been an enforcer at another hive once upon a time, or maybe he had been military, too. And then what the hive called him—a failure. The hive vivisected him and chewed him up and destroyed him.

The hive was trying to make something. Change something. From the sound of it, it didn't work.

Cuttin' up and sewin' together.

In Crane's belly, the baby turns, reaches out with a tiny hand.

"Hurts," Stagger says. His lip quivers.

Crane considers taking the knife and killing them both. Severing Stagger's spinal cord to obliterate the man underneath the worms, then finding the fastest way to off himself so he won't have to sit through the bleeding-out for long. The knife is right there. It's *right there.*

The only thing that stops him is the baby.

Not because he cares about it. But because if it dies, Levi is just going to do this to someone else. It might be Jess. It might be Hannah again. And Crane isn't going to let himself become responsible for that.

So he does not touch the knife. Instead, he leans down, curls Stagger's hands around his own, and together they crush the creature they pulled out of his guts.

Somewhere deep inside him, it is a shock to Crane that this creature dies. That it is capable of something as *mundane* as dying. But as the worm spasms and leaks fluid between their fingers, and Stagger's chest heaves, he thinks, of course it does. Why else would it be so hungry? Why else would the hive be so capable of anger, which is just another word for fear?

Their mouths are so close. Crane can see the vein at Stagger's temple shift and slither, disappearing into the brain, and one day maybe that movement will destroy the part of the gray matter that allows for what little speech Stagger can manage, but today is not that day.

Crane, with bloody hands, signs, *please?* Stagger nods.

The kiss is clumsy, and cold, but still a kiss.

It'll be over soon.

Twenty-Eight

Crane thinks about the kiss constantly. Constantly. When he stitches up the hole and cleans up worm guts. When Stagger washes him every few days. When Stagger sleeps on the floor next to the bed and Crane lets his hand dangle down, fingertips brushing the blanket he's taken.

No matter how much he thinks about it, there is never a second. He wonders if Stagger thinks about it as often as he does but does not ask.

The second wave of winter comes in hard over the mountains, as if the cold season hasn't already arrived hard enough. The channel 10 forecaster stands in front of a green screen, tracing the path of a snow-storm headed straight for Wash County, while a maintenance man lays bag after bag of salt on the sidewalks. The heating's shit out and Crane is pretty sure he can see his breath in the kitchen. He wears gloves to sleep, and sometimes Levi turns the oven on high and leaves it cracked. Utilities are included in rent, he says. If management doesn't want to pay the gas bill—and if they want the local schools to stop reporting unfit conditions to the appropriate government agencies—then they can fix the fucking heat.

Someone calls into the news station to claim this is proof that global warming is a hoax. Someone else calls in to insist that liber-als control the weather. A third says no, it's the space lasers causing this, not carbon dioxide, because carbon dioxide is good actually. The newscaster is baffled. Who said anything about carbon dioxide? Levi turns off the TV.

Thirty-seven marks on the wall between the door and the gun safe. The next time she visits, Tammy places her hand on his belly, checking for the millionth time that the baby won't come out breech.

There's three more weeks until term, she says, but it never hurts to keep an eye on things.

Crane's water breaks at thirty-seven and a half.

Surprise.

It happens while snow comes down heavy, while Crane is *not* writing his suicide note. That's the truth; that is technically not what he is doing. Levi is making lunch (beans to go with the cornbread Tammy dropped off), Stagger is inspecting an instructional manual to make sure he still remembers how to read with what's left of his brain, and Crane has the notebook he'd practiced drawing dragons in, giving himself a task that isn't thinking too hard about how much he hurts.

He's been hurting bad for a while. That morning, he'd woken up early to piss—and also because cramps were bad enough to shake him into consciousness—and found a wretched mess of blood and mucus in his boxers. It was so bad that the underwear wasn't worth saving. Just went directly into the trash. But those fucking cramps haven't let up. More than once he's struggled off the couch to double-check the marks by the door, just to make sure they don't say forty. They don't.

Stagger keeps looking at him. Crane keeps signing *okay*. Gotta work through it is all.

What Crane is doing instead of writing a note is sketching. It's not turning out great, and his memory of the subject is fuzzy. Blame pregnancy brain, and the passage of time. It's supposed to be the main character of a comic he saw in high school, a flimsy wide-eyed twink with a soft face, but proportions are the devil and he turns the page to try again. That said, it does feel like a suicide note. What are suicide notes except a thesis statement about everything that went to shit? Every now and then they include a little memory, a tiny story, just to drive the point home.

Crane's story isn't even a good one.

In high school, the art class Sophie shared with Aspen was tucked away on the top floor, hidden by a set of heavy double doors. Unlike the rest of the school, which contained gleaming tile and shiny lockers, the art classroom had concrete floors and unfinished walls, paint spills and massive windows that turned the place into a sauna during the month before summer break. The advanced art kids took over one corner, scrambling to finish their portfolios, only rarely coming over to ask for knives or permission to use the kiln. The kids who were only there for an easy A, and Sophie, were confined to a collection of tables in the center of the room as they worked on their final project.

The final was a "future self-portrait." *Select one of the following mediums (pencil, ink, acrylic, oil, watercolor, pastel) and create an image of who you hope you will be at the age of 25. Extra credit (10 points)— include a 200-word essay explaining how your use of value, perspective, color, and/or style reflects your prediction.* Sophie was excited. Extra credit meant a chance to show off just how good she was at writing essays. Two hundred words was insulting, actually. She could do better with a thousand.

Plus, the drawing was, on a mechanical level, pretty good for a fourteen-year-old. It was also the most stereotypical, cookie-cutter shit anyone in that art room had ever made. During a check of the initial sketch, the teacher frowned.

"Is this you?" she asked.

Sophie frowned back. "Yeah. See—that's my hair, and that's my mole." She pointed to the drawing's hand. "There."

"That's not . . . " A pause while the art teacher tried to figure out the words. "I mean, is it *you*? It's you, but when I look at this drawing, what am I looking at?"

Sophie squirmed, studying the sketch in front of her. What else was there to add? She was going to grow up, go to college, and get a job, obviously. Any specifics of a future life like that dissolve into static, but don't they for everybody? She's not a psychic. And it wasn't as if she was going to do a whole project on what she *really* wanted. If she drew a picture of herself with no skin on her face, she'd be sent to the guidance counselor's office expeditiously. It's just—she'd drawn what the rubric had asked for, right? Her at twenty-five, if she managed to avoid setting herself alight for that long.

"I don't get it," Sophie finally admitted, pretending she didn't want to cry.

The art teacher was about to try again, but one of the other students started to paint the table out of boredom, and she had to go. So Sophie went back to her own table and stared at her drawing helplessly.

Aspen was sitting across from her, ignoring the project in favor of a comic book they'd positioned themselves against a wall to read. They'd placed a sticky note over what was clearly a big bold **18+**.

"You're going to get an F if you don't start soon," Sophie informed them.

"I already have an F," Aspen said. "Are you crying?"

"No." Then, "I think I messed up the project."

"Okay? Let me see it." Aspen put down the book, the cover featuring two men gazing at each other in a loving embrace, and yanked the drawing closer. "Oh shit. Yeah. This is boring. You have to actually do something interesting." Sophie was not interesting in any way that wouldn't get her locked up. "Draw yourself—I don't fucking know— killing a billionaire."

"I'm not getting in trouble like that."

"Fine. Draw two husbands. Draw yourself as a boy. Whatever."

Sophie yelped. "I'm not a *boy*, either."

Obviously, Sophie was not a boy. She was a girl who just had to try very, very hard to be a girl. She was a girl who looked at pictures of transgender men on social media and got *pissed* because they got to be men and she didn't. If she really was a boy, somebody would have told her. Somebody would've given her permission to do something about it.

"Sure," Aspen said, unconvinced, and slid their book across the table. "Read some gay porn and get back to me on that."

Sophie didn't touch it.

See? It isn't even a good story. *Nothing* actually *happened*. Sophie didn't make a decision or take a risk. She didn't look deeper. She didn't do *shit*. She muddled through her boring final and turned it in and received her first-ever grade of B.

The world was not made for ones like you.

When the swarm said that to Sophie for the first time, she'd sobbed. They were right. She was miserable and trapped. She wasn't a boy until the worms finally told her it was okay, because she couldn't do it herself.

Come with us, come with us, come with us.

The only time Crane decided something for himself was when he put his face into a pot of boiling water.

From the kitchen, Levi knocks on the counter. "Food's ready. You hungry?"

Crane is always hungry. He gives up on the sketch and motions for Stagger to help him up, which he does. Hoists Crane right up, easy as anything.

Pop.

Crane's boxers, and his sweatpants, and the floor are wet.

Now, Tammy had told him there was a chance he'd lose control of his bladder at some point. It's a rite of passage, she explained, the muscles loosening in preparation for birth and the uterus jamming itself into the bladder since there's only so much room in the abdominal cavity. Granted, she'd said it as *you'll piss yourself*, the last word coming out *yerself* like it always does with her, but still. All the preparation in the world doesn't make it any easier when you find yourself soaking wet and sick with embarrassment.

It's still coming out, too. Crane holds his stomach, can't make himself move, can't see his legs but imagines the trickling mess down his thigh.

Levi says, "You good?" He sticks his head out of the kitchen. "Oh *shit*."

Crane needs to go to the bathroom right now, but Stagger won't let him move. Crane whimpers. It's mortifying. Let him *go*.

That's when one of those fucking contractions hit again. A pain in the lower back, a cramp at first before it rises to a sharp point, wrenching across his stomach and squeezing out more hot liquid that soaks right through his pants and begins to drip onto the hardwood floor. He tries to shift his weight to make it stop but it just gets worse. Feels like something slippery, slithering out of him.

"I'm calling Tammy," Levi says.

No. No, Levi doesn't need to do that. It's fine. They still have two and a half weeks. Look, the tally marks on the wall say so. It's not due yet. It hasn't been forty weeks. Ignore the fact that Braxton-Hicks practice contractions don't get stronger like these have been getting. Ignore that these have been getting closer together, more frequent; swear to god, this pressure is pushing the baby's head into the waiting gap in his pelvis and he can feel it lodged there.

He wasn't timing on purpose. He didn't want to know.

Levi, ignorant of or just ignoring Crane's mounting panic, jams his phone between his shoulder and his ear and immediately goes to pack up the food that'd just finished cooking.

"Hey. Where you at? Gas station? Yeah, his water broke." Cabinets thud as he gathers up Tupperware. "I don't fucking know, it's not like he's *said* anything. I'll just—fine. Hold on. Crane, *how bad is it?*"

There is no good way for Crane to admit he has been ignoring actual labor contractions for at least six hours, so he just signs, *Bad.*

Stagger translates, ***"Bad."***

"Bad," Levi says into the phone. "I can come get you. We gonna do it here? Your house?"

The contraction's grip on his stomach loosens and Crane gasps for air. He remembers being in middle school again, lying in bed. Pretending to be an animal in a stall, birthing a calf into the hay.

"Fuck," Levi says. "Alright. Be there soon."

Levi hangs up, jams the containers of food into the fridge, and grabs a duffel bag from inside the makeshift nursery. Crane tries to place it but can't. Levi answers the question without being asked, as he starts plugging the combination into the gun safe: "Apparently, you pack bags for this kind of shit. Underwear and phone chargers, stuff like that. Come on, gas station, let's go. Tammy said the worms want you there."

Crane realizes they never bought a car seat.

What a thought. After everything, they forgot a car seat. He doesn't want this baby, he's going to kill himself, all this is at the behest of a pile of mutant invertebrates and talking flies, and they forgot the fucking car seat.

Twenty-Nine

It's been almost two years since Crane's had to use a menstrual pad, so maybe it's because he's a little out of practice, but when Tammy hands him a folded-up pack of cotton to stick into his new pair of boxer-briefs, it doesn't feel right. As in, the pad doesn't feel correct. He's already embarrassed—nearly to the point of anger—that Tammy won't leave him alone in the cramped gas station bathroom, sitting on the toilet just in case, but she's already clucked her tongue at him.

"You're about to have a baby come out of your vagina," she said, purposefully enunciating *vuh-gine-uh* in three hard pieces to drive her point home. "You're gonna have to get over this modesty thing real quick."

At least it's not Levi in here with him. Levi's out there closing the store.

Crane turns the pad over, inspects it, and gives Tammy a wrinkled nose. *Why is it like this.*

"It's one of them overnight ones," she says. That would be why he doesn't recognize it; Crane hated overnight pads, back when he still had periods. He usually plastered two together before bed and hoped for the best. "You're gonna keep leaking, so might as well catch it."

Crane groans and unwraps the pad to the nostalgic crinkling of plastic, but Tammy has to help untangle his boxers from his ankles and smooth the pad into the fabric. Boxers are most definitely not made for pads, because why would a clothing company for men ever make them that way. Tammy tests the adhesive, frowning at the strange fit. Wait until she learns about how there aren't sanitary bins in men's restroom stalls.

There's a fly on the mirror. As Tammy helps him get his underwear back over his ankles, Crane watches it. It doesn't say anything. He can't tell if it's a hive fly or just a side effect of the general disrepair of the place.

Something starts to bang. Crane winces. He feels like a live wire. Everything is too bright, too loud, veering into pain if he doesn't squint or cover his ears. Tammy had instructed Jess to find a way to turn off all but one singular bulb in the manager's office, and if she couldn't figure it out, to either remove the bulbs or break them. Is that Levi out there, then? Hammering? Crane stares at the door numbly, praying for the sound to stop. Eventually, it does.

"So, the contractions are bad, huh?" Tammy says, still on the grimy floor. "How bad?"

Crane has no previous experience to compare this to. He shrugs.

"They been happening all day?"

That he can answer—he nods.

Tammy sighs, but before she finishes helping him into his clothes, she walks him through checking his progress. Cervical dilation, she calls it. The same steps she took with Hannah. She pushes her fingers into him and prods, face impassive.

"Lord above," she mutters. "All day is right."

Crane gives a half smile in apology, the closest thing he can get to *sorry*. He can feel how far apart her fingers are inside him and he doesn't like what that implies.

But hey. Almost done, right?

They help each other up. Tammy washes her hands and Crane huddles into his new clothes. Loose pants, a sports bra, not much else.

"You ready?" Tammy says.

No.

Outside the bathroom, the gas station is dark and cool. It smells distinctly of rotten meat, and the coppery stink of afterbirth he remembers from Hannah. The door to the hive's closet has been propped open. The worms writhe and the swarm shivers. Stagger stands halfway in the room with them, and the low droning hum of wings must be what people imagine when they talk about wind turbine syndrome.

The little one, the little one is almost here.

Crane desperately wants Stagger to come to him and comfort him, but he refuses to move closer to the hive, so he looks elsewhere.

Tammy has picked up her notepad to jot down whatever his cervix is doing. His vague recollections of the contractions he'd tried and failed to time in the truck are listed there too.

Our little one.

The back door creaks open and Jess fumbles her way through, lugging in pillows and blankets from Tammy's car. Snow blows in around her feet with a whistle. Jess stamps off the slush on a towel before walking in and offering a lopsided smile.

"Hey," she says as she passes by. The heap of fabric is dumped in front of the door to the hive. A fly buzzes too close to Crane's ear and he shakes his head to shoo it away. "Don't worry about messing these up. They were all gonna go in the trash anyway." She sniffs. "Smells like attic, though."

As she shuffles around the blankets, trying to get them somewhat comfortable-looking, another twinge grabs ahold of Crane's belly. He thumps against the threshold. Closes his eyes like Tammy taught him. Deep breath in. Hiss it out between the teeth.

Breathe, the hive croons.

The contractions aren't *so* bad. They're not a broken arm. Or a hammer to the head. He can handle it.

But Jess is still helping him straighten up, his face in her hands, her brows furrowed. "Your lungs working?" she asks. "There we go. I—hey, Tammy. I got him."

The pain, Crane thinks, is getting repetitive. The impotent frustration reminds him of being a child and being told to use his words when he couldn't. He can be mad all he wants, but it won't make it stop.

"Levi's out front," Jess tells him. "He's turning off all the lights, and locking the doors, and putting down the blinds so nobody can see in." She uses the sleeve of her shirt to wipe down his face; the parts of his face that still have operating sweat glands, having survived the boiling water in patches here and there. Mainly across his soggy throat. "He hasn't been alone with me if you're worried. I won't let him be alone with you, either."

Her voice is so soft, so close to his temple. There's so much buzzing. The hive sounds like wet meat, the same thing he heard while rooting around in Stagger's insides, the constant squelching like slogging through the floor of a slaughterhouse.

She says, "Are you scared?"

It's such a simple question, but he can't believe he's never been asked it before.

He can't imagine anyone who goes through this being anything other than scared.

It's not the pain he's afraid of, though. He can handle pain. He's good at pain. He *likes* it sometimes. And if childbirth kills him, if the placenta doesn't come out right, if the uterus doesn't close off its blood flow or an infection takes him out in a few days, then the baby's done the hard work for him. Maybe the uterus will full-on rupture. Straight-up tear and spill little infant feet into the abdominal cavity and kill him. Wouldn't that be convenient.

He is, however, afraid of dying a woman.

He is afraid that he won't be allowed to die at all.

The pain lets go. His eyes flutter open. Jess is so close to him, smiling gently.

"There we are," Jess says when Crane looks at her. "Hi."

She's so kind to him. She doesn't deserve to be here. He should have turned her away from the gas station, he never should've let her step inside. The night Sean died, he should've kept driving her away until they hit Virginia, and then the East Coast, and let her free on the shore of the Chesapeake Bay. He's so sorry he didn't.

"Tammy's here," she says, "and your friend's here, and I'm here. We'll take care of you."

Even half-naked, it's too warm in here. He wants a cigarette and some snowy air to calm his nerves. He can't figure out how to say that, so he shakily mimes a smoke with two fingers to his lips. Jess raises her eyebrows.

"It's freezing," she protests.

"What does he want?" Tammy calls from another room.

"A smoke break?"

Tammy pokes her head into the manager's office. "Girl, you better give him whatever he damn well wants right now. Just make sure he puts on some warm clothes. And good shoes."

Crane doesn't want warmer clothes. He's burning up. He steals Levi's coat anyway.

"Marlboros?" Jess asks. "The red ones?"

The shock of cold is a blessing. It freezes the sweat across Crane's throat, chills the burning of his thighs and cheeks. The blue sky has gone gray and big fat flakes float down between tree branches. There's no one at the pumps; they've been turned off, OUT OF ORDER signs plastered across the screens. Levi must have done that too. Corridor H is silent.

Jess, who is actually halfway dressed for the cold, pulls her hat tighter around her ears as she makes sure the back door is shut tight. Stagger, most definitely *not* dressed for said cold but not seeming to care, doesn't do much of anything.

Crane leans back, lets Stagger hold him steady. Jess watches the road.

It feels strange, now that it's actually happening. He didn't think he was going to get this far.

West Virginia is beautiful in the winter. Just like the weatherman predicted, the flurries turned into massive snowdrifts in a blink. The mountains are smothered and the air itself feels muted. In a storm like this, Wash County is so isolated and lonely that Crane and Jess and Stagger might as well be the only people in the world.

And Washville itself doesn't have a whole lot of time left. Won't be much longer until this place is empty for good and the woods take back everything. The livestock exchange, Tammy's neighborhood, the streets of the town Crane hasn't been to in months—all gone. Returned to the ivy and the deer and the wolves.

Crane pulls a cigarette from the fresh pack, puts it into his mouth, stares at the flame of the lighter too long before lighting it.

No need for fire now. He got what he wanted.

Stagger drops his head against Crane's shoulder. Crane breathes in, tries to savor the precious time in between the pain, is too nervous to manage it even with the nicotine.

Jess says, "California's probably beautiful this time of year."

Crane sighs out smoke.

"Southern California, I mean. Northern California's freezing, I've heard."

She could make it. Out of all of them, Jess would be the one to survive running from the hive. He's not sure if she could've at the start—before she became who she needed to be to survive Sean and Levi, and Crane, and the worms. And it blows she had to *survive* those things, but the world doesn't give a fuck, and now? She could do it.

He remembers to respond to her. Nods.

"Can I try a cigarette?" she asks. Her eyes are fixed on the cold horizon. "Does it help?"

Crane hides the pack from her in Levi's jacket, snorting. *Don't start, it's not worth it.*

Her mouth wrinkles up. "Fine. I guess. God, it's freezing. Do you think we could—" She shuffles a bit, tries to keep her blood flowing while she considers her words. "Do you think we could save the baby? Somehow? Like, get it away from all this?"

Crane obviously thinks the answer is *no*, but he raises an eyebrow at her, a request for elaboration.

"Take it," she says, "and give it to someone who isn't us. Hide it from the hive. Let it grow up normal. Knowing our luck, we'd probably end up raising another Unabomber." She thinks. "No, he had too many degrees. Damn. I can't think of any mass shooters off the top of my head right now."

Crane won't be raising shit, but he can't say that. Plus, this shouldn't be on her. If she tries to take this baby away from the hive, who knows what it'll do to her. Crane can't have that on his conscience. Or, well, his immortal soul. If he believed in that sort of thing, which he isn't sure he does.

He looks to Levi's big black motherfucker of a truck, then to Jess. Hmm.

Crane puts a hand on Stagger's jaw and carefully extricates himself from the man's arms. Stagger grumbles. Crane has never been more grateful for their time together in his life when his stiff fingers spell out Levi's name, then nudge Stagger toward the door. *Be a good boy and fuck with him, will you? Or at least make sure he doesn't come out here?*

Stagger cues in and slips back into the gas station, and Crane starts for the truck.

The snow crunches under his boots. It's thick and heavy and hard to walk through.

"Hey," Jess chides. "Not too far. You're a mess."

Crane just gestures for her to follow him, and when she does, he produces Levi's ring of keys from the jacket pocket. He unlocks the truck, yanks open the door, gets up on the step-bar to look around. The shotgun is gone from the front seat; Levi took that inside. He checks the back next. Jess makes a quizzical noise but doesn't stop him.

Aha. There it is. Crane's go bag, the one that was confiscated when all this shit went down. Crane pulls it out and drops it by the back door to the gas station.

Then he clicks his tongue to give Jess a half-second heads-up before wrestling the truck key off the ring and tossing it to her.

She catches it, and her eyes widen with terror.

"What?" she says. "No."

Crane shrugs. He doesn't care. Get into the truck—the door's already open, snowflakes hitting the back seat—and start driving. Get the fuck out. Levi won't notice until the baby is out, and who knows how long that'll take? She can be far gone by then.

She at least has to try.

"I—" She stammers for a moment. "I'm not gonna just *leave* you here. I can't."

She has to, though. He's literally in active fucking labor, and the hive will chase this baby down to the ends of the earth. But Jess? This is her chance. Levi will be pissed about the truck, but it's not like he can go to the cops. If she's going to go, she has to go now, and she has to go alone.

Jess whispers, "Oh god." He can barely hear her over the wind, the muffling of the falling snow.

Then she steels herself.

"Okay," she says. "California."

Crane should reach for her. Should cram his nose against her temple to wish her farewell the only way he knows how, beg her silently to speed and avoid the cops and pick a new name and get the fuck out. But of course his body won't let him. He feels the contraction tighten before it actually hits, and he grabs the bed of the truck, leans against it. They're so much harder than they were this morning. Lower in the body. The baby's head is a plug jammed into his cunt and it fucking *hurts* and he can't even be embarrassed when that long, low moan crawls up his throat. He drops his cigarette in the snow. He's barely even aware he's doing it.

He's getting closer. It's almost done.

Jess puts a hand on Crane's back. "You need to get inside."

No. She has to leave first. He tries to push away from the truck but only manages to double himself over, gasping for air hard enough it's ripping up his throat. The cold burns. He's convinced the baby has tiny claws and teeth and it's chewing through the organs holding it in place. There's no other reason for it to feel like this.

Jess says, *"Shit."*

Crane looks up, and.

Through the blur of pain and the snow-glare, he can't quite make out the details of the woman walking up to them. There's a car parked haphazardly by the shut-down pumps, a man peering in confusion at the OUT OF ORDER sign.

He can hear what she says, though. With her unmistakable northern Virginia accent.

"Excuse me? Excuse me! I'm so sorry, but the pumps are down, and I can't get service. Do you know where the nearest—"

She stops a few yards from them. The wind whips up her graying hair. Snow sticks to her thick-rimmed glasses.

"Are you okay?" she asks.

For the first time in years, Crane is looking at the soft, kind face of his mother.

Thirty

Crane's mother does not recognize him. She drags her heavy boots through the snowfall toward them and takes a baffled glance from Crane's belly to his face, trying to make sense of it, before Crane's next pathetic sound of pain knocks her out of her confusion.

Her hair has gone gray. That's what Crane focuses on. She finally allowed her hair to go gray. She'd been dyeing her hair since he was in middle school, and he remembers the distinct, thick smell of the chemicals permeating the entire upstairs. He remembers her pinning up her waves in the bathroom mirror to swipe the brush across her temples, the stained towel thrown around her shoulders, the old blanket draped across the couch as she watched the Saturday morning news and let the color take. He remembers being fifteen and admitting over breakfast that she looked good gray. It made her look regal. She should keep it. She'd laughed and said that HR professionals don't need to look *regal*.

Crane remembers a lot of things. Sitting on the edge of the tub while Mom explained how makeup worked, how she always put on her foundation with her fingers and never used black eyeliner because it was too bold—"we don't have bold faces," she'd say, and Crane thought about it every time he picked up the black tube from the drug store. Then there was the time they went to the Humane Society to pick up a cat, and how Sophie probably wouldn't have agreed to follow the swarm if Cici hadn't died the year before. Mom would always insist on splitting a donut when she took Sophie to the grocery store, and Sophie crawled into bed with her when he had a nightmare until she was twelve, and god, Crane remembers his mother beaming during high school graduation, so happy and so proud, with no idea her daughter was planning to set herself on fire that night.

There's no way to sum up nearly eighteen years of closeness like that. Annual shopping sprees the week before school started, reading quietly beside Mom's desk at city hall, scoffing at newspaper articles together, always forcing a smile when Mom asked if Sophie was okay.

Mom turns to the man by the pumps. Crane's father. Crane tries to make out the details: the tight haircut and well-worn clothes, doing that thing where he sticks out his lip in annoyance.

Whatever emotions Crane's feeling about this haven't hit yet. He's not sure what they are. It's like dumping a dozen different paints into a pan and watching it turn into a muddy, thick color, impossible to name.

"Dear!" Mom hisses across the lot. Both Jess and Crane wince in unison. Jess's attention snaps nervously to the back door of the gas station. "Get the blanket out of the trunk."

"What?" Dad says.

"Just do it." Mom turns back to Crane and Jess, her soft face gone tense. "Is everything alright?"

"We're going to the hospital," Jess says. She shows Levi's key. Her smile has too many teeth, warning this strange woman away. "Just trying to wait everything out. The longer you're there, the more expensive it is, you know? We're fine."

"I'm sorry," Mom says to Jess, "do I know you? It's just. You look so familiar—my daughter would have been your age."

As the contraction shows mercy, disappears again like the tide, Crane realizes that above everything, above the confusion of seeing them again and the flood of memories and the pain, he does not want his parents to recognize him.

He can't do that to them. It'd be just one more awful thing he's done, one more knife in the back, for them to see him like this. They deserve to remember Sophie as she left them. Smart and witty and ambitious. The deadpan-funny overachiever who slept on the bathroom floor to comfort foster kittens and designed Easter egg hunts for city hall. He built that mask for his parents and gave them something to be proud of. It wasn't him, but they were good parents. It's what they deserved.

Fuck. Crane never believed in God. Not for a moment. But yeah, he used to pray that his parents would wake up one day and see right through it all. He would get out of bed in the middle of the night and stand outside their bedroom door in tears, trying to work up the courage to tell them but never able to get it past the tongue. Maybe if they noticed the shadow of his feet under the door, they'd gather him up and ask him what was wrong and he would shatter and everything would spill out at once.

I don't know what's wrong with me, I can't do this anymore, I'm so tired and I'm so scared and I'm so sorry.

"You must have the wrong person," Jess says.

Dad tromps up with an old blanket—a blanket that's moved between three cars, a blanket that's probably as old as Crane is—and settles it over Crane's shoulders. Jess stares at this strange man too. She grips the truck key harder.

"I promise we're fine," she says again, pulling Crane closer. Her dark hair sticks to his pain-sweaty face.

Dad's gone still, though. He's stopped, his deep-set eyes narrowed. He hasn't shaved in a while, and apparently he hasn't bought a new coat in four years.

And Crane remembers. Sitting on the back porch on a warm summer night, waiting for the blink of a single firefly as Dad talked about the swarms of them he used to chase as a boy in Pennsylvania. Falling asleep on the couch as a World War II documentary murmured on TV, the back of Sophie's head bumping Dad's knee. Sweeping the sidewalk as Dad mowed the lawn, and playfully squabbling over leftover brownie batter, and sending each other news articles detailing the cruel aftershocks of yet another Supreme Court decision, frustrated but resigned to their fate.

Dad watches him, mouth slightly open, drinking in everything. Crane's hair. His eyes. His tattoos, his scalded face.

Dad says, expression distorting with a thunderclap of pity and fear and heartbreak, "Oh god."

And he begins to cry.

"It's you," he whimpers, putting his hands so softly against Levi's coat. "Nicole, look. Our baby. It's our baby."

Who the fuck knows what Jess must be thinking in this moment: a random couple deciding that a deity has answered their twisted prayers and this silent, pregnant freak is delivering the baby just for them. An episode out of a sex-crime TV show. Even Mom's face screws up for a moment as if she's got no idea what her husband's on about. They lost their daughter years ago; has the weight of grief finally shattered him? Sure, these strangers look so oddly like Sophie, but—

Crane wonders what does it for her. What Mom sees in Crane that makes her get it. Is it the exact color of his eyes? The slightly crooked tooth that slid right back into place after thousands of dollars of orthodontics?

She says, dazed, "Oh."

"Crane," Jess says. "Do you know these people?"

He considers lying. Shaking his head, begging her to take him inside and away from them. Let his parents think for the rest of their lives that they were mistaken, that they ran into a ghost wearing their daughter's face.

But he can't. The pain of labor, the sting of the cold, everything about the past, what, eight and a half months—it's worn him down.

He wants his mom and dad.

He clumsily slumps from Jess's embrace, clutching the blanket tight. His eyes burn and maybe it's the biting wind, but clouds of stuttering condensation betray the hitching of his lungs. Yes, he knows them. He would know them anywhere. He's sorry he left. He's sorry for wasting the money they spent on all those college applications, and he's sorry he didn't say goodbye.

"You're—" Dad attempts, avoiding the obvious horror of the scald. "You have tattoos." His fingers press into the crook of Crane's jaw, finding the tattoo nestled behind his ear. "You're having a baby. You cut your hair."

"Did you think you couldn't tell us?" Mom whispers.

You weren't bad parents, Crane wants to tell them. *You were perfect.*

So why did he leave? Because they didn't read his mind? Because they *believed* their daughter when she said she was okay? Because they *trusted* her?

Let's rewind.

Let's say the swarm never came, but Sophie didn't manage to set herself on fire, either. She chickened out of the flames like she was always going to. She sat there in the back seat of the car with all her supplies, sobbing and gasping for air, and she wouldn't trust herself to drive home; not this emotionally compromised, not with all the graduation parties happening in the neighborhood. It would be two in the morning and she'd call her parents to pick her up, and her parents would come up because they're good parents and they love her. At home, the three of them would sit on the couch, lights turned down low, a cup of water in Sophie's hands, and she would tell them everything.

She would tell them about the fire drill in middle school. Her obsession with hurting herself. She'd explain how tired she was all the time, how she's terrified of college and doesn't think she can do it, how she's not really as smart as everyone believes she is. That she's fooled everyone into thinking that she's a good person. And maybe she'd even talk about the boys in the locker room. Maybe she'd talk about the dog and every awful thing she'd prayed for.

Clutching a snotty tissue in her fist, staring at the wall above the fireplace, Sophie would say she wished she was a boy. She'd say she never wants to speak again, because never once has it been worth it, and she thinks there is something very, very wrong.

Sophie's parents would look at each other over her head and have that telepathy moment.

Dad would say, "I'm so sorry we never noticed," and Mom would say, "Thank you for telling us."

After that? Who knows. College would get deferred for a year, probably. Dad would help make an appointment for HRT on his son's eighteenth birthday, and Mom would pay for a therapist who clocks Crane's autism thirty minutes into the first session. In a few years, he'd see Aspen and Birdie again. And Levi never would have fucked him, and this baby wouldn't be tearing him apart, and he would never know what the inside of a shattered skull looked like, and he would use a safe word if he needed it.

If Crane hadn't been such a coward, and asked for help, he could've avoided it all.

But nobody ever told him he was allowed to.

So look where he ended up instead.

Crane presses his face into Dad's hands, and reaches for Mom, and he's crying too. They can't help him now, the same way Aspen and Birdie couldn't. He's putting them in danger. They are all separated from Levi and the hive by a door and a prayer.

"What happened?" Mom says. "Who did this to you?"

Dad dives right into it. No time for questions. "We need to get to a hospital, then." He's in fix-it mode, visibly sorting through the options. His attention lands on Jess: Jess, who is standing away from them, mouth open in visible confusion. "That's what you said. Right? Our car is almost out of gas but—is that your truck?"

Jess clutches the key. "It is."

But Crane shakes his head. Not because of the truck, but because they can't be a part of it. It can't happen like this.

"It's okay," Mom says. "We're here now. Whatever happened, we don't care." She visibly fumbles through a mental list of worst-case scenarios. "If the father isn't around, we can help with the baby. If there's drugs, we have savings. We can find a rehab center."

"Nicole," Dad says, a whispered attempt to get her to slow down.

"Warrants? Are you in trouble?" Mom continues. She fussily readjusts the blanket around Crane's shoulders. "I don't care. We'll figure it out."

Stop. Stop. If they knew what he'd done, they wouldn't be saying this, would they?

He realizes, yes. They would. They're looking at him—disfigured and pregnant and silent and male—and pleading for him to come home. Promising they'll overlook any and everything. Just so they know he's okay, just so he'll come back with them where he belongs.

It feels like something cracking in the back of the head. Something shattering.

Everything he's told himself about never being able to go home to them suddenly feels like an excuse.

Crane knows he doesn't deserve Jess's help after everything he put her through. After everything he did to her, the truck and this tiny chance to escape—maybe ruined now—isn't nearly enough to make up for it. But still, he turns to her in a panic.

Help me.

She steps in. Gestures Mom and Dad forward, tucks them in close.

"You're Crane's parents?" Jess says.

"Crane?" Dad says. "Like the bird?"

Mom, though, is undeterred. Crane watches her face, the little wrinkles that have sprung up in the corners of her eyes since he left. She still uses the same brand of lotion. "We are."

"Right." Jess nods sternly. "Like the bird. Look, I need you to listen to me. The baby's father—he's a piece of shit. Real motherfucker." Dad's eyes narrow. "No. Absolutely not. He's an ex-Marine with half a foot on you, sir, I'm not letting you do that."

Mom puts a hand on Dad's shoulder.

"We're trying to get away from this man," Jess continues. She's smart, and magnetic, and such a good fucking liar. "We don't want him to get even a whiff that the two of you are involved. If he gets any idea that you're around, we're all in trouble."

"So—" Mom looks helpless. "What do we do?"

Jess points down the road. "There's another gas station on the other side of town, if you have the tank to make it a few more miles. You give us your phone number and then you keep going. You do whatever you were headed through here to do, and you stay away until your son tells you it's safe."

"When will that be?" Dad asks.

Jess says, "I don't know."

It is bizarre and ugly and terrifying to be offered a way out. Knowing that his parents are actually capable of loving him despite what the hive has turned him into, despite what he's been all along. Look, the hive was right, the world is not made for ones like him—but, fuck, neither is the hive. He won't survive here, either. And what *is* the hive, anyway, except a bunch of sweet-talking bugs? They need people to do the dirty work for them. They're not special, they're not magic, they're *bugs* that can *die*.

And Crane doesn't want to die. He just wants this to be over.

He wants to go home.

"It's been a bad few years," Jess says. "He can tell you about it when he's safe."

"Okay," Mom says. "Okay."

Mom and Dad write their number on a napkin and the grease pencil taken from Levi's truck, and Crane tucks it into a pocket of the coat. They kiss his face and squeeze his hands.

"We missed you," Dad says.

"We love you," Mom says. "Whatever happened, we can fix it."

They do not want to leave, but Jess points a look toward the road, like she thinks Levi is out there and might arrive any minute.

Crane whispers, voice raspy, "Bye."

Mom whispers back, "Bye, baby."

And then they're gone. They're in the car and driving away. The snow fills up the tracks in moments, and they disappear into the haze.

Jess says, "Jesus Christ."

No more delays. No more wasting time. Crane points to the truck, can feel another contraction coming on. If Jess is going to leave, she needs to leave now.

When she doesn't move, he grunts. Pulls the blanket off his shoulders and starts the process of folding it up tight. It'll fit into the go bag, he thinks. He glares at her the whole time. *Leave.*

"I feel bad," she says.

Crane doesn't budge.

She groans, frustrated, then grabs Crane's face and kisses the corner of his mouth. Her teeth chatter.

"You gonna be okay?" she says.

He nods. He'll be more than okay.

He's going to do something he promised he'd do a long time ago.

Thirty-One

I was about to come get you," Tammy says as soon as the back door slams shut. "Lord, you're freezing. Where's Jess?"

Crane drops the stuffed-full go bag just inside the door.

Levi and Stagger have situated themselves by the hive, the shotgun leaning against the wall; both of them have taken off their shoes so as not to mess up the nest that Jess had so carefully built. It's in a horrible, voyeuristic place. Right in the doorway to the closet so the worms and the flies can see it all. It makes the word *childbirth* feel less accurate than an emotionless, unhuman alternative: *parturition,* or, why not, let's use the word that's really lodged in his head, *whelping* like a fucking dog.

Tammy says, "Jess, boy. Where is she?"

Crane does not answer. He watched Jess climb up into the truck, adjust the seat, and fumble with the key. She's pulled out of the parking lot by now. On her way gone. To wherever. California. Somewhere a hive won't find her.

And his parents, they're gone too. He keeps thinking about them. Mom let herself go gray; is that because he said he liked it gray years ago? Is Dad using the same aftershave so Crane would recognize his father by smell?

He can't help it. He sniffles, wipes his eyes, tries to pretend he's not crying. The pain, the adrenaline. The *realization* of it all.

It'll be over soon. He just has to be able to do it.

"Shit," Tammy growls, gathering him close. She's watching Levi, and for a terrible second Crane thinks she's going to tell, but she doesn't. "Okay. Okay. Let's get this baby out of you."

After the cold of outside, it's too hot in here. Crane is sweating. His clothes stick to him. He's wrestling out of Levi's jacket as Tammy walks him to the blankets and towels laid out on the floor, as Levi catches him by the elbows and helps him down. In the nest, he shucks his bra and fumbles to kick off his pants. He's burning up and making a low animal noise in the back of his throat.

"Easy," Levi chides. Stagger whines with concern, settling onto the floor to brace Crane against him. "Easy now."

Tammy snaps for Levi to help with Crane's boxers, says she needs to check his dilation again. He barely feels her fingers in him. Levi doesn't watch. Stagger brushes Crane's hair from his face, has an arm around his torso, holds him up and breathes steady, to remind Crane to breathe too.

"Everything look good?" Levi says.

Tammy doesn't answer his question, instead catching Crane's eye. "I know it don't feel like it," she says, "but this looks like it's gonna be the kind of labor most mommas would kill for." She wipes her hands. "Fast and easy. You lucky sumbitch."

Crane almost laughs. *Easy?* Motherfucker. *Easy.* He's going to scream. Tammy is taking notes again. His stomach is in a strange shape now—it's not round like it had been, now deflated without all the amniotic fluid that trickled out of him, the bump clinging to the shape of a baby. The buzz of the hive is starting to get into his head, makes it feel like a bug is crawling around in the narrow gap between his brain and his skull. This is what must have been crawling in Harry's head the day he died.

Oh child, you're doing so well. It's beautiful.

Tammy is talking again. "If you don't feel the urge to bear down yet, we can wait until the head is further down. No use tiring yourself out."

Crane doesn't want to be sitting anymore. Not with his legs spread like this. Too exposed. He gets onto his knees, braces his hands on his thighs. The contraction leaves and he feels hollow in the wake of it. He isn't getting enough rest between them.

"There you go, get up, make yourself comfortable. Drink." Tammy brings him water. "It's coming. You're doing good. You're okay."

"Where's Jess?" Levi asks.

Tammy says, "Pay attention to your damn baby."

Your baby. Levi's baby. This creature currently trying to rip its way out of him. All he can think of are those women in, Jesus they were *comedies* of all things, wailing at their husbands: you did this to me! That had never been funny to Crane. He didn't know how it could be funny to anybody when it was objectively the truth. Levi did this to him. The hive did this.

Thank you, child, the hive whispers. Crane groans. *Your womb is a gift, we are so lucky, we are so blessed to have you.*

He doesn't have long until the next one hits. He needs to drink and conserve energy for the incoming wave.

But these wriggling, weak, crushable sons of bitches. These bugs that tore Stagger open and crammed themselves inside him. These creatures that whispered in Levi's ear and told him what to do. This mass of little black bodies and intestine-shaped *things* spilling across the floor and walls of the room.

The day Harry died, Crane found him in the manager's office, beating at the door to the hive. Rattling the chain. Screaming. His hands were bloody. Levi had just dropped Crane off for his shift and he'd come into the back to get another box of coffee grounds before opening, but also to figure out what that banging noise was; he'd been convinced Mike had left the back door open the past night, and it was slamming open and closed in the wind.

Pathetic ape, the hive said.

"You sick motherfuckers." Harry left red handprints on the metal. His hair had grown long, and he had the gaunt paper-paleness of someone starving. He hadn't been doing well for a while, Crane had thought, but not this bad. "You did this to me. *You* did this."

Crane froze in the doorway, but it was too late. Harry had seen him. "You," he gasped. Crane took a step back. "You. Where's the key."

The key? The key was supposed to be at the register. Was it not?

Crane would later learn that Harry had started talking like this to Mike the night before, and Mike had absconded with the key to prevent exactly this. But right then, Harry didn't know that, and neither did Crane.

Crane shook his head. No key.

So Harry grabbed Crane instead. "Can you feel them? Can you feel them inside you? Jesus fucking Christ, you're just a kid. You shouldn't be here. They're going to do it to you too."

Levi had arrived then, and the rest of the shift was spent on his hands and knees with a bucket. No bleach, no cleaning chemicals, because the hive hates those. Just the reek of vinegar and copper, scraping pieces of bone and brain out of pits in the old concrete.

Now, on the floor, Crane sees it, where Levi's shirt has ridden up just a little bit as he paces, checks his gun, paces again—the scar.

Under it, something moves.

Crane wants to laugh. He wants to scream until his lungs give out, but he can only cough and splutter against the phlegm in his throat. The hive did this to all of them, huh? Their rotten bone-nests weren't enough. They had to find their way inside everybody.

Cuttin' up and sewin' together.

Thank you, child, thank you, this will be so beautiful.

And after all this time, there's still no answer as to what the hive wants this baby for. Why it wants this so bad that it was willing to destroy Crane's trust, his body, his life for it. What can he give the hive that nobody else could? What could a *baby* give the hive now that it could not before?

Levi grabs the shotgun, circles the room like a frustrated animal. Tammy tells him to sit, but he doesn't listen. Stagger rubs circles into Crane's back.

It feels like the pressure of the head in Crane's pelvis will crack the bone in half. Crane reaches between his legs as if he might be able to touch something already, as if he'll find a lock of hair with the tips of his fingers. Nothing yet. His hand only comes away wet.

You suffer and labor for us in your glory.

We are so grateful for you.

The hive can go fuck itself.

Our little one will soon see the sun.

For the first time, Crane feels—so foreign, so strange he barely knows what it is, but so instinctual that he would never be able to disobey—Crane feels the urge to push.

Birth

Thirty-Two

Jess must be doing twenty over the speed limit on Corridor H, chewing on a hangnail as the blizzard buffets the stolen F-150. She has nothing but the clothes on her back and the blood in her veins and maybe a wallet in her back pocket if she's lucky, if she thought to grab it before stepping outside with Crane. Does she even have her phone? He can't remember the outline of it in any of her pockets.

But—she mentioned California, right? That must mean she's driving west, toward the sinking sun barely visible through the snow. Eventually she'll have to turn on the headlights and pray the roads don't get slick in the night. Crane doesn't want to think about that, or the fact that she'll have to get past the Tennessee hive enforcers, or that the price of gasoline might stop her before she gets out of the state at all. He wants to think about her in a motel in boring middle America, drinking shit coffee on a ratty bedspread, cutting her hair to a bob in the bathroom and studying the scar on the inside of her wrist, wondering if it will ever go away.

It will, though. It'll fade with time, like Crane figures most things will once you make it past twenty-two, or whatever age Jess is, close enough to his own. She'll reach the West Coast—he doesn't know shit about California, but if he had to pick, he thinks she'd like Santa Cruz, probably, or San Diego—and step out onto a beach that is seventy degrees in the depths of winter and stare in awe at the rush of water at low tide. She'll sit in the truck bed and watch the sun rise, or set, whichever. Maybe she'll send a letter back home to Cleveland, but more likely she won't, and she'll sell the truck for cash and scrape together enough money for the *worst* room in the *worst* apartment complex and get the *worst* job, and every morning she'll sit by her window with a cup of coffee and watch the sun. She'll go to the beach every weekend and never get sick of it, no matter how many times a seagull swoops too close or steals her food. She'll probably adopt a cat. Maybe she'll get a nerdy boyfriend fleeing the Cali tech sector or realize she's a lesbian in a hot butch's bedroom. She'll make friends. She'll take shots of cheap liquor in cramped kitchenettes and play stupid card games, sleep on warm couches, and make dinner for protest-buddies getting out of jail and discover she's actually a great cook, she really has a knack for it, would you look at that.

For the rest of her life, for all the sixty more years Crane prays she has, she'll step on every fucking worm she sees on the pavement after a good spring rain.

"We're pushing, we're pushing," Tammy says. She's sitting beside him because her knees can't take the kneeling anymore. Levi continues to pace. Stagger reminds Crane to breathe. "I know it sounds like horseshit but, swear to god, your body knows what to do. Just do what it tells you."

It's infinitely cruel that his body has been keeping this secret from him—that it knows something he doesn't. The head is so low in the birth canal that it feels like it's already out of him, but it's not. It's got to be the third time he's thought that, but the head just keeps getting lower and it keeps not being out yet.

The hive has gone quiet. The pile of slick mucus membranes and calcium piled in the closet is silent. It breathes with him.

What about Mom and Dad? Crane can't think of why they would be passing through Wash County of all places, but it's hard to think anything at all. Catching a thought is like trying to hold loose brain matter, slipping between his fingers but still coagulating under his nails. Did Dad's job have them driving to Morgantown for some reason? Do they still have family in Ohio, or Michigan?

Mom and Dad must've gotten their tank filled by now, and maybe they're—*push*, Tammy says, *don't waste the end of the contraction, just like that*—sitting in the parking lot of that other gas station, debating if it's safe to drive with the snow coming down this hard, with both of them crying this hard. They can't pay attention to storm-blurred road signs when they're busy reconstituting the last several years of their life from scratch.

Had they always held out hope that their daughter was alive out there somewhere, or had they found more comfort in an imagined corpse? Are they fully capable of comprehending the new version of this child they met? Perhaps they're testing the name *Crane* until it comes as easily as *Sophie* did, updating their mental image of their baby's body with tattoos and broken fingers and burns and short hair, wrapping their heads around being grandparents. Together, they vow they will take their phones off silent, and they will not turn down the volume until they finally, finally get that call. Whenever it comes.

The lizard-brain urge to push stops, and Crane collapses onto his hands, fingers wrenching into the blankets and towels. The towels are soaking wet. Stagger whines.

"Lucky motherfucker," Tammy is muttering, taking Crane by the back of his neck. He can't decide if, once this is over, he'll miss her or not. "Hey now. Stop holding your breath. Not gonna have you passing out."

Crane does as he's told like always. Tries to take advantage of the lull to clear his throat, wipe his eyes, get air into his lungs. He feels like he's been running for hours. He tastes copper in the back of his throat.

And Luna—oh, Luna is probably asleep right now, taking a nap, cuddled up in her low-set princess bed with the gauze canopy, tucked happily between a plush unicorn and a blanket made out of her dad's old sweater. Her hair has to be longer now, the kind of mess that Birdie carefully untangles every morning with a wide-toothed comb. A few strands would stick to her tiny lips as she sleeps. Aspen can't leave her side sometimes. They're on the floor beside her, making sure her tiny lungs are working.

Birdie would come in, holding a mug of hot chocolate, and settle onto the floor with them in silence. What do they talk about? Nothing good. They're both exhausted and rudeness gets the better of them. "You really think the FDA's going to go?" Birdie might ask, borderline snappish after reading an upsetting news article Aspen forwarded an hour ago, and Aspen will retort with, "You're the one that thinks Crane will text us."

She gets quiet.

Aspen probably thinks, by this point, that Crane is dead. Or that he might as well be. Can't work for journalists so long without returning to that baseline pessimist bitch they'd been in high school. Still, sitting on the floor of their daughter's room, they consider picking up their old college smoking habit, and switching from L&Ms to Marlboro Reds because Marlboro Reds are, were, Crane's favorite and, fuck it, they're allowed to be pathetic sometimes.

Push.

Levi has a palm on Crane's collarbone, Stagger holding Crane's hand. Crane's vision is swimming and if he's making noise he can't tell. Tammy wipes sweat from his shoulders and pours cold water on a cloth to press to his temple, and checks between his legs one more time.

"We've got a head up there," she says.

The contraction peaks and it's the worst one he's had. Crane vomits. It's all burning stomach acid. Levi recoils, but Tammy grabs him by the shirt, tells him to clean it up, whispers to Crane that this happens sometimes, it's okay, it's okay. Almost there. Does he want to reach down and feel the head? Feel the baby for the first time? No, Crane doesn't.

Levi balls up the soiled towel and removes it from sight.

The hive murmurs, ***You're so close you're so close.***

"Nothing to be ashamed of," Tammy says. "Every midwife and labor nurse has seen more puke and shit than you'd ever imagine." Stagger hums, rubs Crane's back, refuses to leave his side. "When you're pushing, damn near everything comes out. It's how you know you're doing it right."

Crane tastes bitter juices down the back of his throat. He wants to grab Levi by the face and crack open his jaw and spit it all down Levi's tongue so he has to taste it too.

Push.

Scrambling. Levi is saying something. "Hey," Tammy says, "hey. Careful." She's touching him. "The head is about to come out. It's right there. It's gonna start burning, you hear me? Ease up, don't hurt yourself." Crane can't hear her until she grabs him by the hair. "If you push, there's a chance you're gonna tear. You hear me? Just take it easy. Let it happen."

Okay. He stops pushing. Not pushing is the hardest thing he's ever done in his life. He times his breaths to Stagger's. He almost vomits again, but there's nothing left to come up, just a gross dry heave.

"Almost here," Levi tells the hive.

Almost here.

He's right. Crane repeats it over and over. It's almost over. Almost almost almost.

He finally reaches down and, oh, just like Tammy said. There's the head. Wisps of hair, wet mucus, too-soft butterfly skin. It's bulging out of him. Liquid trickles over the head and drips all over his thighs and the blankets.

He wants to push. He's so close.

Oh our child, you're so close, we see our little one.

Fuck it, *fuck it*, who gives a fuck anymore, he doesn't care if he tears, who gives a *shit*.

He bears down.

The head comes free, and then Tammy's taking hold of a tiny pair of shoulders and pulling, and it's like she's wrenched everything out of him at once. All the water and baby that had been inside him is *outside* in a gush and it's over.

It's over.

The baby makes a gurgling noise. Tammy passes it into Crane's arms. It's burning hot. It smears insides and phlegm across his bare chest.

"What is it?" Levi demands.

"Hold on," Tammy says, leaning in.

"What is it?"

It's so small. The choking cry turns to a wail.

Tammy says, "A girl."

Thirty-Three

A *daughter,* the hive cries, *a daughter, how beautiful, how perfect.*

The baby—Crane's baby—is the color of a bruise and scrunched like balled-up paper. She's smeared with waxy pith and blood. Her head is a strange shape and her patchy dark hair is plastered to her flat, ugly face. Her crying isn't even real crying. It's a desperate croaking noise as her lungs expel amniotic fluid and fill with real, true air for the first time.

It has to hurt. It has to be so strange and so cold out here, outside her father's body.

Crane's next breath comes out as a shudder. He collapses, falls against Stagger's chest. On instinct, somehow, he cradles the back of her head, supports the weak chicken-neck tendons as if he knows she'll break if he doesn't. She's so soft too. So much sturdier than the twenty-week creature in that grocery bag. A twisting blue cord protrudes from her belly and leads right back between his legs.

She croaks again. Wails. Nuzzles her tiny face against Crane's bare chest.

She is so so so small.

Crane watches her. He's waiting for worms to crawl out from under her skin, for her to open her mouth to show festering rot and putrid meat. But there's none of that. He presses his nose to her temple and she smells like salt and insides. Like a human. Not a worm. No distinct stink of *dead.*

There has to be something. He smooths back her hair, inspects her tiny face to find it: some sort of horrible transmutation, a physical manifestation of why she's here. But Hannah's baby had nothing wrong with it, and there's nothing wrong with this baby either. She's just a baby.

"Looks healthy," Tammy says, checking his daughter's fingers, counting to make sure she has all her toes. Levi can't look away. Stagger leans over Crane's shoulder to peer at the fragile creature he helped Crane birth. "Sounds healthy, too."

Oh, little one.

The towels and blankets make thick wet sounds as Crane tries to find a more comfortable position. He is exhausted. He is ripped-open and sore, he wants to sleep for a thousand years, and she's so warm against his bare chest.

She is alive and she is not a maggot or a beast or—or—

She keeps moving. Waving her tiny arms, bright-red feet tucking up protectively to her belly. Opening and closing her weak-muscled mouth. She's so much bigger than he thought she'd be. How did this come out of him? He puts a hand over her ears to keep them warm, but his hands tremble. He's shaking. He didn't realize he was shaking so bad until Stagger reaches up to hold his jaw.

"He okay?" Levi asks.

"Happens sometimes," Tammy replies plainly. "Get over here, help me cut the cord."

Crane wants to give her a name but can't come up with one that isn't tainted somehow. He wouldn't be able to tell it to anyone anyway. Levi will probably name her without him.

He hates that.

Tammy is tying things around the umbilical cord, telling Levi to make sure Crane doesn't accidentally nudge her while she has the scissors.

This little girl isn't the one who did this to him. None of this is her fault. It would've been a kindness to excise her from the body months ago instead of letting her be yanked from oblivion to end up here. She didn't want this, she didn't ask for this. She deserved to be born to someone capable of loving her, defending her, making the world better for her. Not him.

She's so helpless and it's not right.

She is perfect.

"Crane," Tammy whispers. Crane barely manages to tear his eyes away from his baby. *His* baby. *His.* The brain has latched on to that word and won't let it go. "You did good. You hear me? You did good. There's gonna be a few more contractions, though, yeah? Have to get that placenta out of you so it don't rot in there."

Crane's head swims. There's more? He has to go through more?

"It won't be as bad," she assures him. "It's just an ugly jellyfish.

A big clot. Ain't no head or shoulders to push out, so it should be a breeze. Just rest."

He nods. Behind him, Stagger makes an animalistic snuffling sound.

"There a name yet?" Tammy asks.

"Still working on that," Levi answers for him.

Levi is getting close now—the first time he's gotten this close since this all started, almost stepping into the mess of amniotic fluid and whatever mess of liquid comes out during birth. Stagger growls.

"Fuck," Levi says. "She's tiny."

Apparently that's the only thing either one of them can think. Levi skims his fingertips over her dark hair. It has the tiniest hint of a curl to it, a wave. Like Crane's hair. Crane wonders if he was born with a full head of dark hair. Or if Levi was. Thinking of Levi as a baby is so deeply, heart-shatteringly depressing that he can't hold it in his head for long. Levi's thumb brushes her little nose, then the divot that makes up her spine. In response, the baby just makes that same choking sound and struggles against Crane's chest, as if gaining control of her limbs is painful. Crane imagines it'd be like pins and needles all over, after being cramped up for so long.

"Is she hungry?" Levi asks. "Is that why she's crying? Do we have to teach her or—" He looks to Tammy. "Does she know?"

"No need to rush her," Tammy says. "She'll figure it out. But if you want to try . . ."

Tammy shows Crane how to position the baby against his breast so her mouth can find the nipple, but she isn't interested. She's upset and tired and getting used to breathing air. Tammy says that's normal. Give her a bit.

Eventually—Crane doesn't know how long it takes—the placenta comes out too. It doesn't hurt nearly as bad, and Stagger and Levi and Tammy help him sit up, make sure gravity does most of the work.

When it comes out, it looks like a slab of raw meat, or an excised deer liver. Levi wraps it up to stick in the cooler, to give it to the hive later.

And then it's done. It's really done.

Tammy says, "Hey, baby. You okay?"

Crane doesn't know. He hasn't let go of his daughter (*his daughter*) since she was placed in his arms. She's finally latched to nurse, and it's a bizarre feeling. Reminds him of the semi-painful tingling in his jaw when he bites down on a piece of fruit, saliva glands rushing to fill the mouth with spit. He keeps wincing, but it's not that bad.

When she's done, Levi says, "Alright, let's introduce her."

It takes Crane a second to understand what he means—*introduce her.* To who? His head is sticky and slow.

But the flies lift their shiny wings and the worms slide across each other, chattering their jaws and, oh.

Our little one, the hive whispers in the same voice they use to draw in the hungry, desperate people they feed on. **She's beautiful.**

No.

Crane growls. Levi can't have her. The urge to protect her borders on animal. It's not her fault that half of her is made out of Levi, it's not her fault that half of her is made out of *Crane.* None of that matters. Levi doesn't get to touch her.

She's perfect, the hive says. **Let us see her.**

"C'mon." Levi takes a step closer, but Crane jams himself against Stagger's chest, can feel himself baring his teeth. "Don't do this shit. She's out of you, your job's done. Thought you didn't even want her."

He—he didn't. Of course he didn't. This is fucking awful, and he is so aware that this obliterated some part of him he's never going to get back. But it's not *her fault,* and nobody else is going to protect her, are they? Nobody but him.

Let us see her.

Levi sighs. Gets himself down on Crane's level. Snaps his fingers to get his attention.

Crane is going to kill him. The moment the strength is back in his limbs, the *moment*, Crane is going to grab that shotgun and put a slug through his head and fucking kill him.

Oh child, she will not make it without us.

She needs us just as we need her.

Levi says, "Look at me."

Levi lifts the hem of his shirt to show the scar.

Under the skin, it's moving. Just like it was before. The baby snuffles and coughs like she knows something's not right, like she can feel Crane's panicked heartbeat through the skin of his chest. She probably can. She's been listening to it for so long.

"See?" Levi says. "They did it to me. I took it fine."

Is that what happened in McDowell? To Stagger? In the workshops Irene talked about?

We have tried so many times, the hive says, **to make ourselves as perfect for this world as we can. To make ourselves in the image of our children.**

To walk among you instead of hiding in dark rooms.

To see the sun on our faces.

Levi lowers his shirt. How many times was Crane eye level with that scar when he was sucking Levi's cock? How many times did he accidentally brush it when they were naked together?

"Barely even hurt," Levi says. "Our friend over here, though—" His eyes slide to Stagger. Crane realizes there is a version of all this where Stagger was the father. He chews through the scenario in a heartbeat, swallows it whole, wonders if this would have been easier with someone who treated him gently. "Not gonna lie, I thought he was going to manage it. Guess not. Fucked him up pretty bad."

The father's compatibility with our flesh; the mother's bitterness and hunger and submission.

She will be perfect. She will be beautiful. She will carry us into the sun.

Crane is biting the inside of his cheek so hard the thin membranes pop between his teeth.

His child is a little girl, and he sees the writing on the wall.

This is no universe in which they don't do to her exactly what they did to him.

There is no way out of this. He swallows down bile, and he's shaking again. He just keeps *shaking.* As long as she's alive, the hive will look for her. He cannot destroy every worm, he cannot kill every fly and every hidden maggot in every dark corner in West Virginia. She will never be safe. She will never be allowed to grow up happy or whole, because the hive will always want her and her body and her ability to create more people *just like her.*

"Give her to me," Levi says.

Crane presses his face against her cheek, tucks his head against her shoulder. She knows who he is. She knows his smell, the texture of his skin, the rhythm of his breathing.

If the world was better, he could bring her to Aspen and Birdie's doorstep and collapse there, push her into their arms and beg them to keep her away from him. All he'll ever be able to see in her is Levi and everything he did, and that is so unimaginably cruel. Or he could take his parents up on the offer. Mom always did want grandkids. Maybe she'd be okay raising her without him. All he'd have to do is ask, and his parents would tilt the world off its axis to help.

It would be beautiful, if that was possible.

But it's not. She can survive the infestation. She can carry the worms and not be eaten alive from the inside out. Just like Levi. She will be broken down into the same breeding bitch they made out of Crane, because that is what she was born to be.

Crane needs to do the right thing for once in his life. His silence may be consent, but hers is not. He remembers—his face pressed to his daughter's skin, watching the wretched hive wait in baited silence— that up until the, what, late 1980s? Doctors thought newborns couldn't feel pain. Or didn't have the capability to remember it after the fact. And so they performed surgery on them without anesthesia, only muscle relaxers to paralyze them.

If Levi opened her up to cram a beast inside her, she would feel every agonizing moment of it.

Do the right thing.

It's the only kindness he's ever been capable of giving.

Thirty-Four

There's no other way to do it. Nothing else that will work, nothing that can't be stopped. Nothing that makes her a part of him again, that lets him save her and keep her all at once.

Crane devours her.

The most merciful spot is the jugular. Right under the delicate skin of the throat. His daughter squawks pathetically for a single ear-splitting second—how could anyone have thought they don't feel pain, how could *anyone*—before what's happening rips beyond her capacity to experience it. The skin tears and the veins pop between his teeth and the blood fills his mouth, pours down his chin, chokes him with the sudden heat and salt. He swallows it. The chunk of flesh that comes off in his mouth, the tough stringy arteries, the cartilage that hasn't hardened yet. It clogs his throat and lodges in his esophagus. He forces it down. His body revolts, attempts to regurgitate it, but he won't let himself lose any of the meat, not one shred of it. It's hers. He made her and he won't let them have her, she's his she's his she's *his*.

Thirty-Five

WHAT HAVE YOU DONE?

His daughter has stopped moving. He holds her against his chest like he can turn his rib cage into her tiny grave.

Tammy screams.

WE SAVED YOU, WE MADE YOU, UNGRATEFUL FUCKING BEAST, AND THIS IS HOW YOU REPAY US?

And Crane is laughing. He won, motherfucker. She will never know what it's like to be scared, she will never have that bite on the inside of her wrist, she will never know the crunching of feeding worms or the betrayal of a body becoming something it wasn't meant to be. They'll never be able to hurt her. He is naked on the floor, thighs smeared with afterbirth and bare chest dripping with gore. His stomach is hollow and sagging. He's laughing.

Fuck you.

Levi is the first to get his shit together.

He lunges for the baby, a feverish snarling attempt to wrestle the ragdoll-limp thing out of Crane's arms as if there's a possibility he can save it, reverse the damage, offer it to the hive anyway. But Stagger catches him. Hits Levi like a bull. Stagger the protector. Stagger the loyal, terrified man with worms crawling in between the folds of his gray matter. He slams them both into the door with the dull *clang* of bone on metal, and they fall to the ground. Stagger has Levi's head between both his giant gloved hands. Squeezing. Going to pop him like a piece of rotten fruit.

Up, get up. He has to get up. Crane can't get his legs under him, can barely move them. If he couldn't see, he would've guessed somebody had taken a chain saw to his cunt, ripped it open navel to tailbone. He fumbles away, drags himself backward. Baby held to his chest. Once. Twice.

He bumps into Tammy, who is hunched over with her breakfast splattered on her shoes. Her eyes are blown with panic. Froth gathers at the corner of her mouth. He's never seen her panic before; Crane didn't think she was capable of it. She's gotten pissed, she's gotten mad as hell, but she's been alive as long as him three times over. She's not supposed to be this scared.

It takes Crane until that moment to realize that what he did was insane.

But it wasn't. It was the clearest, sanest decision he'd ever made.

"You—" she gasps.

Levi grabs the shotgun. Racks it.

Stagger bashes Levi's head against the door, and the shot goes wide. *Bang.*

Loud enough that Crane's hearing howls into static, obliterates everything else, sends him reeling.

Tammy's torso rips open. Gut shot, slug, close range. It's a monstrosity. Takes a chunk of meat out of her body and flings it across the manager's office. Obliterates the lower ribs, shreds the flesh, grinds the organs into a useless pulp.

Chuck-chuck.

Tammy hits the ground. Gurgling. The woman who took him in and protected him, the woman he called Ma, even though he never said it out loud, the woman who refused to help him just because the hive told her *no.* She splutters.

Bang.

Second shot. Stagger's shoulder disintegrates. It doesn't stop him. The arm goes limp and writhing worms screech away from the wound, and Levi's head hits the door again. There's no noise except the screaming in Crane's ears, but it has to be a wet, meaty sound, like something shattered. A crunch.

This place is going to eat itself alive. Crane tastes gunpowder. His baby's head lolls against his breast, the neck wound gaping open into a dark mouth. He tries to use Tammy's shoulder as a prop to get on his feet, but holding his daughter, the ruined fingers on his left hand, he can't get it. He slips.

Chuck-chuck bang.

The third slug hits home. Stagger's skull splits. Half of it is gone. His head a waning moon of worm pieces and bone.

Stagger reels back. Stumbles, tries to hold his dripping, collapsing head up. Can't. Half a worm falls out of the crevice chewed into his brain and thumps onto the ground. Stagger crawls on his hands and knees for only a second, remaining eye darting around like it can see the damage if it just strains enough.

The shotgun slumps to the ground, out of Levi's hands.

Crane watches Stagger die on the bloody, freezing floor. Can't get to him before he sags into the nest of blankets as if attempting to crawl underneath them after a nightmare. The worms writhe in confusion. The body is abandoned, destroyed, useless. The man behind it is gone.

Maybe it was a mercy. Maybe that body wasn't Stagger's body anymore—the hive moving him without him, manually forcing each joint and muscle. Or maybe the man was still there under the worms, hoping there was possibly, please god, a way out. Perhaps he hoped that if he sat down with Crane long enough, if they used enough knives, they could take out all the parasites one by one. At least have the chance to find out if his body could function without them, let his body be his own again.

Crane is sorry he couldn't help.

He gets one foot under himself.

Then another.

Crane, finally standing, holding the baby, *his* baby, looks down at Levi.

Levi looks up at him.

Part of his head is dented, Crane realizes. Like Sean's. Levi is trying to get the shotgun back into his hands, but he keeps fumbling it. Struggling. Making these ugly noises in the back of his throat.

Crane slides the shotgun away with his toe. Levi slaps his hand after it and succeeds only in rolling onto his side. God, it's bad. The skull is cracked.

What does Levi see, looking up at him like this? A naked, mutilated woman, or the man he did this to?

Not that it matters much anymore.

Crane casts around the room for the safest place to leave his daughter before settling her snuggly against Stagger's side. Stagger isn't moving anymore, except for the worms, all trying to figure out what to do. *There*, Crane thinks, tucking her by Stagger's hip. *Take care of her for me.*

He picks up the shotgun.

Levi taught him how to use this, once upon a time. Behind the gas station. A cigarette dangling from Levi's mouth, smiling as he pushed each shell into the gun and handed it off. The model holds six shells plus one. Levi used only three. Crane is trembling as he lifts it up, props it up against his chest, has to use his broken hand to pull back the action.

Shit. He remembered this being easier than it was. He can't get it all the way back before he has to release it. There's a quiet *chunk* sound. That's not right.

Levi slurs out something that might be, "Jammed."

The sliding part, the forestock he thinks, isn't sitting right. He pulls the bolt back to open the chamber, finds a shell stuck halfway in. That's not—no. That's not supposed to happen. He shoves a finger in to get it unstuck but he's shaking too hard, can't get any leverage on it.

"Jammed," Levi says again, and he's grinning, and there's blood all over his teeth.

Crane drops it. Fine. He'll do it the hard way.

He stumbles out. Over Tammy. Through the manager's office door, into the back hallway, and opens his go bag.

There's the hammer, under the blanket. He grabs it and adjusts it in the hand until it feels just right.

"You ain't gonna do that," Levi says when Crane makes it back into the room, blood trickling over his thighs with every step. It's gotten

313

so hot in here. It smells like metal. Crane watches Levi brace himself on the floor, struggle to lift his head. "C'mon. Put it down."

Levi says that like it's not easy. Like it's not muscle memory.

Grab Levi's head, don't react when he squawks and tries to squirm away, bring the clawed end of the hammer down on the open wound again, and again, and again, and again. Until it splits all the way and the head falls open and it's a soupy, chemically mess left in the skull cavity.

Crane breathes hard. Sucks in the disgusting air. It feels correct, doesn't it. Inflicting one fucking half of what Levi did to him, a fraction of it. And at least Levi gets to die, right? Crane's not going to keep him alive for months, struggling and choking. Crane put him down. Crane is merciful.

Crane thought he'd feel better, looking at the broken skull. He doesn't. He's just tired, and empty.

So he goes for the scar.

It's easy enough. Smash the clawed end into the keloid, get the hooks into the meat and wrench it open with all the strength he can muster. The worm underneath shuffles away, but it's too slow. Crane reaches in and pulls it free.

It's not even a particularly big worm. Nothing all that great, or impressive. It twists in the air like Stagger's did, panicking at the sudden lack of shelter.

And there's only one.

It dies as easily as the others.

Through the doorway, the hive refuses to move. None of the worms crawl over themselves. The flies have gone still. Like Crane is some sort of predator that can only sense movement; like he's so out of his mind that maybe he's going to let them go, after everything they've done.

They're just a bunch of stupid bugs.

That hive comes apart as easily as Levi's skull.

It's a mess in here.

Crane shuffles to the pile of clothes he'd stripped during labor, but it's all unusable. Stained and splattered with insides. Tammy's, probably. Fuck. He goes back to the go bag, leaving red footprints across the concrete floor, and pulls out socks, underwear, sweatpants, a shirt. He struggles into clean clothes, digs through Tammy's belongings for an extra overnight pad, smooths it into his fresh boxers. He steals Tammy's snow boots too.

Then it's Levi's jacket, hung up by the door. There's only a bit of blood on this one. Also Tammy's. He shrugs it on, then pulls a cigarette from the pocket, pops it into his mouth, lights it.

Crane takes a drag and picks up his baby to wrap her in Mom and Dad's blanket. Up we go, that's it. Her limbs dangle helplessly from her tiny body, so he makes sure she's swaddled tight. He's sorry he had to set her down. He was busy, that's all.

Postpartum

Thirty-Six

It's dark. It's stopped snowing. The only illumination in the parking lot is the emergency light, a flickering yellow bulb that's always given Crane a headache. But the clouds are low, and the snow is undisturbed, and the night is almost bright enough to read by. Everything has that unreal orange-gold tinge, as if he'd walked out of the gas station and into another world. Maybe he should check the news, see if the articles line up with what he remembers. See if he doesn't recognize the name of the president.

The cigarette is down to a nub. Despite the blanket's best efforts, his baby's corpse against his chest is getting colder.

He *really* should feel something by now, he thinks. Besides a little sick. Raw meat on an empty stomach is making him queasy. But there's nothing. His brain has shut that off. If he feels everything now, all at once, he'll rip back into the gas station and find a way to unjam that shotgun and put a slug between his teeth. He'd rather not do that.

He has Levi's phone, though. Took it off his body. And he has Mom's number, too. It's there, in the pocket.

It takes a few tries to get the passcode through, with his fingers so cold and shaky against the touchscreen. In the meantime, Crane can't decide between naming his daughter Jess or Sophie. Sophie is a pretty name. It deserves a better fate.

Finally, the passcode works. He types in Mom's phone number.

Hits video call.

Holds Sophie against his chest, her face pressed safely into his coat, and lifts the phone just enough to hide the blood.

It's Dad who answers. His face appears with an electronic *ding*, grainy video quality and bleary eyes and all. It takes him a second to realize what he's looking at. Crane's own face appears in the small rectangle at the bottom of the screen: a blur of shadows and blood and dark, sweaty hair.

Off-screen, Mom says, "Is that—"

"Crane?" Dad says.

END.

Acknowledgments

Before we get into the meat of the acknowledgments, I need to thank my Sophie.

My Sophie—the girl I was for nineteen years—didn't have a lot of nicknames, but fuck me if I'll let my deadname end up in print, so let's dig one up. A manager at my old job, a shitty cramped gas station, called her *KitKat*. Can't use that; too silly. But the older kids at Girl Scout horse camp called her just *Kat* for half a day, so we'll make that work.

You also need to be picturing her properly. Kat was a short, skinny girl with white-blond hair and egregious snaggleteeth wrangled by years of orthodontics. As a kid, she refused to wear anything but torn-up jeans and black T-shirts; in college, she made an attempt at woman-hood via Forever 21 dresses, fishnets, and makeup tutorials. Take whatever version of her you'd like. It doesn't matter. It's all the same.

Kat grew up knowing the words *autistic* and *transgender*, but they didn't apply to her, obviously. She wasn't autistic. Sure, she was con-stantly overwhelmed, brute-force memorizing social rules and avoid-ing social interaction to keep from getting sick with exhaustion. But that was her own weakness of will. She just needed to get over it. And she wasn't transgender, either. Sure, she was jealous of trans men because they got to be boys and she didn't, and she wanted to burn herself up if it meant her girlhood would go away. But if she was a boy, she would've known already. Right?

Instead, all Kat knew was that she was tired. She wanted to stop feeling so *incorrect* all the time. But without an understanding of why, the only thing she could do was grit her teeth. Keep her grades up, struggle through extracurriculars, bury herself in video games and stories and—

Look. You've clearly read the book. You know what Kat really wanted. It's what Sophie wanted. It's what Crane eventually did.

If you're one of the people in the world who love me, and you're feeling ill at this information, don't worry. I'm better now. Deep in-side, I will always envy horrible things I know I shouldn't, but I don't dream of refusing reconstructive surgery nearly as often as I used to. Transitioning, and recognizing my disability, saved me. So thank you, Kat, for holding it together long enough for me to make it to adulthood.

With that out of the way:

Jennifer March Soloway. Hey, what possessed you to represent a manuscript where the main character eats part of his own baby? Like, I'm not kidding. I genuinely thought I wasn't going to get away with this. But here we are. This book needed one hell of a champion, and you pulled it off; thank you for that, and for everything else you've done, and for being a rock-star agent. I'm always floored by your positivity, generosity, and openness. You're the best.

Joe Monti. Gonna be honest, I thought I used up all my luck getting an agent for this book, so imagine my surprise when you actually wanted to buy it. Holy shit? My copy of *Lost Souls* is still right next to my desk, by the way, getting all the attention it deserves. Thank you for the R&R, and for convincing me to let Jess live, and for giving this book a place I wasn't sure it'd get.

My incredibly small pool of friends. I'm bad with people. This is such a short list I'm not sure I want to print it. You know who you are, though. Thank you for being here, on earth, at the same time as me.

Bri. I've said it before, but I deeply appreciate all of your support and input during the early stages of this manuscript. I can't believe Crane got this far. Whew.

Mom, Dad, and Mamaw. Look, I told you already—this is nature, not nurture. I was always going to end up like this. It's nothing you did, promise! Thank you for not being too embarrassed or nauseated to tell people what your son/grandson writes about. (Maybe. This book's a doozy.)

Splatoon 3. I'm aware this is a video game. It's also one of the few reasons I survived edits. By extension, thank you, *Margarita*, for sending it, because dear god did we need something fun in the house during those weeks.

Marissa. When's the next time you can come over? I'll make cinnamon rolls if you want, and we'll make sure there are strawberries and pomegranates in the fridge.

Alice. How many of my readers know that I met you when I was thirteen years old? We attended the same young writers' seminar. You didn't want to be there because you were afraid of being laughed at, and I didn't want to be there because I thought I was better than everyone else. And then we were writing novels back and forth over email, and then we went to the same college for the same degree, and then I was eighteen and I kissed you after our ASL final and the timing was so fucking bad, but hey, it worked, didn't it? Thank you for making it a little less painful for Kat to exist, and for flinching only a little bit at the mess when I had to claw myself out. (I could've worded-slash-timed that text better, though. Sorry for ruining that *Jurassic World* movie.) I got really lucky with you.

.